GUARDIAN

A DARK MM GUARDIAN/AGE GAP ROMANCE

BELLE ARGO ESCORTS

BETH CHRISTOPHER

I0835780

Copyright © 2026 by Beth Christopher

ISBN: 978-1-969810-09-1

All rights reserved.

No portion of this book may be reproduced in any form without written permission from the publisher or author, except as permitted by U.S. copyright law.

No portion of this book may be used to train artificial intelligence.

This book is a work of fiction. Names, places, and situations are fictitious or are used fictitiously.

This book is licensed for personal use and enjoyment, and may not be re-sold or given away. Thank you for respecting the efforts of this and all authors whose work you read.

NO Bot / No AI – the author prohibits the use of this book in training any generative artificial intelligence tools and no generative artificial intelligence tools were used in the writing of this book or in the creation of the cover. The author reserves the right to *license* this work for use in training generative artificial intelligence tools in the future.

This book was written by a human, one with a super twisted brain, but a human nonetheless.

Editing by Sydney Feron at Just Spicy Romance Edits

Proofreading by Lea Vickery PA and by Kate Wood Proofreading

Cover design by Babski Creative Studios

For questions/comments or to report typos, please contact bethchristopherromance@gmail.com

010526

About Guardian

AND CONTENT WARNING

The one he wants is the only one he can't control.

Ravi

When my parents were killed almost four years ago, I went to live with Liam.

For two years, I've been in love with him.

I've also hated him nearly that long.

He's overbearing, controlling, and lately he tracks my every move.

I can't take it anymore.

I've saved some cash working as a companionship escort, but it's not enough to escape.

So, I decide to auction myself off. It'll give me the money I need to leave this town—and Liam—in my past.

Except nothing goes to plan, and my escape goes up in smoke.

Liam

I'm not a good man. I'm certainly not one who should be charged with someone else's care.

But I promised my old friend—Ravi's safety is my priority.

Even if I'm protecting him from me.

But the more I work to keep him out of danger, the harder he rebels.

The harder he rebels, the harsher my punishments.

Then I discover his ridiculous, harebrained auction plan.

If I can't stop the auction, I have little choice.

Ravi will not become a stranger's plaything.

Not while I have a plan of my own.

Guardian is a dark MM, enemies-to-lovers, kink awakening romance featuring a tortured vigilante hero who's met his match in the sunshiny male escort he's been charged with protecting. This story contains a significant age gap and consensual non-monogamy (after all, sharing is caring).

Reader discretion is advised. Possible triggers include: revenge sex, spanking, imprisonment as punishment, stalking/tracking, use of restraints, off-page military trauma, on-page torture and murder of bad guys, accidental drug overdose, attempted kidnapping, forced OHs, bondage, and some of the consent is a bit dubious.

If you've picked up this book, you are my kind of people. Welcome. We're a little bit twisted, and we like it. Jump on in, the water is fine.

Musical Inspiration

If you're like me and enjoy pairing your reading with music, the following songs helped to inspire Guardian:

- "Run" - Snow Patrol
- "Hemorrhage" - Fuel
- "Mouth" - Bush
- "Live Forever" - Oasis
- "Blurry" - Puddle of Mud

NEWSLETTER

Want to keep in touch? Sign up for my newsletter to stay in the loop about future releases.

https://sendfox.com/BethChristopher

PROLOGUE

Ravi

I think my biggest mistake was going barefoot.

When you see people streaking in movies, they don't show the person stopping to put their shoes back on, right? But I guess they must, because right now I'm running across a gravel lot and regretting the rocks under my feet almost as much as the bullets whizzing past my head.

At least, like, equally as much.

Every shot makes me flinch. Every rock makes me stumble.

"What the fuck is that stupid son of a bitch doing?"

Ordinarily I'd find it hurtful being called stupid. Considering these men work for an asshole who's been trafficking people and drugs, I won't take it personally.

They probably had difficult childhoods or something.

"Jesus Christ, Ravi, what the fuck are you thinking?" My

boss, Brennan, is somewhere behind me. Behind the bad guys. Brennan is also a bad guy, but the ones chasing me are...badder guys? Worse guys?

"I already told you!" Since I'm running away from him, I don't know if Brennan can even hear me, but isn't it the principle of the thing? He came to this warehouse where some rival worse guy is holding people who've been taken off the street, people to be sold, and the plan is to release the people and burn the place down.

"Somebody fucking grab that fucking kid!" Worse guy. Gotta be.

I mean, yes, Brennan did tell me to wait in the car. When someone needs help, though, I can't *not* help. And those people being held here need help. Brennan needed a distraction. He'll appreciate my help in the end. He will.

So, you know. Streaking. It seemed like a good idea at the time.

Liam, my guardian, would call it reckless. I prefer to see it as taking initiative. Or, like, a public service. I'm being useful, dammit.

"Someone fucking grab him and just fucking shoot him!"

They've tried.

Honestly, it's exciting. I'm flying right now. Liam once told me it's a lot harder to hit a moving target, and I'm a fast runner, so mostly they're wasting ammunition. I've been sort of zigzagging to make it harder for them to aim.

I'm passing an open loading bay when something flies close to the left side of my face and embeds itself in the edge of one of the bay doors. I fight the urge to duck when the heat of it brushes my cheek. So I zig right, into the brightly lit warehouse. There are voices in there. People.

The guys with guns won't shoot with their own people around...right?

More yelling behind me. Not words I can understand, mostly grunts and thumps and a bunch of swearing. Maybe that means Brennan's guys got them all?

When I look over my shoulder to check, there's still one dude behind me. He's not shooting, but he's tall. Long legs. And he's gaining on me.

"Shit," I breathe. There's a noise in front of me—some guy carrying a wrapped bundle of some kind. He pulls a knife. He sees me, but there's nothing I can do to stop.

Then my toe slams into a seam in the concrete. "Ow."

Now I'm really flying. Toward the guy with the knife. The bundle.

You know how you put your hands out to catch yourself when you fall?

Well, my hand hits the knife.

Which hits the bundle.

The bundle explodes. I get a face full of powder.

Drugs, my brain supplies. *These are bad guys. Worse guys. They deal drugs.*

Bitterness coats the back of my throat. I gasp like a fish, but my lungs won't fill with air.

My heart, already racing, races faster. Dizziness hits.

Get up. The worse guys are coming. Get up, get up, get up.

"Ravi? Fuck." That sounds like Brennan. He's poking at my neck, slapping at my face. "Jalen, grab him and get him outside. We're going to need to call a fucking ambulance. Jesus, Ravi, you're a fucking menace."

My lips and tongue are weirdly numb. I can't make them move. It feels like I'm dying. I don't want to die.

I was only trying to help.

I really hope I did. It's the last thing I think before the lights go out.

CHAPTER ONE

LIAM

"PLEASE. I swear. I don't know anything else." After hours of begging, the man's voice is raw, cracked by desperation. Good.

Everyone in my line of work plays favorites with their tools. Some have pet names for their knives and guns. My favorite knife doesn't have a name. Just a purpose.

"Reece. Give me the fillet."

My employee hands over the blade.

The man tied to the stainless-steel chair starts thrashing. Water drips down his face with the steady, annoying cadence of a broken faucet.

Thunder claps outside the East End warehouse. Storm season in Belle Argo, Florida lives up to the name. Comes in handy. The drips from holes in the roof aggravate the interrogee. Thunder muffles their screams.

The former bartender we tracked down is good looking, pretty even, with his blue-gray eyes and artsy, new-school tattoos. Or he was before we got hold of him. Between my knife and my employee, Reece, who smashed the guy's head into concrete when we picked him up, he's not looking so pretty now.

"Okay, let's go over this again." I place the tip of my knife at his sternum and press in. Not a lot. Never go big when you can go small, I say. It's enough to get this guy's lower lip quivering.

"Several wealthy young men and women were taken from parties over the span of a few months' time, and the interesting thing is you just so happened to bartend at almost all of them. You're telling me your interactions were only ever with the party promoter. He's the one who gave you the money and the drugs and told you who to slip them to. Nobody else?"

He bobs his head. "Yeah. Yeah. Exactly. This guy, Tony, he seemed to be at all the parties. Always used the catering company I worked for. He'd slip me a grand and a picture. All I did was put the shit in their drink like he asked me to. I don't know who was paying him or who he was working with. I sure as fuck wasn't the one shipping them out of the country. I just needed the money, okay?"

My knife "slips" a little. The sound he makes is more of a whimper than a scream, but I enjoy the way the tendons stand out on his neck.

"What'd you need the money for?" We're probably going to kill this man anyway. Even if he was desperate for the cash because his little sister needed a kidney transplant or something, he could've gotten the money some way that didn't traumatize people and tear up families. Still, it's worth asking.

"Man, I had gambling debts, okay? I moved here to try

and lie low while I made some cash, but the dude I owed sent a guy, and I was running short on time."

I glance at Reece. He raises an eyebrow, thinking the same thing I'm thinking. We're definitely killing him now.

I crouch down so I can look into the eyes in his sagging head. "Here's the trouble I have with all that, my friend. You knew they were drugging people. You probably knew exactly what they were going to do with them, and you still sold them out for a measly few thousand dollars."

Over to the side there's a stainless-steel table where I keep my tools and my phone. The device is on silent, but the screen has been lighting up with notifications.

Ravi has left home.

Where's the little shit going when he doesn't have class for hours? I'm going to need to have a talk with him. I take a breath and turn back to the man in the chair.

"I didn't know," he protests. "I didn't know they wanted to, like, sell people or whatever. I thought it was a little harmless fun."

This is where Reece comes in out of nowhere and slugs the guy in the side of the face. "A little harmless fun, you sick piece of shit? Drugging kids? You're telling us you were all right with assault, but kidnapping is where you draw the line?"

I glare at Reece. He's one of my newer guys, so we're still working on communication. "Give me some warning next time, huh? You almost got the business end of my knife."

"Sorry, boss." His face flushes pink as he moves to stand against the nearest wall.

Fucking guy's like a golden retriever with a penchant for murder. We'll have to work on his self-control.

I return my knife to the bartender's chest and continue

drawing a line down the center of his sternum. He grits his teeth, trying not to scream. Gotta give him some points for that, at least. Most guys scream. Even the tough ones.

Especially the tough ones.

"Here's the thing, Brad. Seems awfully convenient that you've only got one co-conspirator, given that trafficking operations tend to involve a lot of people. Multiple people transported those kids who were drugged. Put them in a van, drove them away, and put them on a plane or a boat. Someone made sure you were assigned to work those parties. Who was your boss? Your boss's boss? Who handles scheduling for your employer?"

"I don't know. I don't—"

I drag my knife farther down his chest. Right through a stupid-ass tattoo of a rooster on his chest. It's well done for a barnyard animal. Detailed. That one probably cost some money.

"Okay. Okay. My boss is..." I glance over at Reece to make sure he's getting the names this guy is rattling off.

"Make sure to look into those people," I tell Reece when the bartender has run out of breath.

Not that I have high hopes. For all we know, the party planner simply requested Brad's presence. Still, it doesn't hurt to check. If we keep digging, eventually we'll find someone who knew something. Persistence is key.

I pick up a tool that looks a bit like a gardening claw, but with razor-sharp ends. "Anything you've forgotten to tell us?"

"I don't know anything else. I swear, I swear."

The bartender is bleeding from cuts and scrapes all over his body. We've been working him over for a couple of hours, so it doesn't surprise me when he mutters, "Man, I'm really dizzy."

I sigh. "Was there anyone else at the parties other than this Tony person who seemed like they could've been involved? Anyone else he could have been working with?"

"It's like I already told you. Dude was a social... What do you call them? Butterfly. Social butterfly. He talked to everybody. Liked to go around hugging and handshaking and snorting lines of coke off the coffee tables and whatever. He seemed to know everyone, so how would I know who he was working with?"

"There were a couple of vans we think he used to get people out of the parties. Did you ever see the vans? Ever help him load someone inside?"

"No. No. I never did...any of that. But I did see the van. It looked like one of our standard catering vans, except he usually parked it in front of the venue, which the staff weren't allowed to do. After a while I figured out that was how you could tell."

"Ever see the driver?"

"Fuck no. Tinted windows."

The bartender's head lolls to one side.

"We've probably gotten about all we're going to get, boss," Reece puts in.

I pause in my carving. "You're probably right."

The guy's head shoots up. Probably calculating for the first time that if he isn't useful, he's dead. "Wait. Wait. There was, uh, another guy. I think he was a cop. I could swear I saw a badge once."

"Did you get this cop's name? Can you give me a description?"

"Kind of tall. Dark hair. White. Uh..." The bartender

squeezes his eyes shut tight. “That’s all I can remember. But, hey, I could go back. Like, if you let me go, I could go work more parties. Keep an eye out for him. For anyone who’s suspicious. I could report back to you.”

“That’s a real nice offer, Brad...” I put my knife down on the table and pick up my phone, which is flashing again.

Ravi has entered the parking lot of Belle Argo University, Lot C.

Ravi is at Campus Coffee.

Ravi is at the BAU Campus Gym.

“Problem, boss?” Reese asks.

I shake my head. “Just my fucking ward being a fucking idiot.”

“So...” Brad trembles in the chair, trying to hold his head up. “So, you’ll let me go, then? You’ll let me go, and I’ll inform for you, like...like you’re the cops?”

“You know we’re not actually the cops.”

“No, yeah, I got that. Cops don’t interrogate you with knives in a warehouse. I don’t care who you are. Just... Do we have a deal?”

“I’m afraid that won’t work, Brad. That Tony fellow you mentioned is dead, and with him that part of the operation has dried up. It wouldn’t get us anything.”

He rattles the cuffs that hold his wrists behind the chair. “Something else, then. Come on, motherfucker. There’s got to be something, right? You can’t fucking keep me here. You’re talking about a bunch of pampered rich assholes. You know how they treat people like me? You don’t get to kill me over them.” The last part comes out in a yell. The big-eyed innocent act seems to have fallen away.

I hold up a finger and then return to my phone, shooting off a text.

Liam: You should not be at the gym so soon after a near-fatal drug overdose.

Placing the phone back on the table, I see movement from the corner of my eye. Bartender Brad is twisting in his chair, trying to work his wrists loose. He's straining forward, eyes on the table, almost like he's interested in what's happening with my phone.

Growling, I grab my pistol from the table and fire off two shots. The bartender, who drugged several twenty-something partygoers and sent them off to be trafficked, is still looking startled when he slumps over.

Then I send a follow-up text: ***Ravi. You're smarter than this.***

A quick check of the bartender's pulse tells me he's definitely gone. Good.

I see the moment Ravi reads the message, but there's no reply. Not even the three dots to tell me there's one in progress. Ungrateful kid.

"Okay," I say to Reece. "Not that we got much, but at least it's one less piece of shit running around. Let's get this all cleaned up."

My employee's eyebrows dip. "You didn't think it was worth trying to get him to give us information?"

"It's like I already said: Tony, the guy who paid him, is dead. There have been no more missing people from that side of town. More than likely they've shut it all down for now. The cop he mentioned isn't enough to go on. I've got a whole list of potentially corrupt guys in the Belle Argo precinct, and probably eighty percent of them match that extremely vague description. It's a dead end."

Still no response from my text to Ravi, so I send another.

Liam: I want you home when you're done with classes today.

"Everything okay?" Reece asks again.

"Fine. This kid's been a pain in my ass since day one, that's all. An even bigger one lately."

"The guys mentioned you had an adopted kid or something."

"Not adopted." Thank fuck. The last thing I need is to be someone's actual parent. "An old friend and his wife got killed about four years ago. We'd lost touch, but his will was old. No local family, so the kid ended up with me."

"Shit, that's got to be tough."

Reece starts rolling up our body in plastic. I get started hosing down the floor and dousing it all in bleach.

Ordinarily, talking to my employees about my personal life isn't something I would do. Lately Ravi's got my frustration leaking out all over the place. Sort of like the blood on this floor.

"He's stubborn like you wouldn't believe. I tried to go easy at first because his parents had been murdered, but I feel like that backfired. Almost got himself killed a couple of weeks ago, and he's still not listening to shit."

My phone lights up, finally, with a reply from Ravi. Not one I was hoping to see.

Ravi: My research indicates that light exercise is fine if I'm feeling up to it, and I am, thx!

With an IQ of one hundred fifty-four, you'd think he could at least spell properly.

"Kid doesn't listen to a damn thing I say," I mutter.

"Teenager?" Reece asks as he tapes up the body.

"Nineteen. Twenty in a few months."

Reece chuckles. "Yeah, they're all assholes at that age. I was. Weren't you?"

"Still am. Hey. How's your grandmother?"

Reece grins. "In remission. Thank fuck. Apparently she's made lots of friends in treatment, too, so her social life is more interesting than mine." He hoists the body over his shoulder. "I'll get this out to the truck. What project am I billing this to?"

"2740."

"That's, like, the internal code we use when we don't have anything else to bill to, right?"

"Exactly. We had a client a few months back who had tasked us with tracking down suspected trafficking victims. The names of the abductees were being pulled from their client list. We tracked down all the victims we could, so technically the project is over. This is us cleaning up loose ends."

This is me needing to cut the head off the monster. I've learned too much to think the world can truly be rid of evil, but I'm sure as fuck going to take as much of it with me as I can before I go.

Even though sometimes I'm one of the monsters.

"Got it." Reece gives me a halfhearted salute and lugs his bloody package out to the loading bay. Meanwhile, I tap out one more text, because I'm tired as hell and I never can leave well enough alone.

Liam: If you don't come the hell home after class, I will hunt you down.

CHAPTER TWO

RAVI

"HEY, Rav, you know you get more benefit from the weights if you're actually moving them. You taking a nap right now or what?" my sort-of friend Troy asks.

Shoving my phone into my pocket, I give an apologetic shrug. "Sorry. Did you want to use this one?"

"Nah." Troy, who's perched on a nearby weight bench, shakes his head. "Trying to make sure you're still with us is all."

Of all my sort-of friends, he's the one who seems to notice me most. I'm not sure why, but it's kind of nice. He's right though. At the moment all I'm doing is taking up space.

If my mother were here, she'd pinch my ear and tell me not to laze around.

"Oh. Uh. Thanks. Texting my guardian?" Calling him that feels weird. Calling him anything feels weird. He isn't a parent. He isn't a friend. He's... I don't know. He's Liam.

"Is he on your ass about the warehouse thing still?" Next to Troy, his roommate, Adam, pipes up.

"He doesn't think I should be here working out." I shrug again, because I'm not sure what else to do. Liam's always been sort of protective of me, but it gets worse as I get older, not better. "At least he hasn't found out I'm failing biology yet."

My friend PJ looks up from the mat he's been stretching on. "From what I've heard so far, this Liam guy sounds like a prison warden. You didn't OD on purpose. It's not like you have an addiction. Guy knows you're an adult, right?"

"I wish he'd understand I was trying to help people." I sigh.

There were innocent people being held in that warehouse. Trafficking victims. Liam can bluster all he wants, but one thing I'll never do is ignore people who need help. It hurts too much to do nothing. Especially after what happened to my parents. After knowing I was close enough to do something, and I didn't.

"Can't you tell the guy to fuck off?" Troy asks.

Sometimes I'd like to. A lot of times, really. But. Well. "He's paying my tuition, right? Until things change, I feel like I kind of have to keep him happy."

There's one small problem with that, though. Nothing makes Liam Masters happy.

I adjust my feet against the leg press and start counting reps again. I try, anyway. I barely make it to ten before my phone buzzes again. Liam's mad because he doesn't like how I answered his last message.

"He's making me stay at his place ever since the accident," I complain to nobody in particular. "He keeps yapping on about where I am. I'm pretty sure he's tracking my phone."

"That's intense," Troy murmurs. Adam nods in agreement, long hair bobbing in a bun.

My lit teacher, Mr. Monroe, seats himself at the pull-down machine next to me. "If you don't mind me asking, Ravi, how long have you lived with this guy?"

Too long.

"Since my parents were murdered." It's not something I like talking about, though. I don't like the pitying looks and the questions. "It was a little before my sixteenth birthday."

One month and four days. We were supposed to spend the weekend in Washington, DC, visiting the museums and art galleries. Dad was going to take us to this café I liked but was too far from our home in Virginia to visit often. Now I'm in Belle Argo, Florida, and my favorite café is nine hundred and two miles away.

I don't know why I bothered looking that up. Couldn't help myself.

"Not that I know from personal experience, but I'm sure it's a big responsibility taking care of a teenager whose parents have died," Mr. Monroe says. "I'm sure this Liam guy is only trying to protect you, even if it doesn't always feel that way."

A plausible argument, right? Except Liam Masters wasn't always like this. And I wish his protection didn't feel so much like iron-fisted control.

"I get what you're saying, Mr. Monroe, but I was already pretty close to being an adult when I went to live with him. He was away a lot for work back then anyway. He's gotten stricter with me since I turned eighteen."

Since the night I told him I loved him. Another mistake,

and like the warehouse incident, some mistakes can't be taken back.

"Ravi, I've told you, outside of class you can call me Fallon," Mr. Monroe says as he gets up to kiss PJ. I guess because he and PJ are dating, he's, like, friendlier with me outside of class? Still, it feels strange.

I'm happy for PJ though. He deserves to be with someone nice. Mr. Monroe is a nice guy. Even if I don't like the homework he assigns.

I don't want to write an essay about the family dog getting killed in *The Grapes of Wrath*, okay? It's so sad.

Off to the side though, someone is not as happy as Mr. Monroe and PJ. Mr. Monroe's brother, Wes. He teaches some class for the hospitality department, I think? Why he comes to the gym with us is beyond me, since he's always scowling at everyone in the group like he's disgusted. Especially by PJ and the openly possessive way he touches Mr. Monroe.

I'm not disgusted. The achy twist in my stomach at the sight of them is envy. What would it be like to belong to someone the way Mr. Monroe seems to belong to PJ?

Some things you can't find out from doing research, and I haven't really belonged anywhere since Amma and Pop died.

"I'll work on it," I say to try and appease Mr. Monroe before returning to my reps. I'm not sure I'm comfortable with it, though—calling my teacher by his first name, even outside of class.

Adam pipes up. "Hey, you said this Liam guy's former military, right? Bet that's why he's such a pain in the ass. Dated a girl who was in the Air Force for a little while. Those folks are all about routine and control."

"That does sound like Liam," I confirm.

For reasons I can't figure out, everyone all of a sudden gets weirdly silent. Troy puts down his weights and Adam puts down his water bottle. Everyone's staring at me. The only sounds are PJ clearing his throat and the rhythmic thud of Mr. Monroe's brother jogging on the treadmill.

"Hey, Rav," PJ comes over to stand next to the machine I'm using. "I know you think I'm beating this to death, but we're all pretty nervous about this auction thing you're planning to do."

Oh. This again.

I'm a male escort. We all are. Well, except for Mr. Monroe and his brother. But I'm sort of unique, I guess? I'm a male escort who's still a total virgin.

For now.

"Look, Brennan said auctioning off my virginity would make me a 'metric fuckton of cash.' His words, not mine."

Brennan's our pimp, I guess? He prefers to see himself as some sort of resource coordinator. Since what he's coordinating is people who want dates or sex with people who are willing to get paid to go on dates or have sex, I'm not sure how that's different from a pimp.

"There are a million other ways to make money," PJ protests.

He's trying to help. PJ always thinks he needs to look out for everyone else. It's nice to be on that list, it really is.

But.

The second I saw the look on Liam's face the night I told him I was in love with him, I knew I needed to get as far away from Belle Argo, Florida as possible. Getting away costs money.

My father loved old Western movies. There's that phrase

they use, something like "This town ain't big enough for the both of us." Well, Belle Argo isn't big enough for me with Liam Masters in it.

"The faster I can get out of town, the better," I tell them all. I focus on managing another ten reps rather than looking around, because I can guess at the looks on my sort-of friends' faces. I've seen it all before.

"Besides"—my body heats. I don't like the growl in my voice or how I can't keep my rising frustration down—"it doesn't make to sense give up my ass to a hundred guys over the course of months. Not when I can use this opportunity to make a bunch of money all in one shot."

Everything's quiet again, except the *clank* of the weight stack as I do each rep. Which makes me finally sit up and look at all of them. Everyone's looking sort of surprised. Or sad. Or in the case of PJ, his face is sort of angry and red?

"What are you all looking at?"

Adam swallows. "We, uh, didn't know you were planning to leave town."

"Oh." I take a breath, standing to wipe the machine. Nobody else does it here, but I can't stand not to. It's rude. "Well, it's for the best. And it's my decision. Not yours."

"Rav, we're trying to help," PJ insists.

It would be easier if they weren't.

Maybe I can travel around the country for a while. Maybe I'll find someplace that really feels like home. Someplace I belong.

When I bend down to the floor to retrieve my water bottle, my hand catches on a rough piece of metal at the base of the leg press machine. It's only a little blood, but the dizziness hits me before I can even straighten up again. My forehead bumps the machine, threatening an even worse problem.

"Not again," I murmur. I hate when this happens. With my hands braced on my knees, I try to steady myself so I can stand.

It doesn't help that after running into that warehouse, I've had some lingering issues. Since detoxing in the hospital, I'm doing better, but I still have weird spikes and dips in my blood pressure.

"Rav, are you okay? Here. Sit. I'll be right back." Troy guides me over to a bench before running out of the room.

Mr. Monroe is checking my forehead for some reason. I don't want to be rude, but I'm sure I don't have a fever.

"Your pulse is a little high," Adam says. I didn't even notice he'd grabbed my arm. I try to shake him off politely, if there even is such a thing.

"Guys, I'm fine." But they keep fussing.

"Here." Troy returns after a few minutes, shoving a green smoothie in my face. "Drink it. The veggies and fruit will help. I had them leave out the honey. I know you don't like it."

"Oh. Thanks." I'm not hungry, but I appreciate the gesture, so I take the drink. Besides, I seem to have the metabolism of a hummingbird. I've learned the hard way that I shouldn't skip meals even when I might prefer to.

"Since when did you become such a mother hen, man?" PJ pokes at Troy.

"Since always," Adam mutters. "Ask me how I know."

"Your body needs nutrients to recover from the damage the drugs did." Troy glares at Adam before returning his attention to me. "Saw it plenty on the street."

"Thanks, Troy." Drinking something green seems gross,

but I take a sip anyway. “Although, I’m guessing the guys you lived with on the street didn’t have access to kale smoothies.”

“Malnutrition is a huge problem, yeah. Which is why I know you need to drink that,” Troy insists.

Well. It’s easier to drink the smoothie than be rude, after he went to the trouble.

“Maybe you shouldn’t be working out yet,” Mr. Monroe suggests.

Even if he’s right, I’ll walk into traffic before I agree. If I agree with Mr. Monroe, then I’m agreeing with Liam. Which is not happening.

“I want to try and put on some muscle before the auction,” I explain.

“I say this with love, Rav,” Adam says, “but that’s not super likely. It takes months to put on muscle, and you’re...”

He doesn’t finish his sentence. He doesn’t need to.

The word is “skinny.” Small. Whatever. I’m five-five and about a hundred and twenty pounds, and that’s after putting effort into bulking up this past year.

“I’ve been making progress,” I insist. “Or I had been before the accident.” That’s what I’m calling it, because it *was* an accident. “The problem is I need to eat, like, three thousand calories a day to maintain my weight, and I haven’t had as much of an appetite this last couple of weeks.”

“The smoothie will help.” Troy nods as if a liquefied salad is the answer to all my problems. After a few sips I decide it actually doesn’t taste as awful as I thought it would, and besides, I am starting to feel a little better. The dizziness is passing.

“Rav. Is this Liam guy honestly so awful that you feel

like you need to leave town?" PJ asks. "I get it, you've got to do what you've got to do, but it'll suck. This auction idea is a nightmare. Besides, we'd all miss you."

They're probably only being nice, but still. I don't know if I'm touched or pissed. I love that they care. I hate how they're treating me like a kid.

"I'm sorry." I really, honestly am. Belle Argo is a nice place, and I'd rather not go. "I'm not sure about literally anything else in my life. But I'm sure about this."

"Is there something we can do to help?" Mr. Monroe asks. He looks side to side then back to me. "I think I speak for everyone here when I say if you're stuck in a difficult situation, you don't have to deal with it alone."

Everyone is still looking at me as if I've announced that I'm dying. I don't know how to answer these questions, and I don't like the squirmy feelings they give me. So, instead, I change the subject. "So, I was researching fetishes again last night..."

Everyone starts moaning and groaning. Which I knew they would. I almost laugh to myself. I tend to overshare in a big way, and lately I've been researching kinks and stuff. But this time it works to my advantage. Everyone has stopped looking at me with pity and quit asking me about the auction.

"Seriously, though, this auction thing could be hella dangerous," Troy says out of nowhere. "If a guy pays fifty grand or whatever to fuck you, what else are they going to think they have the right to do?"

Guess I spoke too soon.

My phone buzzes in my pocket.

Liam: If you don't come the hell home after class, I will hunt you down.

Anger clogs my throat as I flip the screen to show it to everyone. "This is the kind of thing I'm talking about. This is what I live with. It's why I have to do the auction, and it's why I can't stay in Belle Argo."

CHAPTER THREE

Ravi

I avoid making eye contact as I walk into the kitchen, heading straight for the fridge. After working out this morning and then a full day of lectures, I'm starving. Still, I can feel Liam's presence, large and looming on the other side of the room.

"Your last class was over an hour ago. You're late."

Being around Liam raises my blood pressure. Given my recent hospitalization, it's a bit of a problem.

Determined not to let him rattle me, I square my shoulders as I pull bread and jam from the refrigerator.

"Ravi, stop."

It's not a request. He says it the way he'd say it to the guys who work for him. When Liam Masters gives an order, my body responds before my brain.

I turn to face him, dropping my backpack, along with the bread and jam, on the kitchen counter with a sigh. Not that I'm good at staying still for long. When he doesn't speak after a second, I swerve around where he's seated at the kitchen counter to grab a plate and some peanut butter.

"You can't live off peanut butter sandwiches, kid."

Kid. I'm not a child. I turn twenty at the end of November.

"According to my research, peanut butter sandwiches can add approximately thirty-three minutes to your lifespan, Liam."

"Fuck's sake." He nods to a paper takeout bag sitting on the granite counter. "I got chana masala. Your favorite."

When I glance up he's rigid in his seat, with his unfairly chiseled jaw clenched. His dirty blond hair looks messier than usual, as if he's maybe run his hands through it a whole bunch. His blue-green eyes glow under the kitchen lights, sharp and assessing the way they always are. I've read too many fantasy novels. I keep expecting him to turn into something immortal that bites.

His hands are clasped on the counter in front of him, and I can see how tense he is by the way the muscles in his forearms sort of bulge. He's got a tattoo there of a skull with a snake, and the words "memento mori." Right now the snake looks as if it's slithering.

Since I seem to be a constant source of tension for Liam, I pretend not to notice the way his hand slides over his stubble. It's something he does when he's frustrated. Most of all, I pretend I'm not thinking of him slicing open his palm on his razor-sharp features, which gives me a disturbing sense of satisfaction.

Honestly, I try really hard not to be angry. Liam brings it out in me.

No. Stay positive. Silver linings and all that.

I return my focus to my sandwich making. I've got it

down to a science. Well-toasted whole wheat, a thin layer of vegan butter on each slice, peanut butter, and then strawberry jam. Always strawberry. Then a sprinkle of sea salt.

Liam tells me all the time how my way of making a PB&J is an insult to sandwiches, but honestly it's one of my favorite things. It's *so good*, in a place where good things are hard to find.

"Thanks for ordering dinner," I tell him. Because I do realize it was a thoughtful thing to do, even if Liam is generally kind of a dick. "Maybe I'll have some tomorrow."

Not that I can stomach the spices lately. Tomorrow I might.

"Sit down and eat a real meal for a change," he grits out.

"I'd honestly really like to do that, Liam, but my digestive system hasn't been great since the accident. I'm sorry, but I don't feel like I can handle a spicy meal right now."

That sounded mature. Right?

"I talked to the owner. Told him you weren't feeling well. He said he'd make it mild." He glares at me as if I should be grateful for the effort he's gone to on my behalf.

I do have to acknowledge the effort.

Except the owner of Spice Road Grill knows us, and he knows I'm Indian. Indian mild isn't mild-mild, which Liam ought to know.

"Thank you. Maybe tomorrow," I say again.

There's always a sour taste in the back of my throat when I thank him for things, because I'm not convinced he's ever doing them to actually be nice. It's obligation.

I'm an obligation. That's all I've ever been.

"What the fuck ever, kid," he mutters under his breath.

Liam and I didn't always clash the way we do now. At first he at least—sort of grudgingly—taught me things.

How to shoot a gun and some self-defense stuff. How to change a tire. Even hung out with me when I was sick or struggling. Which is probably how I got so attached.

Still, it's always been clear my presence was inconvenient. I'm not sure what it says about me that I developed a crush on him anyway.

I probably ought to research Stockholm syndrome.

"How is your digestion going to get any better if you're eating the same damn food every day?"

"I had a smoothie earlier." At lunch I tried getting a burrito on campus. Couldn't even take more than a bite. Lesson learned.

"Ravi." His clenched fist lands on the counter, bringing my gaze up to his. "When are you going to take responsibility for your actions? What happened to you wasn't an accident. You ran naked into a drug warehouse. You nearly died."

There's a sinking sensation in my stomach. Does he think I don't know? "Newsflash, Liam: it's not like I wanted to die. How was I supposed to know there were drugs in there?"

His face reddens, but he doesn't answer.

I slam the knife into my sandwich a little too enthusiastically, cutting it diagonally into triangles. It's how my mom always used to cut my sandwiches. They don't taste the same otherwise.

Liam yanks open a cabinet door with a huff and starts plopping rice and spicy chickpeas onto the plate he pulls out. The smell of the samosas almost gets me to reconsider, but they're deep fried, and nope. My stomach rebels at the mere thought of all that oil.

"You've got to grow up, Ravi. You keep doing impulsive,

reckless shit like this? You're going to end up like your parents."

He doesn't understand. I do reckless shit *because* of how my parents ended up.

What's the point of being responsible and safe when you might be gone tomorrow?

"I'm not a married man who's sleeping with a mentally unstable art student," I argue. "It's not even close to the same thing."

His hand slams on the counter again. "Don't pretend to be so fucking obtuse. You're more like your dad than you think. Careless. Just because you're not an art professor who's fucking his models doesn't make that less true."

Wow. I know it's rude, but I'm kind of giving him the finger. Mentally.

I grab an orange out of the bowl on the kitchen table and pour myself some almond milk. There's no point in trying to argue. Once Liam's sure he's right, there's no changing his mind. And Liam is Always Right.

Except...one thing bothers me more and more lately. "I don't understand why you even care."

"Your father asked me to look after you. It's my job."

Is that all I am, then? A job?

"I'm not a kid anymore. If my parents were still alive, their job would be done. So is yours. Since I annoy you so much, why don't you let me move back into my dorm room, and then you won't have to deal with that vein throbbing in your temple anymore?"

It's admittedly a little bit satisfying when he scowls and rubs at the side of his head. As if that will stop his actual blood from flowing. I may be failing biology, but even I know the answer to that one.

I hook my backpack over my arm and gather up my almond milk and my plate.

I make it a total of two steps before he asks me, "What's your association with Brennan Doyle?"

I freeze where I am. "How many times are you going to ask me that?"

When Liam picked me up from the hospital a couple of weeks ago, Brennan happened to be in my room. It was nice of him to visit me, but not the greatest timing. Liam's been like a dog with a bone ever since.

"Until you give me an honest answer."

Here's the problem: I've never lied. Not about this. It's not my fault Liam won't believe me.

I'm pretty sure this is an interrogation tactic. Asking me the same question over and over to see if my answer changes. Too bad for him, *I'm not lying*. Also, I've learned his tactics by now.

"Look, he pays me to dance at parties. Sometimes dinner dates, but those usually go to the taller guys. I'm not having sex with anybody. Even if I was, I'm old enough to have sex with whoever I want. It's not illegal, and it's nobody's business."

Least of all yours.

Anger and want make my pulse race. There was a time when I'd have given anything for it to be Liam's business. Maybe it's a simple fact that teenage hormones caused me to crush on the sentient marble statue who swooped in to rescue me when my world turned upside down? That's all long gone, though, believe me.

I mean...more or less.

I'm working on it.

"It's illegal if you're getting paid for it, kid."

"I'm. Not. Having. Sex. With. Anyone." I practically spit each word through my teeth. "One client likes me to hang out and play chess with him. There's nothing illegal about that."

I don't know why I bother. He's never going to listen.

This is another problem with Liam. When I'm around him, I'm practically a different person. Not at all who my parents raised me to be.

I'm not mentioning the auction. That part is definitely a legal gray area. Brennan is good at getting around these things, though. That's why I chose to let him handle setting it all up. Sure, he's going to take a cut of the money, but with that comes security.

Like peanut butter and jelly sandwiches, I'll take security where I can.

Yes, Liam tries to keep me safe. Most of the time, though, it feels more like prison than safety. Like he's my warden, the way PJ said.

There's a special kind of hurt that comes from knowing the person who helped raise you sees you as a burden. Knowing all I'll ever be to him is a child? A job?

It *aches*. Every time he reminds me, it's as if he took his favorite knife right to my sternum.

"Brennan Doyle is a lowlife, Ravi. A criminal. Associating with him is going to get you arrested."

I bite down on the inside of my cheek. Blood adds to the anger coating my tongue. Even though I don't love the sight of it, I strangely don't mind the taste. I'm weird that way.

"How about this? If I get into trouble, I won't call you. Okay? I know you think I do stupid things, so how about we agree my stupid things are none of your business?"

"I'm protecting you from your fucking self, kid. It's my business as long as I'm the one paying for your education."

Asshole. Once I get the money from the auction, he won't be able to hold my education over my head. I'll hopefully be able to pay my own way for everything. Not at BAU, obviously. It's a good school and all, but you pay a premium for the fact that Belle Argo is a beach town. I'll go someplace with a cheaper cost of living.

And no Liam.

I squeeze the orange tucked against my palm enough to squish it a little.

"Nobody asked you to do that," I say quietly. "You announced it was happening with zero discussion. Like everything else."

"It's part of taking care of you," Liam says, almost as quietly. He makes me the most nervous when he's quiet, honestly. When he's quiet, I get the feeling of being in the den of a sleeping dragon. The eye of a hurricane.

I lift my chin, refusing to let him intimidate me. Okay, well, the way my heart is hammering is hard to get past, but I refuse to let him see.

There's this former escort I know. Simon. He's not awkward or worried about inconveniencing people the way I always am. He's sassy and unapologetically himself. Simon wouldn't let anyone make him nervous, least of all Liam.

So what would Simon do right now?

Straightening my back, I march up to him. He's too tall for me to get right in his face usually, but I can now when he's sitting on a kitchen stool. So I do.

When I lean in I can smell his aftershave. The earthy scent has me salivating more than the nearby bag of food.

"I don't need you to take care of me, Liam. I don't even

want you to. You're not my parent." I give him a bold once-over. "But you could be my daddy if you wanted."

The subtle noise he makes, almost like a quiet cough, feels like victory. Ha. Bet that rattled him. I ignore the shiver that runs down my spine. The way my blood rushes south, maybe it rattled me, too.

Take that, Liam.

Vibrating with adrenaline, I take my food and race upstairs. When I get to my room, I lock the door.

Then I eat my sandwich, send a text to the escorts' group chat, and shove open the window.

Carefully, quietly, I grab my backpack and slide out onto the roof that covers the downstairs barbecue area. I may be an adult, but I know what will happen if I try to leave tonight. So, listening for any sign of footsteps, I hold my breath as I slide down one of the support posts and tiptoe to my car parked around the side of the house.

I don't breathe again until I'm on the road.

Fuck you, Liam.

CHAPTER FOUR

LIAM

RAVI HAS LEFT HOME.

Jesus fucking Christ. "Goddamn kid never learns."

"What was that, boss?"

I'm cleaning up the kitchen. Putting away the food I bought for an ungrateful little shit who wouldn't even eat it.

I reach over and mute the speakerphone, letting out a string of expletives. I swear to God this kid tries my patience at every turn.

With a deep breath, I unmute the call. "Sorry about that, Sal. Ravi's been getting into some scrapes lately." To put it mildly. "I have a feeling he's about to get into another one."

"Something you need help with?"

"Not at all." No, because if Ravi gets himself into the kind of shit that requires my entire team, I'll murder him myself.

He's lucky. I didn't know about him tagging along to Brennan Doyle's little "Set Fire to the Competition" warehouse party until it was too late. I was on my way back from a job in Europe at the time. If I'd been here, I would have stopped him.

Part of this is on me. I should have paid better attention. We'd been clashing for the last year and a half or so, and I'd thought it better to give him his space. I gave him too much.

When he first came to live with me, I hated how Ravi constantly followed me. The responsibility weighed heavier than a chock-full tactical pack. Now, I'd take back those days in a heartbeat.

The days before Ravi climbed into bed with me and made it clear he didn't see me as anything resembling a parent. Because after? Well, I keep pushing away the questions that night created.

Sal continues. "Uh, okay, so I wanted to make sure you were up to speed on the three of us heading out tonight to Mexico, and then Bev's got some sort of..."

While my employee gives me a rundown on everything I missed while I was out of the office today, I climb the stairs to Ravi's bedroom.

There's more swearing on my part while I hunt down the spare key to his lock and bust in to find what I already know. The room is empty; Ravi's gone. The window, which leads onto the roof of the covered back porch, is cracked open.

The part I didn't expect? His phone is on the bed.

Did he leave it accidentally, or does he think that's how I keep tabs on him? It would be a reasonable assumption.

"Boss?"

Fuck.

"Didn't catch that, Salvatore. Say it again."

"Since some of us are going to be out of office for the rest of the week, are there any priority items that need to be addressed before wheels-up?"

As I scan the room, looking past anime posters and one for a band called Young the Giant, in the hopes of finding some clue as to where my missing ward might have gone. While I'm flipping through some spicy looking romance novels on the bedside table, his phone starts pinging like a cash register.

Brennan: Got the date nailed down. Two weeks from tomorrow.

Brennan: Hope you're ready. Gonna be a big night.

Brennan: Any questions or concerns you talk to me immediately, okay?

Brennan: We're laying out a lot of money for this, so I don't want any cold feet. Play your cards right, and you could walk away a millionaire.

A million dollars. What the actual fuck for? I'm already spinning up ideas, and each one makes my gut tighten.

Brennan's texts are vague enough that it could be anything, but anything Brennan Doyle's asking Ravi to do for that kind of money... I don't even want to think about it.

"Boss?"

"One second, Sal."

Taking a chance, I pick up Ravi's phone and unlock it with my face. I set myself up as an alternate facial ID ages ago. I'm glad I did.

Then I reply to the message, in the hopes of drawing out more information.

Ravi: I can't remember if you already told me where.

It's a risky question. It could be the thing that tips Brennan off to me not being Ravi if Ravi already knows the answer. But the kid's got ADHD, and his brain seems to prioritize random facts about penguins and peanut butter sandwiches over things like appointments or when he last ate.

Brennan: Still TBD, but I'm working on Shadow for the venue.

My stomach turns at the thought. Shadow. A very private, very exclusive kink club. For damn sure it's not a place where a kid like Ravi should go. Ever. He's too innocent for whatever Brennan Doyle's trying to mix him up in.

I've killed men for less.

Jaw clenched, I throw out one more lure to see what it gets me.

Ravi: Do you really think this will work?

Brennan: You think I'd be putting in this kind of time if I didn't? You said you wanted to make big money fast. This is the way to do it. Just putting out teasers for the auction, we've already got enough interested parties to fill a concert hall. Nothing brings the perverts out of the woodwork like wafting a virgin who's kink curious right under their noses. It's better than waving a red flag at a bull.

My fist tightens so hard my short nails dig into my skin. A virgin. Interested parties. A million dollars. This has got to be a sick joke.

Rereading the text, my brain snags on the word "auction." Is this kid really stupid enough to try to sell his virginity to the highest bidder? Is that what the hell this is about?

If it were anybody else, I'd dismiss it as ridiculous. But it's Ravi, and he's got his father's charming but terrifying combination of fantasy thinking and impulsivity. This is the exact sort of mess he'd wander into simply because he spotted something shiny.

One of these days his wandering will get him killed. It already almost has.

Nothing much scares me anymore. I've seen and done too much twisted shit. I'm not afraid of the monsters because I am the monster. The thought of Ravi doing something this dangerous fills me with icy terror.

Bringing myself under control, I send the one response that I know for sure Ravi would have to Brennan's last message.

Ravi: Bullfighting is animal abuse

Brennan: Ha. Fucking bleeding heart. You're a goddamn unicorn, you know that? Let's meet up tomorrow so we can hammer out details.

I send a thumbs-up before exiting out of the message thread and then deleting it entirely. Ravi won't be meeting with Brennan, but I will. This lowlife's got his hooks too far into my ward. It's my job to get them out.

A subtle throat clear from my phone's speaker reminds me my employee is still on the other end.

"Sal."

"Yeah, boss?"

"You hear any chatter about an upcoming auction at Shadow? Something about someone auctioning off their virginity?"

The thought of a bunch of slavering old men with older money waving their fists full of cash, all for the opportunity to be the person to destroy a nineteen-year-old twink? While he's being paraded around like livestock? No fucking way. Makes me sick.

"Uh, sure, boss. You've always got us keeping feelers out for possible trafficking shit, so that was an immediate red flag. Only this time it didn't sound like the product was unwilling."

"He's not a product. He's a fucking human being."

Sal's quiet for a second. "We know, boss. You know how it can be in this business. Apologies."

Right. Detachment. Dehumanizing. Gallows humor. It's all common in our line of work when you see the things we've seen.

"Understood, Sal. Just trying to keep some perspective."

"Yes, sir."

"I need anything further you guys can dig up on that auction. Anything."

"Absolutely. I'll pass it off to Bev. No doubt there's something online somewhere. If there is, she'll find it, sir."

"Much appreciated, Sal."

"No problem, boss. Anything else?"

While he talks, I do a quick pass, carefully but thoroughly tossing Ravi's room. He's mostly been staying in the dorms since the school year started, but he's left a lot here. And I brought more of his belongings here a couple of weeks ago after his impulsivity landed him in the hospital.

As I rifle through drawers and flip through notebooks and sketchbooks for any other sign of what else he might be up to, I get a notification that Ravi has arrived at a destination in the East End. I know the place. Some shitty apartment complex where the landlord is known to take payment in cash, among other things. It's the sort of place people live when they don't want anyone to ask too many questions.

Dammit, Ravi.

Sliding my hands under his mattress turns up nothing, but my hands hit something hard under his pillow. Lube. And a fairly large dildo. Christ.

Before I know what I'm doing, I find myself running my shaking fingers along the silicone, tracing over the veins and down to the base. Which has a suction cup.

Fuck me.

Clearing my throat, I fight to wipe away the instant mental image of him *using* these things. I drop the pillow like it's a live grenade, hastily scooting the stuffed bear Ravi's mother gave him back into its place on top.

"One more thing," I say at last, deciding to let Sal off the hook. "Get me Brennan Doyle's current location. Immediately."

"Understood. You want me to send backup, sir?"

Fuck, no. The last thing I need is my entire team finding out that the kid whose welfare I'm fucking responsible for is the one out there selling off first dibs at his ass.

"Not this time."

CHAPTER FIVE

Ravi

"Do you think I need to tell Brennan? About all of Liam's questions?"

My fellow escort, Dean, is behind me, pretending to grind while I lean my head back against his chest. Or sort of more like his stomach? He's at least a foot taller than me. It's awkward.

The party we're performing at tonight is quiet enough for us to talk. Unlike some of the parties rich college kids and twenty-somethings throw, there's no pounding music or flashing lights.

It's strange. Gleaming hardwood floors and a baby grand piano. Lots of drinks and cigars and low lighting. It's what I imagine a stuffy cocktail party would be like, only someone decided to toss in some go-go dancers.

Oh, and the attendees are all men. So are all the catering staff, as far as I can tell.

Dean chews his lip as he considers my question. "When

in doubt, always talk to Brennan. If you even think a little bit that something might be an issue, it's better if he knows first. Trust me."

"Got it. You're right. That makes sense." The thing is, I don't want to start a fight. Brennan Doyle is a criminal, and Liam hunts criminals. That could be bad.

Dean makes a good point, though, and I trust his opinion. A lot of the other escorts think he's not the brightest star in the sky, but he's wise in a way a lot of people aren't. Probably because he's got a kid, so all of his decisions are based on what's safest or most practical.

Liam would probably disagree, but I'm actually good with doing the safe thing so long as it's practical. Liam, on the other hand, likes safe and impractical.

Speaking of impractical... Usually these parties have some kind of a stage or something. A platform for us to dance on. This one is different. We're in some rich guy's condo; the music is sensual and drum-based but fairly quiet. Reminds me of the "chill-out room" they had once when I went to a rave. But the lack of a designated space for us means sometimes the customers creep in a little too close.

Adam and Troy are a few feet away, dancing on the other side of the piano. They move almost like they're one person.

It's a small crowd, with all the attendees in business attire. Which makes it feel weirder that I'm over here dancing in nothing but a pair of skintight shorts.

In front of us is a cluster of older, wealthy men drinking cocktails and studying us all with naked interest in their eyes. They all speak too quietly for me to hear what they're saying, but I know it's about us based on the way they nod and stare.

They're sizing us up. Appraising.

"Try not to think too hard about it," Dean murmurs from behind me. "We're basically here to be art. Furniture. Like that weird carved table over in the corner."

Occasionally the group of men will edge closer, one at a time or gathered in clusters. Brennan made it clear to the party host that there's no touching allowed, but occasionally one will stuff some cash into our shorts and use that as an opportunity to cop a feel. So far tonight I've had five guys "accidentally" brush their hands against my dick while they were tipping me.

The good news? I haven't seen anything smaller than a fifty. It's all going into my travel fund.

"What lovely specimens," one guy says as he comes forward. At first I assume he's talking to himself. Most of the guys don't address us directly. We're performance art, as Dean said.

Then he says, "I'd love to see the two of you kiss." He holds up some cash. "A hundred for each of you."

At first, the idea feels weird. Dean's kind of a friend. Sort of older-brother-ish. But if there's one thing I've learned about this group, it's that the boundaries can get sort of incestuous, especially if we're getting paid for stuff.

So, I glance up at Dean to see what he thinks. He shrugs and leans down, pressing his lips against mine. At first it's really chaste. No different from the time Penny Mackenzie kissed me at my old school's fall festival during freshman year of high school.

Still, it feels good. Makes my lips tingle.

Then the guy with the cash goes "Come on, boys, you can do better than that" so Dean slips his tongue into my mouth, stroking it against mine. He slides his hands under my ass, lifting me off the ground some.

With a yelp, I wrap my legs around his waist. More to steady myself than anything. But even though Dean is supposedly straight, I guess the friction of me rubbing against him has an effect, because we're both getting hard. For a while I close my eyes, letting the sensations wash over me.

This is officially the furthest I've gone with a guy.

It's pretty good, too. Dean's body is big and solid, which I like, and with my eyes closed I can pretend he's someone I'd be more attracted to.

Honestly, I like older guys. Daddy issues or whatever. My working theory is that every escort in our group has them.

I'm squirming around as Dean hikes my ass upward to get a better grip, my erection sliding up his and back down again a couple of times. Enough that I'm suddenly feeling an orgasm building.

Which is when Dean lets go, setting me down somewhat haphazardly on the floor.

"Sorry," he murmurs against my ear before straightening. "Can't risk making you come in front of everybody. Brennan would murder me. Besides, we don't want to give the vultures an opening."

He glances toward where the one guy was standing in front of us. Only now it's an entire group. As in, everyone except the kitchen staff seems to be gathered around out here, watching, panting, and eyeing the two of us like a pack of hyenas ready to set into some baby zebras.

"What do you mean?" I whisper to Dean. "About giving them an opening?"

"If they see me dry humping you into an orgasm, they might think you're on the menu. And you're not, at least not until your auction. Plus, no offense, but you're not a big guy. And those guys?" He nods to the crowd. "They always think the little guys are easy for them to step on."

Oh. Yikes.

See what I mean about Dean being wise? "I hadn't thought about it like that."

"No worries, buddy. I'll keep an eye out for you."

Then the guy who was grinding his hard dick against mine less than a minute ago pats me on the head as if I'm a lost child who needed help finding his parents.

"That was even better than I thought it would be." The man with the cash steps forward, shoving what appears to be more than the original hundred he promised into our hot pants.

Once again, he "accidentally" strokes my cock. This guy's not even subtle about it. He's not attractive, either; at least not to me. He's sort of bald, with that thing where they try to comb their hair in a way that hides the baldness, but it really doesn't. And he's a little paunchy, which is fine. He just doesn't look like someone who spent twenty years in the military and still does push-ups every morning.

He's not Liam.

Okay, never mind. The point is that even though he's not the sort of guy I'd choose to sleep with, I'm already hard, and I can't help the way his touch gives me a shiver.

It's probably a good thing for me to get used to. As I look around the room, I realize there's a better than average chance that anyone who has the kind of money to win an auction for my virginity is likely to look like one of these dudes. Or even be one of them. I don't see anyone who looks younger than fifty.

"Uh, thanks," I say when the guy pulls away. Not that I'm thanking him for stroking my dick, but you know.

My mom would kick my ass for disrespecting my elders. She never addressed the situation of my elders groping me, but I don't know. Habit?

Across the piano from us, Troy makes a drinking motion. It's nice, I guess. He keeps reminding me to stay hydrated. Keeps reminding Adam to check his blood sugar. He's awfully goofy a lot of the time but then also seems to worry about taking care of people?

"Come on." Dean tugs on my hand. "Troy's right. Good time for a water break."

Maybe it's my imagination, the way all the guys seem to be watchful of me. At first I'd taken it to mean they thought I was too soft and too weak for the business. Maybe it did. After I was in the hospital from a face full of some new street drug, they were even more protective. But Simon, who recently quit the business after getting his nursing degree, told me that the escorts in Belle Argo take care of their own.

It's the first time I've ever felt like I fit in anywhere. I've even started thinking of them as friends. Whether they think the same of me, I'm not sure. I'm not sure whether friendship is the same thing as loyalty.

Hopefully I'll find a place to fit in wherever I end up moving to.

Dean drags me to a closed bedroom where we've all stashed our stuff, pulls out a bottle of water from his gym bag, and hands it to me. Then he also hands over a granola bar. Must be a dad thing, because Dean's always got snacks.

"It's the kind that has veggies hidden in it," he explains. "My daughter loves them."

"Oh. Thanks. That's nice." It's sweet, is what it is—the

way Dean probably searched around for healthy snacks for his kid. Sweet in a way that slices into the tender skin on my stomach.

After a few sips of water and scarfing down the bar under Dean's watchful eye, we leave the room to get back to the party.

We're stopped in the hall by a man I haven't seen before. Maybe he arrived late? He's younger than some of these other ones, maybe a little older than Liam, with darker hair and a straighter nose (Liam has the look of a guy who has definitely been in some fights, including a slightly crooked nose).

"Very hot out there, the two of you," the man says. He's nice looking but also seems a little too slick. Like the guy I bought my crappy old car from. Maybe this guy also "forgets" to tell people about previous accidents and the fact that there's no spare tire.

For some reason Dean's hand is clamped down on my shoulder. Painfully. It's hard not to want to squirm away, but the tension in his body tells me something's not quite right.

Or maybe it's the vibe from this guy, who definitely seems shady. Maybe not in a used car salesman way, but in a way I can't quite put my finger on.

"Dylan Beck," he says, holding his hand out.

"We need to get back," Dean insists. "Mr. Oak doesn't like it when we take long breaks."

"Oh, of course," this Dylan guy says. "Gotta give everyone their money's worth. Speaking of which..." He turns to me. "You're the one Brennan's holding an auction for, is that correct?"

"Uh, yeah?"

I don't know why but he seems to find that funny. "Wonderful." He looks me up and down. God only knows what he's thinking, but I can make some guesses. "What would you say to a preemptive bid? Two million. I'll write you a check right now and you can skip the hassle of the auction."

Holy shit.

I'm struck speechless. I'm pretty sure my mouth is hanging open. Two million is an awful lot of money. An awful, awful lot. More than Brennan said I might make, and enough to cover college tuition pretty much anywhere even after I gave a cut to Brennan.

It's the kind of money I'm afraid to turn down. Looking at this guy though? The idea of saying yes makes me queasy.

Before I can formulate an answer though, Dean is hauling me away. "I'm so sorry, Mr. Beck, but any offers have to go through Brennan Doyle. I'm sure you understand."

Usually Dean has a slight southern accent. He was born in Georgia, but I think he said his family had moved north for a while before he came to Belle Argo. All of a sudden, though, his accent's a lot thicker and more...syrupy?

"Of course. I understand completely," this Beck guy says with a smile that doesn't actually look all that friendly.

He's not moving aside so we can get back to the party though. The weird thing is, he's almost supernaturally pretty, if you discount his vibe. I guess his eyes are a bit cold. Still, he doesn't strike me as a guy who needs to pay for sex. Maybe he's into some of the more fringe stuff? I shouldn't be curious, but I kind of am.

"Dylan, there you are." Another man comes up from behind this Mr. Beck guy, slapping a hand on his shoulder.

"We should really go and sit down with Mr. Silva. He doesn't like to be kept waiting. Sorry about my friend here; he forgets his manners sometimes." Whoever this new guy is, he directs the last part at me and Dean.

With a last look at me, Mr. Beck reluctantly turns away to follow his friend down the hall.

"I may not know about much," Dean whispers as we make our way back into the main room of the party, "but almost nobody in our group has worked for Brennan longer than I have. A few years ago one of our guys had a weekend boyfriend experience with Dylan Beck and afterward turned up in a downtown alley bleeding out with a broken jaw. After he got out of the hospital, the kid went back to Ohio like his ass was on fire. There was never any proof that Beck was responsible, but if you ask me, he's someone to stay the heck away from."

"Thanks," I tell him, both grateful for the information and grateful Liam isn't here. It's exactly the kind of story he'd use to slap me with a giant "I told you so."

As if thinking of Liam conjures him, there's movement in one cluster of men over by the condo's entrance. I'm convinced I can see his ocean eyes through the crowd. Then I blink again, and I realize the blue is light glinting off a wall hanging and I need to get a grip. Liam wouldn't be caught dead in a place like this. Anyway, I left my phone at home so he couldn't track me.

What I do see, though, is Dylan Beck glaring at me from the far wall. Yeesh.

Wait. Wasn't he supposed to be meeting with someone?

The same old man from earlier returns, waving more money at me and Dean. "I want to see you kiss him again."

Dean sighs quietly.

"We don't have to do it just because they ask us to, do we?" I ask quietly.

He shakes his head. "It's fine. I've done worse for less."

My stomach drops. What does that mean?

Suddenly making out seems a lot less fun. A glance at my watch tells me it's a little after midnight. Hopefully this thing is over soon.

CHAPTER SIX

LIAM

WHEN I FIND Brennan Doyle at Belle Argo Executive Links, one of the private courses here in town, he's still playing his first hole.

"I thought this place closed at seven." By the time I finished searching Ravi's room and got the call back from Sal about Brennan's location, dusk was bleeding into the sky. Now, it's past the time when most decent people would be turning in for the night.

Brennan Doyle, whose neck tattoo makes a liar out of the neatly pressed khakis and golf shirt he's wearing, gives me a shit-eating grin.

"For other people, sure. You gotta be willing to tip well," he says. "And you gotta know the right people."

When he nods his head at the person playing with him, I realize he looks familiar. Ty Danes. The fucking county prosecutor. Of course.

No wonder Brennan Doyle never sees the inside of a cell.

All my intentions of going into this calm fly out the window when I blurt, "What the hell do you think you're doing putting a kid up for auction like a piece of meat, you sick bastard?"

Brennan lowers the driver he'd been about to swing and cuts his gaze over to Ty. "I am definitely not putting a child up for auction," he says slowly. "I am facilitating a charity auction in which the prize is a twenty-four-hour-long date with a legal adult, and there is no expectation of sex."

Jesus, that's rich. Like throwing out the word charity makes dirty old men bidding for the kid's innocence any less disgusting. I'm itching to break this guy's fucking face.

"A charity auction? Are you fucking high? What's the charity? You?"

Brennan's grin raises my hackles. It's sharp and smug and has a heavy dose of I-know-something-you-don't-know. He probably does. That's why I'm here.

Still, I'd like to take a chunk out of his flesh or break his kneecap for that smarmy, self-congratulating look of his. Not to mention his ridiculous fucking baby face. Brennan Doyle is a couple of years older than I am, but he's got the look of a man half his age. Can't even see any stubble from here. Surely that would justify shooting both kneecaps.

Brennan plants his driver in the grass, leaning on it like a cane. "It's an education fund. A private education fund. Proceeds go to the young *man* being auctioned." The way he leans heavily on the word "man" doesn't help my mood.

Before I know it, I've drawn my gun, barrel aimed at Doyle's smug face.

"I'd be careful if I were you, Mr. Masters." He gestures to the two caddies off to the side, one of whom is obviously security. He's taller and leaner than Brennan and more heavily tattooed. He's got a golf bag over one shoulder and one hand holding the pistol that's aimed my way. The other caddy is a lanky redhead who looks barely able to handle the thirty or so pounds of weight in the golf bag he's carrying. But he's also pointing a gun in my direction.

Brennan Doyle's not only selling kids. He's also arming them. Big fucking surprise.

This is what I get for charging in here without clearing my head. Ravi drives me so fucking crazy I can't see straight. With the odds against me and the course exit half a mile from this tee, my only move is to holster my weapon.

I study Brennan, debating how to proceed. It's impossible to live in Belle Argo without knowing who he is, but our interactions until now have been minimal. Thank fuck.

"How much would it take for you to call it off?"

"More than you've got." Brennan laughs, making me want to shoot him anyway and damn the consequences.

Piece of shit.

"How the hell would you know how much money I have?" My general wardrobe may be a T-shirt and tactical pants, making me look like nobody special, but my company is doing well. Only three years after retiring from the military, I've got nearly a dozen employees, and we make a premium by taking on investigation cases, search and rescue, and even the occasional hit that's too hot for anyone else to handle.

"Seriously?" The look I get from Brennan suggests he genuinely doesn't understand my question. "I know your line of work, Liam Masters, so I *know* I don't need to tell you how many sickos are willing to pay for an innocent kid on the black market. Now you take a young man like Ravi, all legal and shit, but also super naive, with big anime kitten eyes and the physical stature of someone who's not yet old enough to drive? What the hell do you think is going to happen?"

"You disgusting piece of shit." Reducing Ravi to a cartoon fantasy for pedophiles? My gun may be back in its holster, but I haven't taken my hand off the grip. I should empty my clip into him for that line alone. "They're going to tear him apart like a pack of rabid dogs."

The thought compresses my lungs. I try not to picture the kind of damage the wrong buyer could do. I've seen too much not to.

"They'll pry open their bank accounts like it's a goddamn fire sale." He raises one speculative eyebrow. "You know, you don't give the young man enough credit."

No, I do. I give him exactly enough credit. I know what he's capable of. And that's the problem.

"Your text said he could be a millionaire. I can pay you a million."

I hate the words and myself as soon as I've spoken. Bargaining for Ravi makes me no better than the rest of the sickos. But I'm doing it for his protection.

Brennan tsks. "Funny, I don't remember texting that information to you." He gives his driver an experimental swing. "For the record, I think it's going to go higher. Didn't want to get the young man's hopes up, but it will." He gives me a knowing look. "For some reason Ravi's in a real hurry to get out of Belle Argo."

Fucker. Ravi hating me enough to run away? It hurts worse than any bullet I've taken.

We've butted heads more lately, but that seems extreme. Besides, Brennan is an instigator. He loves to stir up shit. He's lying. He'd better be lying.

"Whatever you may think, Brennan, Ravi's still a kid. It wasn't that long ago that his parents were murdered. You know as well as I do how trauma messes with people's heads. Among other things, it negatively impacts their decision-making."

He laughs. "Unless you're about to show me a court order letting me know the kid, as you call him, no longer has the legal right to make his own decisions, then this has all of jack and shit to do with you. We both know that wouldn't happen, because Ravi's too fucking smart. No judge in the world would hand you legal guardianship of him now. You've got no say here. That's probably eating you alive, isn't it?"

I stand there seething as he repositions his driver at the tee, frowns at it, and then holds it out to the taller, tattooed caddy. "Jalen, give me the Calloway, if you would, please."

Please. Brennan Doyle, gentleman. I almost laugh.

Except I'm having some trouble shaking off his comment. *You've got no say here. That's probably eating you alive, isn't it?*

On the outside, I won't dignify that with a response. Inside? He's right. It's burning in my veins like battery acid.

"You know... I have to say I'm surprised, Masters." Brennan lines himself up and takes a swing. We all follow the path of the ball as it sails down the fairway.

I've had too many years in the field to be gullible enough to take his bait. But I chomp on it anyway, like the desperate man I am.

"Surprised at what, Doyle?"

"Surprised you haven't fucked that kid yet yourself. He's practically begging for it. If you did, then all of this—" He makes a motion that I assume is meant to indicate our conversation. "—would be a moot point."

"Are you fucking crazy? I'm his guardian."

Deep down where my shame lives, my body stirs. Peering cautiously from behind the part of me that's horrified by the suggestion of fucking Ravi, something I've made every effort to suppress wakes up. There's bile in my throat even as my cock thickens against my will.

Images fill my head. One of Ravi with his legs wrapped around another man at that party, his tongue down his throat. The veiny, realistic dildo under his pillow.

The night he turned eighteen comes back to me full force. The night he climbed into my bed. *I don't want you to be my friend or my parent, Liam. I don't love you that way. I want more.*

You're not my parent, but you could be my daddy if you wanted.

"You're fucking disgusting." I'm scolding Doyle as much as myself. Then, to twist the knife, I add, "I guess you can't help seeing kids like him as nothing more than someone to use. To sell. I guess he's lucky you haven't tried to use him yourself. Rumor is, you like to sample your own merchandise."

Brennan gives me a grin that makes me want to tear his face off. "Because I'm not too stupid to recognize an opportunity, even if it's standing in front of me all curious and horny as hell. And that *kid*—" He gives me a pointed look. "—is going to make us all a lot of fucking money."

He slides the driver back over to his tattooed caddy and gives me his back. "You gonna join us for a game, Masters, or did you want to sling some more pointless bullshit?"

I assess the four men in front of me. I'm a quick shot. I

could probably get a slug into Brennan Doyle before anybody else could react. If I did, it might do the trick. It might protect Ravi.

But Brennan said us. Ravi's going to make "us all" a lot of money.

"Who's us, Brennan?"

"What now?" He turns around, looking annoyed that I'm still here. He's already dismissed my presence. Fuck him.

"You said he's going to make us all a lot of money. Who's us?"

"Oh Jesus, you're full of shit. You know as well as I do these things aren't a one-man operation. There's me, there's Rav, and then there's everyone else involved. If you think I'm dumb enough to name names, you're not the guy I thought you were, Masters."

No, I didn't think he'd name names. I'd also be negligent if I didn't ask.

If I shoot Brennan Doyle now, I won't be alive to find out. His security guard would shoot me in the next second. I'd be dead before I hit the ground.

If I'm dead, I can't protect Ravi from whoever else is looking to make money on his sale. And protecting him is what I need to do.

That's the mission.

CHAPTER SEVEN

Ravi

When I crawl back through the window at Liam's place, it's nearing three in the morning. After the party ended, I had to get Adam and Troy to take me to their place so I could pick up my car and my stuff.

My body's buzzing from the party, but what I really need is a solid few hours of rest.

How tired I am is probably why I miss it until it's too late —that the lamp I left on by my bed is off now.

I'm halfway through the window before something prickles at the back of my skull. I pause, straining my eyes and ears, but I can't figure out what I'm sensing.

A moment later I hear Liam's voice.

"Good of you to finally come home."

Shit. Shitshitshitshitshit.

"What are you—" I topple the rest of the way through the window. Shaking my head, I pick myself up and straighten my glasses before flipping on the lamp. I should have realized he'd check up on me at some point.

In hindsight, maybe I should've crashed at Adam and Troy's place.

"What are you doing in here?" It's Liam himself who taught me that a good offense is the best defense.

"I think the better question is what were you doing out there?"

"Sorry, I must have missed the part where I was grounded. Oh, wait, you can't ground me because I'm an adult."

He stands from where he's been sitting on my bed, tossing Mr. Bear onto my desk.

"Are you really?" he asks as he stalks forward. "An adult wouldn't be so stupid as to put their ass on display for a bunch of drunk old men. An adult wouldn't parade around in booty shorts like a cheap fuck toy."

Fuming, I glance down at the shorts, which I'm still wearing. *I am not cheap.* I bought these custom from a dancer on Etsy. I like to support small businesses.

Liam stops right in front of me, using his finger to tip my chin up to meet his gaze. "An adult wouldn't do something as stupid and dangerous as serving up his virginity to a pack of wealthy jackals for the highest goddamn bidder."

Every syllable is quiet and controlled. The quieter Liam gets, the more enraged he is. And also?

"How did you know where I was?" I glance at my phone, which is still sitting where I left it on the bed. Understanding dawns. "I figured you were tracking me. I guess it wasn't with my phone."

He doesn't answer. I shouldn't be surprised. What he does do is walk over to my bedroom window.

He brushes past me, his aftershave assaulting my nostrils when he's so close. The heat of his body, the quick brush of his pecs against my shoulder... Maybe if Dean hadn't gotten me so horned-up at the party, I wouldn't be so sensitive. But right now I'm kind of on the verge, you know?

The click of a lock makes me jump. "Wait. What the hell are you doing?"

When I turn around, he's securing a padlock that definitely wasn't there before. I'm suddenly freezing cold. The urge hits me to shove him, to try and wrench open the window, but it's too late. It's already locked.

"Installed it while you were out. I had plenty of time while you were shaking your ass for old men with Benjamins."

My chest is tight. Too tight. "Liam, you can't do this. I came to stay here because you said you wanted to keep an eye on me after being in the hospital. Why did I think it meant you actually gave a shit?"

His face softens, which kind of makes me want to punch it more. He settles himself on the edge of my bed as if we're having a friendly chat. "You have no idea how much I give a shit. Why do you think I'm trying to protect you? What do you think your parents would say if they knew their baby boy was auctioning off his virginity to the highest bidder?"

The way my throat gets tight forces me to pause. The backs of my eyes are burning, and I refuse to give Liam Masters the satisfaction of crying in front of him.

My feet are rooted to the floor, but I glance again at my phone. I can only guess how he found out about the auction, but Brennan's been sending texts with information. Should've known a little thing like a password wouldn't keep Liam out of my business.

"They wouldn't say anything, because they're dead." I wouldn't be doing this if they were alive. I wouldn't be here at all. "You wouldn't understand."

His expression goes hard again. The next thing I know, I'm swept off my feet, landing face down across Liam's lap. "What I understand," he growls from above me, "is you insist on continuing to act like a brat, so you obviously need to be treated like one."

In one swift motion, Liam yanks my shorts down to my knees. Cool air hits my backside, making me gasp. I squirm in his grasp, but he's got me trapped. "What the fuck are you—"

The smack of his hand against my ass ricochets around the room, even before the sting registers. "Hey!" I kick my legs. "Is this some kind of—"

Another swat lands against my skin, and then another. Every touch heats my entire body. My protest dies in my mouth when I realize two things: After being kissed and groped and teased all evening, I'm reeeealy turned on. Also, Liam pulling down my shorts freed my dick, which is now trapped between his thighs, my foreskin getting abraded by the rough nylon of his tactical pants.

I squirm again, not sure if I'm fighting for him to stop or keep going.

This is obviously supposed to be a punishment. To be fair, it hurts. I also can't seem to hold back the decidedly non-punishment ways my body is reacting.

The horror dawns slow, and then fast, as my dick gets harder. And harder. I'm desperate to pull away. Desperate to get closer.

Not that Liam seems to notice. He's so wrapped up in his anger that he rains blows one after another until my ass is throbbing. It's not the only thing. Every flinch and jerk causes friction, an awful, delicious heat building with each swipe of my sensitive cock on heavy ripstop fabric.

Every blow forces the air from my lungs. I gasp, dizzy and confused as my blood tries to decide whether it should rush to my head or my hard cock, and my brain tries make sense of how the humiliation only makes me burn hotter. It's not until drops of water land on the thin blue blanket covering my bed that I realize I'm crying.

About to come. But crying. Does that make sense? I'm burning with shame, and too desperate to care.

I need to research humiliation as a kink. Because I think I've got it.

"You keep trying my fucking patience, kid." There's a dark grittiness to Liam's voice. "What the fuck—" Another swat. And then another. "—is it going to take—" Smack. "—to realize I only want what's best for you?"

Right as I'm sure it'll only take one last hard spank to make me come, he abruptly stops. My hips buck and thrust, seeking that last little bit of friction. I'm so close. So fucking close.

My needy squirming is stilled by the heavy press of his hand on my lower back. I can't see him from this awkward angle, but I can picture the way his nostrils flare when he's mad, and the heavy puffs of breath tell me his chest is rising and falling with every breath. Something tells me he's finally fully aware of what he's been doing to me.

It's all I can do to hold in my needy whine. If I let him know how badly I want him to touch me again, it'll only make things worse.

His hand comes down again. Gently, this time. His palm smooths across my burning flesh, and it's all too much—the highly sensitive skin on my exposed ass and my chafed cock, which is already on a hair-trigger when as his leg shifts against it. The too-gentle brush of his fingers over my hole is the last straw.

A loud cry rips its way out of my chest as my body betrays me. My fingers clutch at the blanket on my bed as my body shakes. As I soak Liam's leg with my cum.

Even as some small voice in my head tells me how embarrassing this all is, I'm too lost in sensation to pay it much attention. My body twitches. My nerves sing. The relief flooding through me is so, so sweet.

I'm still floating down from the high of an orgasm a thousand times more intense than anything I've done with my own hand when I'm unceremoniously dumped onto the bed. Liam stands above me, hair mussed and face red. His gaze flicks down to the cum on his pant leg—my cum. He tries to school his features, but there's something on his face he can't wipe away.

His chest puffs. His nostrils flare. He looks...haunted.

"Help me understand about this auction, Ravi." He clears his throat.

I guess we're both going to simply ignore the straining bulge in his pants? The cum on his leg?

Wincing, I pull my shorts up slowly. I'm shaky and spent, forcing myself to stand tall when my body wants to collapse on the bed. Mental note: research what to do after getting a spanking.

Ohhh, even thinking it sounds dirty.

"Help me understand what the hell made you think this ridiculous scheme was a good idea. How would you even think of something like that?" Liam demands. "I spoke with Brennan. He mentioned you wanting to leave Belle Argo.

Why in the hell would you want to get away from the place where you have your college paid for and a safe home to live in? You have no idea what the sort of men who would bid on an auction like that are capable of. What they would want to do to someone innocent like you."

There's a tremor in his hand as he runs it through his short hair. The same hand he spanked me with.

I'm still struggling to catch my breath. But this? This is where I've had exactly enough. More than enough.

I force myself to stand, putting us toe-to-toe. Yes, it means I have to kill my neck to look up at him. It is what it is.

I'm about to poke the bear. But what else can he do to me?

"I know exactly what men like that are capable of," I tell him, "because I've seen it. I've seen what you do when your 'poker buddies' come over and you think I'm not here. I've seen the special setup you have in the garage. I've seen the women, and the young men, you bring in to pass around your circle of friends. So, how about you spare me the hypocrisy and let me make my own decisions? Because *you* are exactly where I got the idea from."

He doesn't realize it, but Liam Masters is responsible for the vast majority of my sexual awakenings.

Well, he's aware of it now.

My chest is absolutely heaving while he stares me down. His jaw clenches. His fingers twitch. For a second I think he might throw me over his lap again.

There's that vein bulging in his temple for the zillionth time.

Is it a vessel? A vein? Artery? Shit, I'm awful at biology. I really need to change my major.

He lets out a heavy breath, saying, "What you're too young to realize is the world is a hell of a lot more fucked up than you've got any clue about. Whatever you think you've seen, you don't know the half of it."

Is he trying to suggest I don't know what I saw? Is he going to tell me next that I didn't come while lying across his lap?

Instead he says, "It's my job to keep you safe, and I take that job as seriously as the one I get paid to do. Since you can't make good decisions on your own, I'm going to have to protect you from yourself until you can."

Then he tosses something into the air, like a ball. The cash I'd been saving. It was hidden in my desk drawer, secured with a rubber band. "What, you're stealing from me now? I earned that money. It's mine."

My fear rises with every toss of the bundle he's holding. There's almost five thousand dollars in there. Right now, Liam is holding my only ticket out. He's holding my freedom.

"You really think I need to steal from you, kid? I'm going to hold on to it though. I don't think you'd use it for anything worthwhile right now."

Like buying a gun and shooting you? Like a train ticket? Like getting you a prescription for the sedative you desperately need?

"You can't make me stay here. I have an appointment tomorrow."

"You mean your appointment with Brennan? That's not happening. While we're at it, you're not going to that auction in two weeks, either."

"You can't stop me. And are we even going to talk about the fact that we just—"

I'm cut off by the slam of my bedroom door.

I'm still struggling for breath when I hear a loud click, exactly like when he closed the padlock on my window. Emotion swirls through me, a mix of confusion and frustration. How does he give someone an orgasm and walk away? Maybe it wasn't anything to him, but it was something to me. He has to know it was.

It's not until I sink onto the bed with exhaustion that I realize my phone is gone. He must have taken it with him.

In a last-ditch effort, I get up to test the door, but I already know what I'm going to find. He's locked it from the outside. He's locked the window. I have no phone. My laptop is gone, too.

Mr. Bear is still here, his empty sideways stare aimed at me from the top of my desk.

Fear creeps up my spine. The auction is in two weeks. "He can't keep me in here for that long, can he?"

But I heard Liam. He thinks he's protecting me.

And that's exactly what he'd do.

CHAPTER EIGHT

LIAM

THE EAST END warehouse my company owns looks like it's past being condemned. From the road it's all peeling paint and crumbling stone. A sign out front that's no longer readable.

Around back? That's where I string up the prisoners.

It's about four in the morning when I drag myself from the car, not quite an hour after leaving Ravi to stew in his own stupidity for a while. The entire drive over here, minus the few minutes it took to order and receive a large black coffee from an all-night drive-through, has been spent wondering how long I can realistically keep him there.

And what the fuck was I thinking, losing my shit and disciplining him like that? The noises he made when he came are still ringing in my ears. The whimpers. The moans. The goddamn screaming.

Fucked up of me? Sure. As much as I want to deny I lost control, I absolutely did.

This is entirely Ravi's fault, though. I told him to stay away from Brennan, and I told him to stay away from escorting. He didn't listen. Worse, he's come up with a hare-brained get-rich-quick scheme that could easily land him in the hospital again.

Or worse. Much worse.

Maybe I need to show him case files from back when my team was hired to retrieve a young man who'd run away from home. He'd left to escape parents who were clearly a bit heavy-handed but landed himself in a worse world of hurt by hooking up with an abusive sugar daddy who got him addicted to drugs to keep him compliant. Or Cam Blakely, one of the initial victims of the trafficking ring we've been dismantling, who hasn't spoken a word since my team found him on an island off the coast of Brazil.

By the time we got them back home, all the therapy in the world wouldn't put those kids together again.

Ravi doesn't understand. There are far uglier things out there in the real world than being asked to follow a strict set of rules.

Kid doesn't get it. I'm doing all of this for him.

I'm slugging coffee by the back door when a Porsche SUV pulls up. Out jumps a medium height, muscular blond, and Sebastian Pierce, a former client.

"Thanks for calling us," Sebastian says. He holds out a hand to shake, which I do, even though I don't like having to juggle my coffee.

After which, Sebastian looks to the guy he brought with him. "You sure you want to do this?"

"Definitely." The blond nods his head. "I want to see that fucker suffer."

Sebastian hired us to find out why people on his

consulting company's client list were going missing. We've completed our obligation to him, and any stragglers involved in the operation were picked off because abusive pieces of shit piss me off.

During our investigating, Pierce's boyfriend was kidnapped by one Pastor Elijah. The pastor owned a farm nearby, in the rural unincorporated area between Belle Argo and Beacon Hill. Only a few miles down the road from my own home, in fact.

Turned out the good pastor had not only been using his private and well-protected religious commune to hide trafficking victims, but he'd been selling teen boys from some of the "less valuable" families in his commune to bring in extra cash. A real philanthropist, this one.

So when our team located Pastor Elijah, I reached out as a courtesy. Pierce struck me as the sort of man who would want to be personally involved in resolving things.

When we get inside, my tech guru is waiting. Bev might be brainy, but she can wrestle a man to the ground as easily as she can hack his email. Which is how Pastor Elijah ended up hanging from the warehouse ceiling with his head lolling sideways. He's conscious, but he doesn't look good.

"Nice to see you out in the field for a change," I tell Bev. Then I nod to the hanging man. "You fucked him up pretty good."

She tosses her thick chestnut braid over her shoulder, boots thudding on the floor as she approaches. "I like it better behind my computer. But—" She shrugs. "—nearly everyone else is out of the office right now. Besides, who doesn't enjoy putting a man in his place once in a while?"

"I appreciate you going above and beyond. I'll keep it in mind when I'm handing out end-of-year bonuses."

She only rolls her eyes and shrugs again. Bev is someone I suspect does what we do for her own reasons other than the pay. Still, I try to take care of my employees.

Sebastian Pierce studies the slumped figure. "Where'd you find him?"

"A small camper not too far from the farm where he'd been running his commune. It was rented in his name. We figure he parked it out in the woods at some point as a hide-away. It sort of worked. The FBI didn't find him when they searched the property, but when the land went up for sale this week, we went back for a final sweep. He was living in a moldy, piss-smelling metal box and eating out of tin cans." I give his limp body a kick, enjoying his pained groan. "How the mighty have fallen."

The blond one, Simon, perks up. "You said the property's up for sale?" He pulls out his phone and starts typing.

"I think he knows someone who might be interested," Sebastian explains.

Nodding, I pull out both my phone and Ravi's, placing them next to each other on the metal table where I keep my interrogation tools. If he does something clever, or if more messages come from Brennan, I want to know. It's a long shot, since Brennan already knows I've intercepted his texts. So far, the only recent ones have been some group thread discussing brunch plans. Plans Ravi will not be there for.

"Elijah, I'm Liam. Nice to see you." I've learned that sometimes politeness throws these guys off their game. They expect me to come out swinging, and then I introduce myself like a gentleman.

Then I start swinging.

After I land a punch to his gut, his eyes fly open. They're piercing and blue, oddly cold. That old chestnut about eyes being a window to the soul? This guy hasn't got one. Still, the retching and pained gasps are real.

"Okay, here's how this goes. I'll start with what I know, and you're going to fill in any blanks," I tell our prisoner.

"We know about a guy named Tony, whose bright idea it was to start trafficking well-off entrepreneurs and sometimes their family members. He's dead now, in case you forgot. We also took care of the bartender he'd been paying off at parties to drug certain attendees. Also dead. Then, of course, there are the two guys who were hired to put select kidnapping victims on private planes and fly them to wherever they'd been purchased. Those guys are also dead. Are you sensing the theme?"

Pastor Elijah's stare is sharp and hard. No begging or pleading. Nothing but a bit of labored breathing.

"See, the trouble with these operations is they're like a hydra. So many heads, and we'll keep cutting off as many as we have to. I will happily remove yours as well." I lean in, close enough that he can hear my lowered voice, but not close enough that he could manage to headbutt me. "We know you guys were working with at least one member of law enforcement. We know a shell company with the operating initials TMI was transporting these victims overseas. We know your farm was used to store and transport victims. Someone was bankrolling this whole fucking thing. Who was the money guy?"

"You're going to kill me. It doesn't serve me to tell you anything."

"Good point, Pastor." His observation pleases me so much I feel my cheeks spreading with an unnatural grin. "But the easier you make this on yourself, the easier I make it on you."

"Hmm." He sounds the opposite of impressed.

"I don't think you should make it easy on him at all," Simon says with his arms crossed over his chest.

Sebastian leans over to his boyfriend. "Baby, anything they get from Elijah could help them find the other people still involved. Which helps the chances of making sure this sort of thing doesn't happen in Belle Argo anymore."

Elijah, for his part, simply smiles and manages a sort of shrug, killing any notion that he's anything more than inconvenienced by this entire situation.

I gesture to Sebastian and then at my tools. "You want to get started?"

He turns to his boyfriend. "What about you, baby? You want to be the one to hurt him?"

The blond wrinkles his nose. "I don't want to even touch him. Will you do it for me, Sir?"

Sir.

An unexpected memory hits me like a brick to the face. *You're not my parent. But you could be my daddy if you wanted.*

Of all the fucking times. I'm a breath away from shoving the table full of knives and implements sideways. If I get hard in the middle of an interrogation, I'll hang my own self from the damn ceiling.

Sebastian smiles, pulling a pair of brass knuckles from his pocket, and gets to work. Ignoring the steady thumps and groans of a man getting beaten, I pick up the two phones to check for notifications. The tracker in his watch tells me Ravi's staying put at home for a change, and there's still nothing on his phone aside from brunch plans and dick jokes.

When I look up, I'm surprised to see Simon regarding me

and not watching his boyfriend pummel the man who kidnapped him.

"Why do you have Ravi's phone?"

"Whose?"

The blond crosses his arms over his chest. "I know it's his. What are the chances that anyone else in the world has a blue glitter phone case with the initials RN on the back in magic marker? I tease him about his initials all the time. I'm a nurse. You know, RN?" I don't answer, but after a minute, he reaches a conclusion. "You must be Liam. I remember now, seeing you at the hospital. And he's talked about you."

My eyebrows jump into the air. "Has he?"

Probably nothing good.

Simon shrugs. "Some. Doesn't sound like the two of you get along too well."

That would be putting it mildly. "He's a teenager with his head up his own ass," I growl. "It's not my job to be his friend. It's my job to keep him out of his own way."

Simon's frown pulls me up short. *Rein it in, Liam.*

"Sometimes people butt heads," I add, trying to smooth away his apparent suspicion with a softer tone.

The way Simon's looking at me, he seems to have come to some sort of conclusion. There's a knowing glint in his eye. I don't know what it means, and I'm not sure I want to.

"Yeah, they fucking do," he says after a while. As if that makes any sense.

A pained groan tells us Sebastian is still at work. From past experience, he tends to work in a pattern of hitting the guy a couple of times and then asking a question. The pastor, little that he's willing to speak, seems to be giving the same information I got from the bartender.

I hesitate before saying, "All roads seem to lead to Tony."

I study the man, waiting for his reaction. Tony was Sebastian's husband, after all.

"Fuck." Sebastian straightens up, cracking his back. "Now I kind of wish I hadn't killed him."

Jesus. Even I'm not that cold. Tony caused a fucking shipping freighter's worth of trouble though, to be fair. Betrayal runs deep.

I think of the way Ravi looked at me right before I locked him in his room and try to rub the icy spot in my chest away. Betrayal.

"This is the third person who's said their only interactions were with Tony," I agree.

Some alert on Simon's phone brings his head up. "Hey, Sebastian, we need to get going."

Sebastian nods, wiping the blood from his brass knuckles and sliding them into his pocket. "Whatever you want, baby."

Simon stomps up to the limp, barely alive body, stopping close enough to put his middle finger in the pastor's face. "I hope you rot in hell," he whispers before storming out.

Sebastian gestures to me. "You mind finishing him off?"

I glance at Ravi's phone when it pings again. There's a text from Brennan asking for two guys who are willing to do a "joint performance."

I can guess what that means. Fucking piece of shit.

Fucking Brennan Doyle. Fucking Ravi.

Brennan's smug face in my head makes my hands curl into fists.

I've seen what you do when your 'poker buddies' come over and you think I'm not here. I've never seen someone so unsteady and so cocky at the same time as the moment when Ravi called me out. Especially not post-orgasm. The thought makes my breath come faster.

I look to Sebastian and then back at the pastor, who's hanging there like a bloody punching bag.

"Yeah, I can finish this up."

My knuckles crack when I flex my fingers. It's been a long fucking night. Ravi's face flashes behind my eyes again. His tearstained face and puffy lips.

Before I know what I'm doing, my booted foot plants on the leg of the steel table, sending the whole thing to the floor. Bev's eyes go wide. Even the pastor almost looks startled.

Fuck it. Sebastian Pierce had the right idea. I could use a punching bag right now.

Maybe if I hit this guy hard enough, I can get Ravi's flushed face and dilated pupils out of my mind. The memory of him shuddering in my grasp when he came.

"Let's fucking finish this," I say as my fist sinks into the man's stomach.

CHAPTER NINE

Ravi

Against the odds, I managed to fall asleep.

When I wake again I jerk off, because I always wake up horny, so of course I do. And after Liam's rage-fueled early morning spanking session?

I don't know if rage-jerking is a thing, but that's pretty much the shape of things this morning.

The first time I knew about Liam and the things he was into, it was senior year of high school, and I'd gone out to see a Batman movie.

Except I needed gas, and I'd forgotten my wallet on the top of my dresser. The place I'd stopped at didn't have a way to pay with my phone. I turned around, only to see a light on in Liam's garage. The garage was the one place I'd been told to stay the hell out of.

Sneaking around to the side door where there was a small window, I finally realized why. Liam had friends over.

Or at least a small group of acquaintances who didn't mind getting naked together.

Strapped to a table in the middle of the room was a woman. College age at the time, if I had to guess. Liam and three of his friends stood around her, all fully clothed at first while the girl was completely naked. I watched, fascinated, as they took turns touching her. They pinched her and slapped her, sucked her nipples, used dildos and other things I didn't recognize, eventually taking turns fucking her and covering her with cum until she looked as if someone had thrown a meringue pie in her face.

At the time I was so confused. About the fact that she seemed so into the way they treated her, and the fact that it had made me hard. Well, it wasn't her so much. It was the guys. The things they did to her. The sight of Liam, the golden tan of his back as his muscles bunched, his ass clenching and flexing while he fucked her. The other guys too, but most of all Liam.

It took a while to realize I'd wanted to be in the girl's place. I'd wanted Liam to touch me the way he'd been touching her. I'd wanted him to hurt me in the way that blurred the lines between pleasure and pain.

I pulled out my phone to buy a movie ticket for a different weekend and then jerked off standing there outside the window like a stalker.

Eventually I figured out that when Liam was "having the guys over to play poker" it didn't mean a card game. It became a habit, lying to Liam that I was leaving when his friends came over and then doubling back to see what was happening in the garage. It wasn't every weekend, and a lot of times he had to travel for work, but I got quite an education.

The biggest surprise? One week, instead of one of a revolving selection of college girls, it was a college boy. He was lean with dark skin. Tall and muscular, with a strong jaw that clenched when he got on all fours and braced himself. Liam whipped him with some sort of strap and then fucked him. Liam always went first. Whatever this group was about, Liam was clearly in charge.

And clearly he didn't mind fucking guys. It gave me hope.

That was then, though. Before Liam had done things like tracking my every move and locking me in my room.

"Shit." With my hand covered in cum, I look around the room and realize I've got a problem. The door is still locked. Which means I can't go clean up in the hall bathroom.

For lack of a better option, I lift up the blanket on my bed and wipe my hand off on the sheet. If Liam wants to lock me in here, he can be the one to wash the cum off my sheets.

I feel like I should be sorry about that, but I'm not. After cleaning up as best as I can and searching my room, I come to a depressing realization. While I was gone last night, he must have eliminated everything he thought I could possibly use to bust out of here.

"He stole all my stuff," I mutter. To Mr. Bear, to myself, but mostly to the universe. Because honestly, I'm not sure what to do right now.

It's not only my phone and laptop that are gone. My keys are gone from where I dropped them on the bedside table. So is the portable screwdriver set I keep in case I need to take apart my computer case. The adjustable kettlebell set I keep in my closet for when I can't get to the gym is gone. Annoying, since sending it through the window would've been an easy way to get out. My eyeglass repair kit is missing. Even the pens from my desk drawer are gone.

But the one thing he didn't take?

My backpack. I had it on me when I climbed through the window early this morning. Given that Liam is too calculating not to realize I might have something in there he'd want to take, my guess is he was too busy lecturing me to even notice.

Or too busy turning my ass red.

Thunder rumbles outside. Dammit. Normally I love a good rainy day, but not now.

My backpack search turns up some school supplies, a spare pair of booty shorts from last night's party (because you never know what might happen), a spare shirt, and a bottle of water. Another one of Dean's granola bars. He gave me an extra on our way out.

Oh. Wait.

I've also got a paperback of *The Grapes of Wrath*, which I've been reading for lit class. I've been using a paperclip to mark my pages. Ha.

"Point for me, Liam."

Falling down research rabbit holes is kind of my thing, and once upon a time I got obsessed with videos on how to pick different locks when I couldn't sleep. Handcuffs. Bedroom door locks. Padlocks.

I've only ever picked the lock on a bedroom door, and only ever from the hallway side. That was easy, but it won't work here. Liam's locked it from the outside. Another padlock, I'm guessing.

So, I get to work on the window. Which is not, in my opinion, as easy as the guy in the video I saw made it look.

It takes long enough that I'm getting discouraged as I

work at the window lock. My neck and back start to hurt from bending and squinting. My palms sweat from nerves.

Every couple of minutes I stop to listen, sweating as I strain for the sound of a door or tires on gravel. I don't know when Liam will be back. Will he come storming in to check on me and catch me trying to escape?

Do I want him to catch me? Will he try and spank me again? My cock thickens at the thought.

Honestly, is it awful that I sort of wish he would? The trouble is, he probably wouldn't now that he knows I liked it.

I've nearly given up when something pops and the lock springs free. "Yes!"

"Oh. Wow." I hold the lock up for Mr. Bear as I stuff him into my backpack along with some extra clothes. "Did you see that? I got it open. Yessss."

It's silly, but Mr. Bear has become something of a confidant over the years.

I should really get moving before Liam comes back. Which is going to suck, because there's a storm absolutely raging outside. Still, I don't have much choice.

I grab whatever I think I might need for at least a few days while I cram my single granola bar into my mouth and use the water bottle to wash it down.

Liam may have taken the cash I had saved up in my room, but I still have the tip money from last night's party hidden in my pencil case. It's only about a grand, but it'll get me by until the auction. Then I should be home free.

Where I won't be is here.

I'm soaked by the time I make it out the window. Then there's the challenge of getting down the post I usually climb, which is mossy and slippery now that it's wet. Not knowing how much time I have, I try to hurry.

About halfway down, my hand slips. Gravity yanks me to the muddy ground, knocking the breath out of me. It takes a lot of wheezing and coughing before I can get up onto my hands and knees, and when I do, I'm a mess.

Also, there are feet in front of my face.

There's a second of panic mixed with...am I actually getting turned on again? Then I realize these are not the black military-issue boots Liam wears. They're a pair of high-end dress shoes, which means, probably Michael?

I stand to face my fellow escort. He's wisely wearing a rain poncho over his designer khakis and buttoned shirt, but the dark skin on his hands and face are splattered with rain. Which probably means he's been standing out here for a minute. His expensive-smelling cologne wafts my way as he looks at me with concern.

"Hi. Uh. I didn't expect to see you here?"

I don't mean to talk in questions. I don't even like that I do. It just sort of happens.

Michael smiles patiently. "I'm driving rideshare this weekend. Simon sent a text. Said this Liam guy you're staying with had your phone, and he was worried something might have happened. I volunteered to come check things out. Is everything okay? Why does someone else have your phone?"

Okay, well I'm not touching that last question. I squirm a little, standing there in the rain, scratching my cheek in my nervousness. Which I think got mud on my face. Ew.

I look down at myself. At my mud-spattered clothes. The cut on my shin that must have happened when I fell. "I won't lie to you, Michael. It's been better."

I give him the briefest, too-long-didn't-listen version of my last twenty-four hours. Minus the spanking.

"I don't think he's tracking my phone since he took it with him," I finish. "But he keeps finding me."

Michael points to my arm. "What about your watch?"

I hold up my arm. "It was a gift from my dad. I never take it off, except to shower."

Michael looks at me as if I might be stupid. Which maybe I am, because it takes me a second. "Right. Why didn't I think of that?"

Of course Liam would hide some sort of GPS locator in the one thing other than my phone that I always have on me. Something with sentimental value, no less. Of course he would.

I take it off, hesitating because I really don't want to leave one of the few things I have left from my parents. I've got the watch, and I've got Mr. Bear. Everything else got sold off. It's not even a nice watch. The band is plastic. But I'm used to the solid weight of it on my arm. It's practically a part of me.

Except, if Liam finds me again, I'll be stuck in that bedroom until I'm thirty. After a beat, I slip it into the top of the barbecue grill. That should keep him guessing for a while.

"Can you give me a ride? Liam took my keys and phone. I can pay you with cash, though?"

Michael clicks his tongue and shakes his head at me again. "Friends give friends rides for free, man. Let's go. Brennan's got his panties all in a twist. You were supposed to be at Shadow, like, an hour ago."

As we head to his car, I resist the urge to look back. If I do, I might not be able to go.

CHAPTER TEN

Ravi

The inside of Shadow smells like furniture polish and latex. The converted mansion is almost entirely open on the bottom floor, with a stage at the back wall and a gleaming giant birdcage to the left, and I sure wonder what goes on there. Or on the raised platform to the right. Or in the rooms upstairs.

The small rectangular bar, gleaming with cut glasses and polished wood, is the most elegant thing I've ever seen. Michael has wandered over there, admiring the glossy surface and tracing the golden trim with the tips of his fingers. It definitely looks like the sort of place wealthy people would drink. Not people who simply have a lot of money, but classy people, stylish people. People who are friends with politicians and who use their money to pull strings from the shadows.

If I listen carefully, I can almost hear my mom chiding me for my overactive imagination.

Honestly, though, I don't belong here. My clothes are damp and muddy, and even though the place isn't open for business yet, the few employees milling about are all polished and well dressed. Over at the bar, Michael has seated himself to chat with a guy who looks like he's stocking bottles, his clothes somehow pristine even after slogging through Liam's muddy yard.

Trying to tamp down my envy, I turn to take in the rest of the massive room, gasping at what's in the middle of the floor. There are clusters of comfortable-looking chairs and loveseats, each surrounding a sort of padded table, a low bench similar to what I've seen in Liam's garage. One group of chairs is situated around a hanging contraption that looks as if it's maybe meant to tie a person to it? If I had my phone, I'd take a picture so I could look it up later.

The carpet under my feet has a dark, abstract kind of pattern, sort of like at the movie theater. Absurdly, I remember an online video about what the carpeting of pricey hotels looks like under a blacklight. Would it be the same here? Worse? People have sex here, but they have sex in hotels, too. People who aren't me, obviously.

I make a circle in the middle of the room, picturing it with the lights low and full of people. Do they come here dressed in cocktail attire like the employees, or black latex like I've seen in the movies?

Guess I'm about to find out.

"Like what you see?"

"Ah. Sorry." I'm certain my feet leave the ground when I spin around to find the voice. It's the quiet growl of a guy who has power and money but doesn't need volume to get people's attention. Like Liam, sort of, but this guy looks more refined, and he has an accent. Not sure what kind. British-ish? But not quite. I don't know.

"You must be Ravi." He's looking me up and down, and immediately I wish I could sink into the floor. I know what I must look like. Soggy. Dirty. At least I had the foresight to clean my feet off on the mat out front. Now, though, I realize I should've asked Michael if he could take me somewhere to change.

It's real work, fighting the urge to turn around and slink back out the door.

"Mr. Corvus? Hi." I hold my hand out, see a smear of mud on my palm, and then pull it back. "I-I'm sorry we're late. I was kind of...being held prisoner?"

He raises one eyebrow. He won't believe me, I know he won't, but I wasn't sure what else to say. Anything else would be a fake excuse and would probably sound like one.

From living with Liam, I know how easily some people can detect lies. I'd bet my stolen moving fund the owner of Shadow is that kind of guy.

Still shouldn't have told him you were a prisoner, dumbass.

Daniel Corvus stands close enough that I have to crane my neck to make eye contact. He's as built as Liam muscle-wise, and he's got the same calculating look in his eyes. Like even if he sounds friendly and casual he's probably already thought of how to pin you to the floor if you step out of line.

The thought makes me shiver. Or maybe it's the air conditioning on my wet clothes?

He's also very...I don't know...stately? Like, I could picture him on the back of a horse with a helmet under his arm. His voice makes a weird rumbly sensation in my chest. Not sure what to do with that.

I do my best to hold still as he circles me, his feet silent on the dark carpet beneath our feet. Whatever he's looking for as he sizes me up, I don't know if he'll find it.

"Held prisoner? I don't see a tattered dress or long, flowing hair."

Shaking my head makes my glasses slip down my nose. I push them back up again. "I'm sorry? I don't understand." Was that sexist? Should I be offended?

He tilts his head to one side and then the other, examining me. Self-consciousness has me wanting to shrink back, but then again, I'll have more than one person staring at me on the night of the auction. It's probably something I should get used to.

"You don't look like a helpless maiden."

"Oh. Uh, I'm not? I had to pick a lock, though. I'd seen videos of it but never practiced on that kind, so it took me a while."

Why am I even blurting these things out? Why does he keep staring at me like that? I don't like the way he pauses and stares after every sentence. It gives me this squirmy, uncomfortable sensation that he's rooting around in my brain or looking into my soul or something.

God, imagine if someone could really do that. I'm not sure they'd like what they found.

"Ravi...Novak. is that correct?"

"Is that correct?" Wait, he's asking me. "Uh. Yes. Sir."

I don't know why I tack on the last part, only that it feels important.

"Your parents are Polish?"

"My father. My mother's from Jamshedpur. India." I cough to clear the tight feeling in my throat. "Was."

He takes a breath that's deep and slow, and for some

reason I find myself doing the same thing. Which is good, I suppose. Now my shoulders aren't so tight.

"This auction. Are you certain it's something you're willing to do?"

"Oh." I straighten my spine. "Yes. Sir. Very certain."

"Are you certain it's something you want to do?"

I open my mouth, about to repeat my previous answer, wondering why he's asking me the same question twice. But then it hits me. I don't think he *is* asking the same question.

Do I want to do this? As in, is it something I desire? "It was my idea."

"Hmm." It's impressive, really, how he packs so much skepticism into that one sound.

Maybe I haven't hidden my mixed feelings as well as I thought.

Deep down inside where nobody can see is this little burning ember that still glows with all the hopes I've ever had about Liam and what I wish we could be to each other. About having a family. Belonging.

Doing this auction means snuffing that ember out. Pouring cold water on it. Stomping it to dust. When I think of killing it, my stomach feels like it's full of battery acid.

It also feels necessary. How else will I ever move on?

I mirror Mr. Corvus's breaths by taking another slow and deep one of my own. "I'm certain that I need the money, sir. I'm also certain that I'm willing."

The corners of his mouth lift a little. From the look on his face, I could swear he understands what I'm saying and everything I'm not.

It's almost nice to feel like someone understands. Even if that someone is as intimidating as Daniel Corvus.

He pulls a clipboard from behind his back. How did I not notice he was holding it this entire time?

You were too distracted by the way he's eyeing you up like a prize-winning purebred.

"Fill this out. It'll be useful in weeding out the applicants for attending your auction. There's been a great deal of interest, and we have limited space."

Once again, I scan the room we're in. It's huge. I can't see how they would fill it, much less have to turn people away.

"The final page is a contract," he continues. "Dotting our i's and crossing our t's, legally speaking."

A contract. For the auction. I can't decide whether that's terrifying or awesome. Maybe both, from the way my heartbeat is all scattered.

When I take the list and scan it, I can see what he's getting at. It's a list of kinks, with a row of checkboxes next to each one. A box to mark if I've tried it, a box to mark if I haven't, and a box to mark if it's something I'm definitely willing to do, maybe, or definitely not.

"There are things on here I've never even heard of," I say with a hard swallow. "I've been doing a lot of research but..." Clothespins? Sensory deprivation? "Why is kissing on here?"

Kissing? Like Penny Mackenzie at the fall festival? There wasn't even tongue. Her dad's a pastor. Like Dean at that party? None of that seemed kinky at all.

I'm going to have to look all of this stuff up later. If I had my phone I could take a picture.

"Kissing isn't always as vanilla as one assumes, and it's not something everyone enjoys. Explicit consent is best."

I think of Liam throwing me across his lap and pulling my pants down at three in the morning. Did he know he didn't need my consent because he already had it? Because when I offered myself to him at eighteen I was willing to give him every part of me, and everything I had? Or did he simply think it was his right, because I'm his "job"?

Probably the second one.

Which burns, honestly. As much of an asshole as he's been, there's never been anything I wouldn't do for him, except stay in a cage. That's much worse than a crush, I know it is. My therapist would certainly have some things to say about that if I'd ever admitted it to her.

"Got it," I tell Mr. Corvus. At least I think I do?

When I get to the line item about spanking, I suppress a shiver and try my hardest to keep my thoughts from wandering. I don't need to confuse myself any further now, and I definitely don't want a hard-on in front of the owner of a sex club. I squeeze my eyes shut and picture a bloody scene of lions eating a giraffe before checking "no" that I haven't tried it and "no" that I definitely don't want to.

That'll be easier. I think?

Maybe it's stupid to want to keep my first and last orgasm with Liam sacred. Maybe I won't always feel this way. But yeah, for now, easier.

"A word of advice," Mr. Corvus adds.

I swear my blood flow screeches to a halt. Does he know I just lied on the form? God, imagine if Liam saw this list. Would he be mad I lied? Would he punish me again?

I force another hard swallow. "Yes, sir?"

"For the purposes of this auction, if you're uncertain about something, check the box for no. You'll be in an intense situation with an unfamiliar person whom you may or may not trust. I've already made it clear to Brennan and to my employees who are handling logistics that there will be no body modification allowed."

"Body mod—" The heading jumps at me on the list. "Branding. Scarification... Tattoos? People get off on that stuff?"

Hopefully his frown isn't really as judgy as I'm making it out to be when he says, "You have no idea."

Clearly, I don't.

But I'd like to. I make a mental note to look that up later.

My eyes drift shut for a second, picturing the knife Liam always keeps clipped to his belt. Or the long one with the thin blade he uses when he's interrogating people.

He doesn't think I know about that, but when I first came to live with him, I didn't like being left by myself. One night I hid in his back seat, following him to a warehouse in the East End. It was the first time I'd had a response to blood that wasn't getting lightheaded. Maybe because I knew if Liam was hurting the man, it must have been something he deserved.

My breath hitches when I picture Liam over me with that same knife, slowly and carefully bringing up a line of blood on my chest.

Oh, fuck. That's... A shiver hits me hard.

I might need some help.

Daniel clears his throat.

My eyes fly open, and I shake myself, trying to clear the thought. "You're right, I don't think I'd want to do that with someone I didn't trust."

Unpacking the idea of trusting the man who locked me in my room this morning? That's a problem for Tomorrow Ravi.

"I've done plenty of these auctions in the past. For charity, but never before for a person's virginity. I think it's a strange obsession humanity has with that sort of thing. Still, this event has the potential to bring in a great deal of money. Mr. Doyle and I are both investing time and resources, with the expectation of a substantial return. It would be unpleasant for everyone if you were to have a last-second change of heart."

I know it's the lighting, but I swear his eyes flash with the threat. And I definitely hear a threat.

I think I get what he's saying. And everything he's not. If I changed my mind now and walked away, they'd be pissed. If I change my mind after signing this contract when I'm about to go on stage and he's got this club filled with people who are expecting a show, I'm going to be in a world of trouble.

Probably massive trouble. He's definitely reminding me more of Liam. And, well, I've seen Liam tie a guy up and carve him into pieces for doing something wrong. What would Daniel Corvus do?

With a nod, I roll my shoulders back, lift my chin, and meet his eyes. "I won't change my mind."

Saying it out loud, I can hear the nail being hammered into my coffin. In spite of my certainty, it makes my stomach turn.

"Good." His smile is unsettling. "Then there's just one more thing I need from you."

CHAPTER ELEVEN

LIAM

"SIR, YOU LOOK LIKE SHIT." Bev spins the chair across from me and straddles it, folding her arms across the back. "Same thing still eating you as before?"

I drop the piece of label I've been peeling from my beer bottle and meet her curious gaze with a "back the fuck off" glare.

"Leave me the fuck alone," I add for good measure.

"Your face is too pretty for such an ugly look, boss. You've been extra edgy lately, and everyone's starting to worry." She gestures to the room behind us, where the rest of the team are either playing or betting on a game of darts. My friend and business partner, Zed, has for some reason taken his shirt off and is circling it in the air like a lasso.

"After you beat a man of God to death in our warehouse, we figured you could use a night out to decompress," she adds with a humorless smile. "Doesn't seem to be working."

I take a healthy swig of my beer. "Can't call him a man of

God when he was trafficking his own followers, if you ask me."

She shrugs and tips back her IPA. "If you ask me, God doesn't exist, so it doesn't matter what you call him."

Thirty seconds into this conversation and I already want to go back to being left alone. "You didn't come over here to discuss whether or not God exists."

"No, sir. I came over here because you've spent the day biting everyone's head off. The little boys are all too nervous to talk to you about it, so somebody had to woman up. Since I'm currently the only woman on the team, here I am."

A shout comes from the far wall, where Reece has managed a bull's-eye. Zed pumps his fist and holds his hand out to Yannis, who forks over some cash. Fred and Callaghan keep glancing over my way, trying to act as if they're minding their own business.

"They placing bets on why I'm in a bad mood?"

"Odds heavily favor your boy, Ravi. Reece said you were ranting about him at your last job together, and Callaghan said—I want to be clear that these are his words, not mine—last time he saw the two of you together, the boy looked at you 'like he'd crawl naked over glass if you asked him to.'"

"I think Callaghan needs to keep shit to himself before I cut out his tongue."

She continues as if I hadn't spoken. "Sal and Marcus called in from Mexico, and they're thinking this goes back to months ago when that recovery job went tits up. Yannis has fifty on the fact that none of us did anything for your birthday last month."

Fuck that. I never celebrate my birthday. Why do I need to, when I've got a college freshman in my life to remind me exactly how old I am? Besides, birthdays are hard for Ravi. No need to put him through that shit.

"Yannis should stop betting on things. He's already broke from two divorces."

Bev raises her eyebrows but says nothing.

"That recovery job is done and buried. We don't win them all. Can't change the past."

Honestly, Bev's an amazing hacker but she could pull the truth from anybody with nothing but her eyebrows. No fillet knife needed.

I've had interrogation training. Twenty years in the Army, ten of them in special forces. Nobody can break me with the power of a stare.

Usually.

I'm tired as fuck. I'm strung out from that spontaneous spanking session in Ravi's bedroom. Still sensing the smoothness of his ass under my palm, the way he orgasmed from the lightest brush of my finger on his hole. The moans and cries he made when I touched him won't leave me alone. There's this ugly thing pacing and thrashing inside me since it happened. I'm trying so hard to keep the beast on a leash.

It's not working. Not when every time I close my eyes I see his tearstained face, flushed with a mix of confusion and sated pleasure. Hear his voice, rough from crying out, asking to discuss what happened between us. I hate myself for what I did as much as for the way I keep wanting to do it again.

"He's not my boy," I growl.

If I could just convince the beast inside me. The one who took over when I grabbed him and threw him over my lap as if he very much was mine. I still can't believe the way I lost control.

"But...you...want him to be?" There's no judgment in her face. Only interest.

"Of course I fucking don't." I rip the rest of the label off my bottle, crumpling the foil-stamped scrap in my fist. "I'm supposed to be protecting him. It's what I do. Protecting people is what I've spent my entire life doing. I've also never been more certain that I'm failing."

She regards me silently, spinning her empty beer bottle in little circles. The repetitive sound has me wanting to stab somebody.

"Sir, you know my ex was an alcoholic?"

Where is this going? "I think you've mentioned it before."

"Spent years trying to fix him. Years. Dumping out his booze, trying to keep him in a good mood, placating him when he was on a rampage. He'd agree to go to a meeting once in a while but never made it more than a few weeks sober before it all went off the rails again. He was set on killing himself, and I kept trying to save him."

Ah. I see now. "This is a teaching story."

"Damn right it is. See, I learned the hard way that you can't help someone who isn't interested in taking it from you. Whatever you think you owe this kid, or owe his parents, you've done your job. When you were his age, you were dodging missiles in Afghanistan. If you ask me, it's time to let go before you drive him away."

After locking him in his room and taking his phone? "Not that I did ask, but I'm pretty sure that ship has sailed." Hell, it's halfway to the Kamchatka Peninsula by now. I try to shake the earlier memories from my head. "The whole thing's thoroughly fucked at this point. I tried to help him. He pushed back. Then I pushed harder, so he sneaked out, and I lost my shit and padlocked his door and window."

Her eyes fly open wide. "I'm sorry. You did what now?"

"Didn't work. He picked the lock on the window and climbed out."

When I went home to change, I found him gone. Found his watch hidden under the cover of the fucking barbecue grill. "I've spent all day wondering who's more screwed up. Me for trying to lock him in his room, or him for constantly sneaking out with the apparent mission of putting himself in harm's way. So, you can go tell everybody who won the bet. You can also let them know I intend to get my shit together ASAP."

Not a clue how I can promise that when I feel so far out to sea, but Bev seems to accept it. I don't like the way she seems to be mulling over everything I just said. Mostly, I don't like that all of it was true.

She turns her chair and props her feet on the table. Our waitress, Annie, comes by and swats the back of Bev's head with a bar towel. Bev only grins and swats Annie on the ass as she walks past.

My chair scrapes on the floor as I push it back. "Time for me to go. Don't think I'm in the mood to stay and watch you get laid."

I'm drowning in prickly, itchy shame since what happened in Ravi's bedroom, but probably not enough. Hasn't stopped me from jerking my dick raw. My balls are still so blue they're on the way to purple.

I can't even stand that I'm thinking of him this way. By the time I came back to myself in the middle of spanking him, I was already in the midst of crossing the line. My shrieking conscience hadn't been able to stop me from that dangerous moment when I let my finger wander into territory I couldn't explain away.

My control has been shredded into tiny pieces of confetti. I never should have let things go as far as they did. Never mind the way I can't stop...*craving* him.

The kid's phone pings on the table in front of me, where it's still sitting next to my own. A notification about an upcoming test from one of his teachers.

I've told myself a dozen times to quit looking at the damn thing. The group chat, the messages from Brennan, have all gone silent. The abrupt lack of communication from the people he talks to most tells me they've probably been informed Ravi doesn't have his phone.

Any further monitoring is pointless. Like the guilty jerking off, I can't seem to stop.

"Why don't you get yourself laid, then?" Bev's question snaps me out of my thoughts. She tips her head to the side, flicking her gaze over toward the bar.

When I follow the path of her attention, I realize there's a man there who isn't doing much at all to hide his interest. He's close to my height, a little leaner. Dark hair. Dark eyes. Nervous.

No chin dimple, no full lips, no tight, barely legal ass. Probably doesn't use bubblegum-scented bodywash.

Most importantly, he's not half my age. I can see the gray at his temples from the weathered table where Bev and I sit.

Yes, I could probably have some fun with him tonight. I could probably even call up my buddies and get a group together. Zed would be happy to come over and help me escort the guy home. Seems like the type who wouldn't mind being shared.

"Not in the mood right now," I tell Bev.

"Aaand this is because of the kid?"

"He's not a fucking kid."

My brain flashes back to the day he arrived at my house, wide-eyed and silent, with a Jujutsu Kaisen anime backpack slung over his bony shoulders. No. As much as I try to ignore it, the young man who defiantly called me Daddy and climbed through his bedroom wearing spandex shorts is not a kid anymore.

"You're the one who keeps calling him a kid."

"I'm keeping this insubordination in mind at your next review."

She responds by giving me the finger.

"Fuck." I run a tired hand down my face. "He's been living with me since he was almost sixteen. It's a little..."

"Weird."

"Twisted. Incestuous. Fucked up."

"You know, you're not his actual parent." The right side of her lip lifts into a sneer. I don't know if she's disgusted with me or something else. I'm not presently interested in asking.

"I'm responsible for him. I'm not supposed to be..."

Pictures flash across the back of my eyes. Ravi calling me Daddy. Ravi grinding against another dancer at Mercer Oak's cocktail party. Ravi coming across my goddamn lap. "Doing anything more."

Whether Ravi believes me or not, I did take my promise to look after him seriously. Have I already failed, after what I've done?

"Is this a you thing or a him thing? Like, are you all frustrated and guilty because you want a little barely legal ass? Because that doesn't make sense. We all know work isn't the only place you and Zed like to collaborate, and we also know it wouldn't be the first time you've fucked a college student. Is he not interested?"

So much for thinking I've been successfully keeping my personal life private.

"He seems to be doing anything he can to get away from me as fast as possible. Including auctioning off his own virginity."

In my head I've gone over asking Ravi to stay a thousand different ways. I've even pictured him saying yes. But something tells me that yes would cost something I'm not sure I can pay.

She lets out a low whistle. "Shiiit, I heard about that. That's intense." Her fingers swim around in a bowl of peanuts on the center of the table, cracking one and picking it apart with a singular focus. "You want my advice, boss?"

"No, but here you are giving it to me anyway."

"Damn right. I've seen his file. I know what happened to his parents. That's a Grand Canyon-sized void to fill. If you aren't interested in taking that on, or you don't think he wants you back, then you gotta let the bird fly the nest. He's an adult, whether you like it or not. Nobody understands better than I do why it is you insist on flogging yourself every day, but this young man isn't your responsibility or your salvation. Let him move on with his life so you can move on with yours."

I nod. It's good advice. A smarter man might even take it. The crumpled beer label finds its way into my hand again. I go to work shredding it into smaller and smaller pieces.

"It isn't entirely one-sided," I finally admit. That's as far as I go, because I've already said more than I wanted to, and because saying "he started it" is a ridiculous cop out.

"Hmm." She leans back in her seat, hands at the back of her head like she's about to knock out a round of sit-ups. "I get it. This is punishment."

When the burn of her laser-focused stare cuts into the side of my face, I'm forced to look up. "What are you talking about?"

"A few years ago I drew the short straw on driving Zed home when he got white-girl wasted after the office holiday thing."

Fuck. I press my palms to my eyes until colors burst behind my lids. "What are the odds I can teleport myself to a different bar right now where everyone leaves me the fuck alone?" And also: "White-girl wasted?"

"You went home early that night. If you'd seen him, you'd understand. After causing considerable damage to my back seat, he spilled an ugly crying confession about some shit from back when you two served together. Pretty brutal."

Fuck. "Jesus, I don't want to talk about this."

"You keep a therapist on the payroll for a reason. Survivor's guilt is a thing. I know you know that. I also know if it was one of us, you'd tell us to get our heads out of our asses over something we can't change. Probably some nugget about how you don't get redemption by living a life of assholish solitude. You're punishing yourself, maybe Ravi too, because you don't think you deserve to be happy after your squad got past-tensed in the desert. Knock it the fuck off. If the feeling's mutual, then maybe stop making everyone around you miserable. Stick to good old-fashioned murder like the rest of us do."

Good thing nobody's nearby to hear her. Though if they

were, they'd assume she's joking. For all her pretty words, she's not the one who saw the people she was meant to be leading lying in bloody chunks in the sand like castoff meat on a slaughterhouse kill floor.

"Order your tacos or let someone else take your place in line, sir."

"Right." I won't touch the rest of that, but Bev's on the money. I ought to leave Ravi the fuck alone. He's made it clear he doesn't want my help. Isn't interested in hearing about the risks of his lifestyle of working for a small-town lowlife like Brennan Doyle. If he wants to put himself up on the auction block like a stud horse and let a room full of old men treat him like one, it should be no business of mine.

Ravi's phone pings again. An email notification. From an anonymous address.

Can't wait to win you. You're such a cute little thing. Make sure you keep yourself pristine. Nobody wants tainted goods, pretty.

Hands braced on the wobbly table, I shoot to my feet. There's no chance in hell the sender's in this room, but still my head whips around wildly. Looking for someone to punish for threatening Ravi.

"Boss?"

"Bev. Sal asked you to look into that auction, didn't he? What were you able to find out?"

"Charity auction, technically. Not unusual in the kink community. Aboveboard as these things go."

"Do they have a location?"

"Brennan Doyle's the one setting it up, and there's been a lot of communication between him and Daniel Corvus, the owner of Shadow. If I were placing bets on the location, it would be there."

"That's in line with what I've heard."

The more I think about it, it's also the only venue that makes sense. I spin Ravi's phone on the table, letting my vision go unfocused as I wait for it to come to a stop. Then I read the email again.

Nobody wants tainted goods, pretty.

My brain's a little slow thanks to the beers I've had, but there's no way this email is anything but a giant, flashing warning light. This is a vague threat, a spider toying with Ravi, waiting for him to wander into a sticky web.

"I'm going to forward you an email. Do me a favor and find out anything you can about the sender."

"Sure, boss. I'll see what I can do. Any background other than the email?"

Nothing I wish to discuss. I've had enough emotional purging for the time being.

I push away from the table and head for the door as Bev shouts "Good talk!" at my back.

CHAPTER TWELVE

Ravi

"I don't understand why Daniel's paying for me to stay here."

I'm in a hotel room that probably costs more a night than what I paid for my car.

Channing, the guy who's supposed to guard me until the auction, comes back from checking all the bedrooms and the bathroom. "Mr. Corvus wants to protect his investment."

Practically the second my signature was on that contract, I was whisked into an SUV that still had its new-car smell and driven to the Premiere, the most expensive hotel in Belle Argo. I can see the ocean from the window of my suite.

My *suite*.

I've never stayed anywhere like this in my entire life. It's got two bedrooms, a spacious living area, and a wide balcony that stretches across the living area and both bedrooms. It's filled with not only fancy-looking furniture, but also vases and little plates on the tables, and various other decorative things I've only ever seen in pictures of rich people's homes.

There's a little table on the balcony where you can eat. So adorable.

Adorable, but... "This has got to be expensive."

"Mr. Corvus mentioned that you had been previously imprisoned in a small bedroom. He wants to be clear that these accommodations are for your protection and comfort and doesn't wish for you to feel trapped. It's extremely important that this auction not be done under duress."

Am I less imprisoned when the setting is nicer and I have a seven-foot-tall guard? "What does it matter? I already signed the contract."

"It's messier." Channing's got one of those smiles that always seems a little bit predatory. Almost wolflike.

I've really gotta stop reading those smutty paranormal novels. They're really hot, though. Like...the one where bosshole billionaire shifter Maddox Remmington turned his subordinate into a wolf *for reasons,* and then they got trapped in an elevator together during the full moon and were forced to have violent knot sex?

Yes, please. If I could, I'd live in that fantasy forever. And I really do wish I could.

That's not the point though...

"I could have crashed on someone's couch for a few days," I tell my new bodyguard. "This seems like way too much."

There's a large flat-screen on the wall in the center of the living area. Not to mention an honest-to-God dining room table. My parents and I only ever used the dining table on holidays. Liam doesn't even have one. The dining room is where he keeps his gun safe.

"Well, I haven't been small enough to sleep on someone's couch since I was twelve, and Mr. Corvus wants me to keep an eye on you. Besides, the more comfortable you are, the better the auction will go." He shows that predatory grin again. "Gotta make sure the merchandise stays in good condition, yeah?"

"Okay, but..." I take a breath, trying to hide the full body shiver I get when he refers to me as "merchandise."

Channing is a big guy. Like, a biiiig guy. Liam's formidable at six feet tall, with the kind of muscles that come from more than using those machines in the gym. I've never seen anyone who didn't find him a little intimidating or at least see him as someone they needed to respect. This bodyguard guy Daniel stuck me with? He makes Liam honestly look closer to average in size.

It's hard not to think, is he really here for my safety? Or because Daniel Corvus considers me a flight risk? Something tells me if I wanted to go for a walk on the beach alone, I'd find out real quick that I don't have much more freedom here than at Liam's.

"Here's the thing, Channing. I really hate to be a pest, but whatever money I make from this auction, it needs to be enough to last me for a while. Hopefully, enough to pay for three and a half more years of college plus expenses. Whatever Daniel spends on this place, I assume it's coming out of my cut. This hotel room isn't something I can afford."

There's a knock on the door. Channing motions for me to stay put before checking the peephole and then opening it to reveal... "Mr. Monroe's brother?"

"It's Wes. Good evening." My lit teacher's brother—Wes

—clears his throat and gives us both a polite nod. "I'm the night manager here at the Belle Argo Premiere. I wanted to introduce myself and check in with you personally to see if there's anything we can do to make your stay more comfortable. I do apologize that I wasn't available to escort you to your room, but please be assured I am available any time of the day or night if there's anything you need. Dinner reservations, a private beach cabana—just let me know."

Whoa. Whoa. *Whoa.*

Holy. Shit.

Mr. Monroe's brother gets a whole lot friendlier when you're renting a suite in the hotel he works for, I guess. When he's at the gym he's usually sneering at me. At all the other escorts. How the hell much does this room cost?

Apparently, enough to keep him from looking down his nose at me for a change.

I've *got* to tell the guys about this. My hand goes to my pocket, and then I remember I don't have my phone.

Dammit, Liam.

"I think we're all good here." Channing's already in the middle of closing the door.

"Oh. Uh. Hang on, please. Sorry." I peer around Channing's blocky body. "Could, uh... If it's not too much trouble, is there a way to find out if you guys have any plant-based options available in the restaurant downstairs?"

I try not to tense up as I wait for his answer, but I've learned some people really get put out if you ask for any kind of special diet accommodations. Me, I really hate putting people out. I just hate eating animals more.

Amazingly, the usually scowly Mr. Monroe's brother doesn't bat an eye. "Of course, sir. I'll have the chef send up a list of options for you. Is there anything else I can help you with at this time?"

While Channing is growling "no" and pushing the door closed again, I manage a hasty thank-you.

"I thought that guy hated me," I say to nobody in particular.

Channing laughs. "When you're a VIP guest, nobody hates you. Also, everyone hates you. Either way, Mr. Corvus made the reservation, and he spends a lot of money in this town. That guy's smart enough to know whose ass to apply his tongue to."

Channing positions himself in front of the dining table across from me, lazily crossing his arms over his chest and one ankle over the other. He gives me the same sort of silent assessment Daniel did—is this some kind of kink thing?—and then he inhales, almost as if he's sniffing the air.

"You're nervous."

Wait, what? Is smelling anxiety a thing?

Not that he's wrong. "Of course I'm nervous," I say with a shrug. "Wouldn't you be nervous about auctioning your virginity to a stranger?"

Channing shrugs his wide shoulders. "I lost my virginity in a drug-fueled rut under the full moon." The guy looks like he's on the verge of laughter.

Well. He may be making fun of me, but based on his answer, I know what kind of books he reads now, so the joke's on him.

I see you, bosshole billionaire.

Honestly, that book was the source of most of my jerk-off fantasies until I realized I had a thing for Liam. If the bosshole started to look a lot like Liam when I imagined him fucking me under the full moon, that's not my fault.

I give Channing a shrug of my own. "Being nervous doesn't mean I'm going to bail, so you can tell Mr. Corvus not to worry. The important thing for me is having enough money to pay for my education and get out of town. This was my idea. I'm not going to back out."

It's really hard not to think of Liam right then. Has he given up on stopping me? Is it super bad that I don't know whether I want him to find me or not?

The biggest heartbreak is knowing he'll never do the one thing that would keep me here.

The more I try not to think of him, the more his stern glare fills my head. His eyes are the same color as the ocean outside my balcony.

Channing shakes his head. "You don't want to leave town, do you?"

I narrow my eyes. "I don't want to. I have to. Not that it's any of your business."

"Fair enough. What's your number?" he asks.

"Like my phone number?"

"The number you need so you can leave town. Your expenses, your education. There's no way you haven't tallied all that up."

Of course I have. I've got my ideal scenario, a more moderate scenario, and a worst-case scenario. What I don't have is any idea how feasible meeting any of them is.

It's an awful lot of money I'm looking for. What if nobody thinks I'm worth it?

I take a breath. "I'm not sure it's realistic, but fifty or a hundred thousand would allow me to move someplace with a lower cost of living, give me time to find a job, and work until either I've got some money saved or I can get access to my trust fund when I turn twenty-five. Maybe even put a down payment on a small house." Growing up, we moved a few times. Then I moved again, to live with Liam. It's kind of a dream, finding a place to stay put.

"Brennan thinks I can get a million," I add, as nerves twang in my body like guitar strings. Even saying it sounds outrageous. "That would be even better. He could be wrong, though. I don't think it's safe to assume either way."

When Channing lets out a shocked laugh, I'll admit it stings.

"A million? You're hoping for a million."

Well, that's hurtful. It's one thing for me to worry I'm not going to get what I want. It's another to be laughed at for saying my wants out loud.

"There's no need to be rude." I may know I'm not worth that much, but what's so wrong with hoping?

Channing takes a step, looking down his perfectly shaped nose at me. I refuse to back up though. I don't need him thinking I'm scared.

I'm not. I'm not scared.

"Hey, chill. You're a good-looking guy. Not my type, okay? I want to know when I go all out fucking someone I won't accidentally launch them across the room."

The last thing I expected was to laugh today. "I guess that's fair. So?"

"So, I may not be into you, but my vision works fine. That nice tight body of yours? Gorgeous brown skin, a killer smile. Chin dimple and all. Don't get me started on the nerdy glasses. Eyes like a baby lemur. Hell, I could give you a long list of people who'd be willing to pay to have those eyelashes. If you think the rich pervs won't open their bank accounts nice and wide to be the first to plant their flag in you, you're on something."

Um.

I fight not to squirm. Am I supposed to be offended or flattered right now?

He reaches out with one big paw and pokes me in the shoulder. "You? Need to be thinking a lot bigger."

"You think I can get more than fifty grand?" That guy from the party pops into my head. In all the, uh, shenanigans that happened after, I'd nearly forgotten. "Some guy at this party... I don't think he was even serious, but he offered me two million to skip the auction. I said no. Even if it was legit, Brennan would rage. The guy seemed kind of slimy, so I doubt it was a real offer. But... you think I could get that much?"

Channing's quiet for long enough that I have to fight not to squirm.

"Why are you looking at me like that?"

His expression turns serious. "That's the exact sort of reason why Mr. Corvus wants you guarded." The way he leans in close to my ear, it's only the fact that he already said he's not interested that makes me think it's not some weird kind of flirting. "You poor, naive little puppy. When I say you need to think bigger, I mean a hell of a lot bigger. Because that guy? He was trying to get you at a bargain."

CHAPTER THIRTEEN

LIAM

AFTER SPENDING a few days running surveillance on every one of Ravi's friends, known associates, and even a classmate who texted about borrowing his macroeconomics notes, I'm coming up empty on his location.

Sunday morning I scoped out the diner where he and his friends like to have brunch, but for the first time since he started going, he wasn't there. Perhaps he knew I'd be looking for him.

I'll get him eventually. Finding people is what I do. It's the not knowing that's making my head hurt.

Like a fucking addict, I keep going back to that email Bev hasn't managed to pin down. Letting it fuel my terror and my rage. Soothing myself by plotting the death of a faceless stranger. The idea that someone out there is seeing Ravi as theirs, as some sort of possession or plaything, has me sharpening my knives every night as the vague threat eats at me from the inside.

Isn't that how you see him?

I bat away the image of his smooth, firm ass, heated by my handprints.

It's completely different.

Are you sure?

"Fuck yes," I growl to myself. "It's completely different. I'm trying to protect him. It's different because..." Fuck it. My conscience has never gotten me anywhere good, so I tell it to take a fucking hike.

The hour is late when I pull up to Shadow. When Daniel Corvus first arrived in town looking to set up shop, I did some digging into him and found almost nothing. No criminal record. No education. Not even much of a credit history. Whoever he is, someone who's deliberately erased their own past is bad news.

Until now, I've never had a real reason to deal with him.

The black-painted door to the club is guarded by a man bigger than my refrigerator and about the same shape. In spite of his tuxedo and slicked-back hair, he's got the posture of someone who expects to get into a fight at any moment. While I see no outward signs of incarceration, no obvious prison tattoos, my money is on ex-con. If my theory about Daniel being a criminal is right? Well, birds of a feather and everything.

Showing my little-used membership card does nothing to make him move.

"I'm here to talk to Mr. Corvus," I tell Gigantor when he throws his arm across the door.

"He's busy. VIPs only tonight."

"How would you know he's busy?"

There's a little earpiece in his ear. This place probably has cameras everywhere. It's possible someone's already recognized me and has given my presence a big thumbs-down. Still, playing dumb works more often than you'd think.

"He's always busy. Mr. Corvus has a lot of responsibilities."

It only takes a brief scan of the overhang above the doorway to spot the small black dome that more than likely encases a camera. Hopefully it has a microphone as well.

Giving the camera a little wave, I say, "Please tell Mr. Corvus if he's too busy to see me, then the next person he's going to see is whichever member of the local SWAT team holds the battering ram, because I'm about to call in a suspected hostage situation. He's got the whereabouts of someone important to me, and I've launched missiles at a building for less."

Big Man only grins. "I'd like to see you try."

In spite of his dismissal, a moment later, he puts his finger to his earpiece.

"Mr. Corvus will see you now," he says, making a growling noise under his breath.

Now I'm the one grinning. This is the first good news I've had in days. "Thank you. I had a feeling he might."

Big Guy throws me a murderous look before turning to open the door. "Stay behind me and don't talk to any of the other members."

As if I'd want to. Tonight, I'm here about Ravi. "Anything you say, Big Guy."

When I'm led to a private room where the man in question is sitting in a high-backed chair like it's a throne and being serviced by a lanky young man with dirty blond hair who's kneeling between his feet, I'm curious. Is Corvus trying to make me uncomfortable, or is he simply multitasking?

For that matter, how old is this kid? He looks about Ravi's age, but with the practiced and performative movements of someone who's been selling themselves for a long time. Christ almighty.

"Told you he was busy," the bouncer says. He ushers me into the room with a wave of his arm, unable to make eye contact with anyone as he excuses himself to return to his post.

Well, if Daniel's thinking seeing another man get his dick sucked will get me flustered, he doesn't know much.

"Liam Masters. To what do I owe the pleasure?"

"From where I'm standing, the pleasure's not on my account at all."

Daniel chuckles. Looking down at the young man between his knees, he runs a hand through that shaggy blond hair with an almost fond look on his face before quietly pulling out of the young man and zipping himself up. "Take a break, sweetheart," he murmurs. "Grab a drink. We'll finish this later."

Now that I get a better look, the kid—boy? Young man? —looks maybe a little older than Ravi. He's skinny, but on the taller side, without the lean definition Ravi's worked hard to pack on this last year. Wearing nothing but a tiny pair of shorts similar to the ones Ravi wore the night I caught him crawling through his window and a pair of boots that could have come from my closet. He bows to me and then Daniel before slipping out and closing the door behind him.

"Sorry to interrupt your important business matters," I say without any kind of sincerity.

Mr. Corvus has a lot of responsibilities, my scarred ass.

"For a man who's seen the world, Mr. Masters, there's a lot you don't know. Some people need regular sexual stimulation. It's air. It's food."

Give me a fucking break. "You're telling me a man of your age can't survive without getting your dick sucked?"

Not that I'm entirely sure of the man's age given the sparse information out there, but local records list his date of birth as being a few years before mine. That he looks several years younger than I do is one more reason I'd like to stab him.

Daniel scoffs at my jab. "Of course I can. I meant the boy. I'm sure you know how...passionate and enthusiastic they can be at that age."

I rub at the sudden throb in my temples. "Jesus Beverly Christ. You've got to be fucking kidding me right now."

Whatever. If Daniel Corvus wants to use his club as a thinly veiled excuse to fuck barely legal young men, it's not my problem. The boy could use fewer blow jobs and more sandwiches if you ask me, but nobody did.

So long as one of those young men isn't mine.

"Where is he?"

Daniel's eyebrows go up.

"Don't act like you don't fucking know who I'm talking about. Ravi Novak. Where. Is. He?"

The smug bastard clasps his hands behind his back. "What gives you the impression I have any idea?"

"He's not at home where he belongs. I've checked out everyone else he knows, including Brennan fucking Doyle. He's not with any of them. Word's out that the auction is being held here. Right now he's an asset to you, and you don't seem like the sort of man who would let a million dollars wander around freely when there are threats against him."

Suspicion crosses Daniel's face. "How do you know there are threats against him?"

"How do *you* know?" I'm assuming he hasn't read Ravi's emails. And if he has, I've got a lot more questions.

"Tell me," Corvus says with his jaw tight.

Leaning against the door behind me, I cross my arms over my chest. "Show me yours and I'll show you mine."

Daniel Corvus stands, having the actual audacity to glance suggestively at my crotch. "I believe I've already shown you mine."

"Fucking hell you're an asshole." My hand goes to my gun holster.

Corvus makes a discouraging noise. "Careful, Mr. Masters. Discharging a firearm in here would be extremely dangerous." He seats himself back on his throne, looking unconcerned in spite of his warning.

A glance up shows me another camera, tucked away in the corner and barely visible. Something tells me security is already on their way.

"Someone sent him an email." I hold up Ravi's phone. "It's vague, but the proprietary tone gives me the creeps."

Corvus nods. "We've had a few attempts at preemptive bids, including one person who approached Ravi himself at Mercer Oak's last cocktail gathering. In addition, there have been a few anonymous messages demanding we shut the entire thing down. Frankly, I wondered if those might be from you."

"Wouldn't be me. If I have a problem with someone, I let them know directly."

He nods. "Clearly. Well. Rich men get astonishingly

turned on by a bargain. Perhaps that's all the notes have been about—not wanting the auction to drive up what they'd have to pay to have him. I see an equally great likelihood that someone out there—" He gives me a pointed look. "—aside from you feels an unreasonable level of ownership over Ravi and doesn't want anyone else getting him."

"I don't feel—"

He cuts off my protest with a wave of his hand. "Let's not waste each other's time here, Masters. Yes, Ravi is under my protection until the auction. No, I'm not releasing his whereabouts. Not even to you."

Fuck if I'll tell Corvus he's right. I do feel an unreasonable level of ownership. And his refusal to tell me where Ravi is, what the kid might be doing... Jesus Christ, who he might be doing it with. I need to fucking pummel something.

There's a frustrated growl building in my throat. "This is completely fucked. Ravi's not savvy about how the world works. He makes these impulsive, reckless decisions. I guarantee he has no idea how dangerous this is. I need to let him know about these threats."

"Do you?"

My fingers clench tight around Ravi's phone before I force myself to shove it back into my pocket. "What the hell kind of question is that?"

"One of my staff or I can alert him about the situation. There's no need for you to do so. You've clearly appointed yourself the young man's protector and savior. Still, I've gotten the impression that while he isn't particularly thrilled at the prospect of giving up his virginity to a stranger, he's very set on the decision and is of sound mind. He indicated needing the sort of money that would allow him to go away and not come back. One can't help but wonder who it is he's running from."

Brennan Doyle said something similar. Later, when I'm alone, I'll take the time to consider why it feels like the man in front of me has plunged a knife into my gut.

"You motherfucker."

I'm known for staying cool in all manner of situations. It's something I've honed over more than two decades. How is it then that I find myself standing over Daniel Corvus with his finely made dress shirt twisted in my fist?

Not that he seems particularly ruffled. He's never seen me carve a man to pieces with my knife. Maybe that would give him more cause for concern.

"You have to know that my security is already on their way. The sooner you let go, the more likely you are to leave here in one piece."

He's not bluffing. Heavy footsteps thunder nearby, coming up the stairs and down the hall toward the room where we're standing. Three people. Maybe four.

Fuck. I release Corvus and take a step back. It's not like me to go into a scenario without backup or to lose my temper to boot, and here I am doing it because of Ravi again. Fucking again. This kid is messing with my head.

Reason enough to stay away. As if there aren't plenty of others.

Am I going to? No. At least I have the presence of mind to know that I should.

With however many seconds I have left, I come the closest I ever have to begging. "Daniel, his parents trusted me to take care of him. Which I can't do if he's getting sold off to the highest bidder like an antique chair. God knows what some creep with deep pockets would do if they had him for an entire night. Tell me where he is. *Please*."

"The deal is for twenty-four hours. It's not exactly an eternity."

"That doesn't make it better. In twenty-four hours he could be dead."

Footsteps come closer.

"We're vetting the applicants carefully. That's a promise, and I take promises seriously. These auctions are supposed to be fun, Mr. Masters. We've got several other club members auctioning themselves for charity on the same night as Ravi. The others will be donating their proceeds to the East End Mission."

"Then you don't need Ravi, do you? I'm asking you to put a stop to this."

"You have to know there's too much invested. I'll give you this, Mr. Masters. In spite of your behavior this evening, I'll instruct my security team to allow you entry for the auction. Don't make me regret that. If you cause a disturbance, my security will tear you apart before you've had time to regret your actions. Oh, and bring a bank statement. Bidders will be expected to prove their ability to pay prior to the auction start."

What the fuck? I take a step back, staring Corvus right in the eyes. "You're saying if I want to take the kid who's already living in my damn house back home where he belongs, I'm expected to fucking bid on him?"

"I'm saying if you don't want your young man spreading himself open for someone who isn't you, then you'll need to win him, yes."

The door bursts open.

When two sets of hands grab me, I don't resist. There's

only one of me, and from the sound of it, a few sets of boots at my back. In spite of holding my hands up in a show of surrender, I give Daniel Corvus a look that tells him exactly what I think of his suggestion.

"Please escort Mr. Masters outside. We'll be seeing him again on the night of the charity auction. And, Mr. Masters, I'll even give you a little help to ensure your finances are in order." He pulls a piece of paper from his pocket and unfolds it. Without reading the page closely, I know it's a consent list. Ravi's.

"Ravi's expressed a willingness to be shared. I see a distinct likelihood that men with those proclivities might be enticed to pool their resources."

Fuck. *Fuck.* That cannot happen.

Over my dead fucking body.

I process this as I'm shoved down the stairs and out into Shadow's parking lot. The truth of Corvus's parting words weigh me down more than the Florida humidity. He's telling me some of Belle Argo's richest and most influential men might decide to chip in on Ravi like stoned kids in a university dorm splitting the cost of a pizza. Bile shoots into the back of my throat.

It's one of my personal kinks, sharing someone. Admittedly, the thought of Ravi being in the center of one of the circles Zed and I have hosted in my garage elicits feelings it really, really shouldn't. Disturbing, beautiful images of him tied down and spread out.

But faceless strangers sharing the kid? Without me there to ensure his safety?

No. He's mine, goddammit. I'll blow up this club and everyone in it before I let anyone else have him.

CHAPTER FOURTEEN

Ravi

"Hey, Rav. What's with the lothario?"

"Huh?" Simon's question filters to me through the haze of near-pornographic "yum" noises I've been making over my breakfast burrito. I'm sooo freaking glad my stomach is finally working again.

Room service at the hotel where I've been staying is nice, but I've been craving one of Gil's tofu scramble burritos all week. I hated not being here last Sunday, but I had homework to catch up on. I'm not letting that slide until I know for sure I can leave Belle Argo.

When I see where Simon's pointing over my shoulder, my face falls. "Oh. Him."

A quick check tells me my giant shadow is indeed still with me. For the past several days he's followed me literally everywhere. Class, the gym, the hotel restaurant, the farmers' market, and, of course, here to brunch. The only place I've had privacy is back at the suite, when I'm behind the locked door of my own room. Weirdly enough, I've gotten so used to Channing I sometimes forget he's there.

I guess it was wishful thinking that if he stood against the back wall of Gil's and didn't talk to anybody, my fellow escorts wouldn't notice a giant at our weekly group brunch.

By the expectant stares they're all giving me, it was definitely too much to hope.

Christian, who's had some past issues with an abusive boyfriend, seems especially wary. He's leaning so far away from Channing he might fall off his chair. I give him my best apologetic smile.

"Sorry. That's Channing. The guy who owns Shadow seemed to think I needed someone to keep an eye on me until the auction. As long as I don't make a run for it, everything is fine."

It still seems like serious overkill. So a guy offered me money to blow off the auction? I didn't do it, did I?

A few of the guys give an awkward wave. Simon's boyfriend has narrowed eyes and tightly pressed lips, as if he maybe doesn't trust the guy. Which I don't blame him for. My bodyguard has been mostly nice to me, but I'm not stupid enough to think he's on my side. Channing responds with a tight grimace that could almost but not quite be classified as a smile.

Nico uses his breadstick to point from across the table. "Is he, like, one of those palace guards? He's not allowed to make facial expressions or whatever?"

"You'd have to ask him." I lift a shoulder and return to my burrito.

Not that there's anything really wrong with Channing. He's been perfectly fine, I guess, for a bodyguard. Staying in the nicest hotel in Belle Argo, nicer than anyplace I've stayed in my entire life, and getting to order room service for the first time ever? I certainly have nothing to complain about.

Staying away from Liam has felt unexpectedly hollow. Even when I was at the dorms I came home to do my laundry and eat on weekends. He'd call or text to check in. Being cut off from him completely, it's almost like when my parents died. Someone I loved, just suddenly gone. Why I miss his presence so painfully after the way he's treated me, I don't understand. All I know is the closer I get to the auction, the more my nerves jangle in my stomach every day.

It's a good thing I'm usually a stress-eater, or I'd risk being skin and bones by the time the big night rolls around. For all of Daniel's predictions that I'm going to "fetch a pretty price," nobody wants to fuck a skeleton.

I mean, maybe someone does? That's probably not something I want to bother researching.

"Hey, you doing okay, man?" Next to me, PJ nudges me with his elbow. "You decide you've changed your mind about this thing, you say the word. We'll bust you out of whatever castle tower they've got you in and fuck that giant bodyguard."

In spite of all the chatter, both here in the back room and out front, Channing clears his throat behind me. I've noticed the big guy has ears like a bat. PJ might be scrappy, but I'm not sure he can take Channing down. After four years of living with a soldier, I know one when I see 'em.

"Really, I'll be fine," I assure my friend. "If you ask me, the security isn't even necessary, but it is what it is."

If Liam were here now he'd be telling me how stupid and dangerous this all is for the millionth time. I'm not as stupid as he thinks. Or as the rest of these guys might think, as well meaning as they are.

I'm aware the auction is a risk. Some guy might want to hurt me or push my boundaries past what's comfortable. Who knows, though, I could like it, right? And even if I don't, it's only twenty-four hours out of my life.

I handled my parents getting murdered. I've handled Liam rejecting me over and over (and over) for nearly two years. I can handle this. Especially for the chance at a huge payoff.

It's only twenty-four hours, right? I can handle anything for that long.

Next to Nico, Dean leans forward. "But, Rav, this shit's no joke. There was that guy at the party who tried to put his hands on you, so maybe a little extra protection for the time being isn't a bad idea."

"Wait, who the hell grabbed you?" Alexis, one of Brennan's female workers, asks as she, well, grabs my arm. Sweet of her to be worried though.

"It wasn't a big deal. Some guy at a party wanted me to take money to skip the auction."

"Oh hell. Brennan would've given birth to kittens. You know he's going to take his cut of your payday." This is from Prince, one of our newer escorts. Unlike a lot of the guys, who do dinner dates and charity events and all sorts of things aside from having sex with clients, Prince pretty much only has sex with the clients, from what I can tell. Given that he's got more tattoos than I've ever seen a person, even on his knuckles and on the side of his face, I can see how it would be hard for him to simply put on a suit and blend in.

I've also heard he's into the "super kinky stuff," whatever that means. I haven't asked, even though I've wanted to. Tattooing, for sure. Kissing? Maybe even clothespins?

There was something on that list Daniel made me fill out about ice cubes. I chickened out and put no because I wasn't clear on where the ice cubes would go. In a drink? In my mouth? In my...?

I've been meaning to research that one.

Either way, pretty much every sex worker I've met—including me—has some sort of pressing financial need that they haven't been able to meet any other way. Prince seems to be the exception. Once on the group chat he said he likes to fuck so might as well get paid.

Makes sense.

"I'm not stupid enough to go behind Brennan's back," I mutter. "I don't know what everyone's worrying about. Dean told the guy no. His friend got him to back off. Aside from being all starey-glarey for the rest of the night he left me alone. Everything was fine."

Troy, whose normally styled hair is all ruffled for some reason, pipes up. "You gotta be careful, though, pip-squeak. There are some real sickos out there. That's the whole reason Adam and I started working for Brennan instead of being freelance." He gestures between himself and Adam, who's sitting next to him eating a cupcake. For breakfast.

"Uh, Adam? Aren't you worried about your blood sugar?" He's diabetic, right? Cupcakes don't seem like a great idea for breakfast.

"It's sort of a special celebration." He elbows Troy in the side. "Don't worry, this guy makes sure I check my numbers and everything." Troy surreptitiously moves his hand over, patting Adam on the thigh.

They're not as subtle as they think, because a look

around the table tells me I'm not the only one who noticed their intimacy. Even I've put a few dollars down on the pool for when the two of them are going to finally admit they're a couple, but they keep swearing they aren't.

Over by Alexsis, Eve tries to ask what he's celebrating, but they both give her a weird look, so she lets it drop.

Then Troy changes the subject by asking Dean how his daughter is doing. Which works like a charm.

"She's in ballet now. You guys gotta see this. I did her hair myself..." Then he's showing around photos of a toothless little girl in a tutu and a bun, who's beaming happily with her two front teeth missing.

Michael's the only one not oohing and ahhing, grumbling something about how Dean's not the one who searched high and low for brown ballet flats.

There's an unexpected heaviness in my stomach as I look at the pretty ballerina picture. I mean, it's nothing against Dean's daughter, who's definitely the cutest daughter ever. It's not even that I'm jealous, because I'm not even twenty yet, and I don't know if I'll ever even want kids. It's more that she looks so secure and happy, and I hardly remember when I felt that way.

The rest of my burrito hits my plate in a scattered mess. I'm not as hungry now.

While I loved my parents, most of my childhood there was constant fighting. Nothing was ever predictable. Then they were gone, shot by my dad's heartbroken mistress, which was worse.

Mr. Monroe is with us today, on the other side of PJ. He leans back in his chair and clears his throat. "Uh, so, Ravi, PJ mentioned you were having trouble with your living situation. Do you need a place to stay? We've been a little lax about getting the new house furnished, but there's a sofa."

"Yeah, and I made sure that shit was comfortable," PJ pipes up. "His old one sucked. Badly. Not like you do, baby," he says with a hand on Mr. Monroe's cheek.

That's, uh... I mean, good for them? Except already I have to see Mr. Monroe in class three mornings a week and pretend I haven't overheard PJ on the phone before telling Mr. Monroe to "get his pretty ass home and have it up in the air."

It's so hard to focus on Mr. Monroe's class lectures with that mental picture in my head.

Out of the corner of my eye I can see my teacher blushing hard, but whatever he says in response to PJ's lewd comment is too quiet for me to hear. Thankfully.

"Uh, thanks, Mr. Monroe? I'm good though. Daniel Corvus is putting me up at the Belle Argo Premiere. It's really nice."

Around the table I can hear some whistles and murmurs of appreciation.

"That place is phenomenal," Michael says from next to Dean. "I stayed for a week once doing a boyfriend experience. Especially nice if you're on the VIP floor. Top-notch service. Don't sleep on the gym and the pool while you're there. Makes the gym at BAU look like that old place where Rocky trained."

"I haven't checked out the pool. Maybe you guys want to come over and swim while I'm still there?" As soon as the words are out of my mouth I freeze, because why would they want to come and hang out with me? But then some of them nod, and I relax a little. Sometimes I'm just not sure if I'm overstepping with people.

"It's a great place," Mr. Monroe agrees. "My brother Wes is one of the managers there. You can get in touch with him if you need anything while you're there. Remind him that you know me."

"Oh, yeah. I talked to him, actually." I don't mention the weird ass-kissing vibe and how different it was from the way he usually stares daggers at us all. Even though I still wonder if the guy had a personality transplant.

"Just don't tell him you know me." PJ laughs.

"He already knows, silly. He's met all your friends at this point." Mr. Monroe gives PJ a playful smack on the shoulder. Then he gives PJ the same look he gives when kids are talking in class before turning back to me. "Seriously, Wes's issues with PJ aside, if you need something he'll be happy to help. He's one of those people who likes to feel needed. He's staying at the hotel temporarily while going through a divorce, so he's there most of the time."

"Thanks. He did stop by the room to ask if I needed anything. I don't want to go bothering him any further, though, if he's dealing with personal stuff."

"You're definitely on the VIP floor if a manager stopped by the room," Michael throws in.

"Honestly, I think Wes could use the distraction," Mr. Monroe counters. "We don't talk about personal stuff as much as we used to, but I get the impression he's having a hard time."

"Hey, remember when your brother followed PJ in here and threatened him a while back? That was kind of hot." Adam asks as he licks the frosting from his cupcake wrapper.

"I wasn't here that day, but thank you so much for the

reminder." Mr. Monroe gives Adam that same talking-in-class look.

Honestly, Adam's comment gives me the urge to look around the restaurant. I'm a little surprised Liam hasn't tried to find me here. He knows it's my favorite place. Maybe he's finally decided he's done keeping tabs on me.

Which is a good thing. Except I don't like the way thinking it makes my heart sink.

From behind I get a tap on the shoulder.

"Mr. Corvus wants to speak with you. We need to go," Channing says.

Just like that, whatever peace I felt being in one of my favorite places with people I know disappears. The look on Channing's face tells me whatever this is about isn't anything good.

CHAPTER FIFTEEN

LIAM

I'M STATIONED outside the building where Ravi's literature class takes place, bright and early on the Monday before the auction. The second I see him, I want to throw him over my shoulder and drag him out of there. That fucker he's with is big, but I can take him. I'm certain.

By the time Ravi notices me standing here, the big guy behind him is already glaring. This must be the security Daniel mentioned.

"What are you doing here? How did you know where my classes are?" Only seconds before spotting me, Ravi had been chatting with the large man next to him and laughing. *Laughing*. I haven't seen him laugh in at least a year.

"Wasn't easy." Bev hacked admissions to get me his schedule. She wasn't thrilled about it, but some situations require creative solutions. "I'd have tracked you down earlier if you hadn't left your watch at home."

"You mean the GPS tracker you put in my watch without even letting me know? That was pretty fucked up, Liam."

A frustrated breath punches its way out of my chest. "Ravi, I've told you—"

"Yeah, yeah, your responsibility to babysit the little orphan because of your ancient friendship with my dad, blah, blah. I'm not your job. You can stop."

My heart's fucking aching right now. Doesn't he understand? Protecting him is the one thing I've done sort of right in all the fucked-up shit I've been part of. I need that rightness, especially now.

"Everything okay here, Rav?"

Rav. His fucking security guard is calling him Rav, as if they're pals. He's walking around with one of Daniel Corvus's oversized goons on his six, but when I try to protect him, I'm an overbearing asshole.

To my surprise, Ravi rolls his eyes and says, "Everything is fine, Channing." When he turns back to me, his expression hardens. "Seriously, Liam. What are you doing here?"

I hand over the bag I've been holding. "Since you haven't come home and you haven't been back to your dorm, I thought you might need some things."

He takes the bag and briefly inspects the contents. Some clothes, his phone, his watch, and a couple of his sketchbooks, because I know he likes to draw when he's having a tough time. A ghost of a smile crosses his face, but he quickly wipes it away.

Ravi spent days on end drawing when he first came to live with me. Wouldn't talk much, but he'd have his pencil scratching on paper for hours. Days. I found the old ones in his room when I gathered his things. Mostly pictures of his folks. Some animals. A new book had pictures of me.

Fantasy images of the two of us together, entwined and sleepy. I'm not proud of it, but that particular sketchbook found a new home in my dresser drawer.

"Thanks," Ravi says. "But...you know I couldn't stay. Not the way things have been."

Once again I'm assaulted by the memory of my hand striking against his ass. The heat of his skin. The way I made him—

Dammit. As much as I hate to admit it, he's right. Things would have gone berserk if he'd stayed. They'd already departed wildly from anything resembling sanity.

"Last time..." *His cries and moans. The way his hips bucked every time my hand came down on him.*

The truth is, that night opened a door I'm having a hard time slamming closed.

"I went too far, Ravi. I don't know what got into me. I'm sorry." Every time I see him sitting on his bed crying, asking me to talk to him, the self-loathing digs its claws deeper.

The way he's looking at me now, I think it's supposed to be a hard stare. Mostly it comes off worried and wary. When the kid first came to live with me, he trusted me. I know he did. In spite of how oppressive his trust felt at the time, I'm cold and empty now that it's gone.

Now that he's gone.

"I know you don't believe me, but I really am trying to keep you safe." I gesture at the bag he's holding. "Your phone is in there. Check your emails, if you don't believe me. You've been getting messages from an anonymous source and they're legitimately worrying. Some guy asking you to save yourself for him. Calling you creepy shit like 'pretty' and 'precious.' They're unhinged, Ravi."

"I already know about the emails," Ravi insists. "Channing dragged me out of brunch yesterday so I could go down to Mr. Corvus's office and hear all about the fact that some insistent potential bidder is pushing really hard to get the auction canceled. I told him it was probably you."

What Ravi doesn't realize is that I was at Gil's yesterday when he and his friends were there. While I stood in the crowded restaurant pretending to pick up a mobile order, Ravi chatted with his friends and looked at pictures of someone's kid. The only thing that stopped me from barging in was that I counted at least a dozen people in the room, along with Ravi's fucking guard dog. They would have circled the wagons, and I wouldn't have gotten near him. Whatever I may think of that group, they protect their own.

What pisses me off most is that Ravi is one of their own.

"I'm not sending the damn emails," I growl. "I'm not that stupid."

What the fuck does he take me for?

When I see him inching along the wall to get to the entrance of the building, I soften my tone. The last thing I want is to make him run again.

"Look, kid, I've made it crystal clear I don't want you to do this auction. You and I both know your parents wouldn't want it for you. I've already tried to get both Doyle and Corvus to cancel by speaking directly to them. I don't need to hide behind some anonymous email address."

He chews his lip. I can see the moment he believes me. Thank fuck.

"Did you look into them? The emails?"

Some of the tension leaks out of my shoulders. For this small moment he's speaking to me the way he used to, before we were always at each other's throats. Not that I appreciate having to talk to him with a bodyguard standing two feet away, but I'll take the win right now.

"My tech guru, Bev, she's looking into it. So far all she's found is a dummy account, which are easy to set up these days and hard to track."

Ravi only chews harder on his lip. "You really think I'm in danger?"

I pull on his lip with my thumb and forefinger, forcing him to stop biting before he draws blood. It's alarmingly difficult to take my fingers off his damp, plump skin. "Ravi, those emails made my blood cold. In my line of work you take every threat seriously. Blowing something off is how you get killed. I can't have something like that happen to you."

He fidgets a little, glancing around before saying quietly, "Channing said some guys were probably just trying to, uh, get me at a discount?"

Jesus, I can't stand the mental image that gives me. "You're not a dented can of peas at the grocery store, kid. It could be a hell of a lot worse than someone who's bargain hunting. What if this is some delusional shithead who thinks they have a right to you that they don't have?"

There's an ugly whisper in the back of my head that the right should be no one's but mine. I do my best to shove it way down into the seething pit where the rest of my ugly shit lives. It swirls in my stomach, threatening to rise up and choke me.

Ravi raises his chin. "I know this might not make sense to you, but I don't actually care too much about being objectified. Whoever wins the auction, they *will* have a right to me. For twenty-four hours. And I'll be getting a payout in return."

My morning coffee curdles in my stomach. "Ravi."

"In fact, I gave Daniel a whole list of things I didn't mind someone else doing to me. I don't care if you have a problem with it. I am an adult, whether you want to acknowledge it or not."

Lately I've been doing nothing but acknowledging how adult he is.

Somehow I'm drifting closer. His puffy, wet, chewed-up lip shines under the morning sun like a homing beacon. Yes, I know he's an adult. What I wouldn't give to forget.

"You said you'd seen what goes on in my garage. Were you spying on me? Hoping to get caught?" Some wicked force has gotten hold of my tongue. "Tell me how you know."

He lifts his chin. For a second, his lip gets caught between his teeth again. "Yeah. I came back early one night and there was a light on in the garage. I checked it out. So?"

"So you should realize it's not your...interests that I have a problem with."

He seems surprised. "Then how come—never mind. I think I get it. It's not about the auction. It's about the fact that you still see me as a child and you can't handle thinking of me doing something like that."

Ravi's hard cock thrusting between my knees while I spanked him. His tight virgin pucker winking at me. His—

"You have no idea what it's about for me."

We're so close now, my toes pressing against his, his back against the wall. I bring my lips close to his ear, whispering so nobody else can listen, including his nosy fucking bodyguard.

"Do you honestly believe I can't think of you as an adult? I can't get what happened in your bedroom out of my head.

It's turning me goddamn inside out. If one of my employees was going out of their minds the way you've got me, I would have forced them to take a leave of absence by now. Of all the people your parents could have assigned to take you in, they chose the one with a checkered military record and a higher body count than the I-4 strangler. Always thought it was fucked up of your pop to want me to have you."

Have him. Lord help me, I'm sick.

Forcing myself to take a breath, I step back. Or I try. The morning has a hint of chill with fall on its way, and Ravi's heat is heaven. What interests me, as I study Ravi's face, is the lack of surprise. My military career isn't something I've discussed with him, but he's simply expectant after my little bomb, waiting to hear more.

A kid walking into the building knocks into his shoulder. Ravi stumbles sideways against the wall while the stocky, pimply-faced prick wearing too many designer labels keeps on going.

"Hey, get the fuck back here, you Prada-wearing piece of shit. Ever heard of apologizing?"

I'm dragging the asshole backward when Ravi reaches for my arm. "Liam. Stop. It was an accident." He glances uneasily at the guard dog, who's on alert now, stepping forward. "Let him go."

What's worse? That I let this minor infraction trip my wires, or that Ravi's guard dog looks more ready to come after me than the careless asshole who bumped his protectee? I make a show of letting the little piece of shit go.

As the guy scurries away, Ravi asks, "Are you okay? You're not usually this touchy."

Am I okay? I shake my head. Probably not.

"I'm fine," I lie. "Just tired."

"So go home. Get some sleep. Stop worrying about me."

Doesn't he realize I can't? I can't stop breathing. Can't stop worrying about Ravi. Soon he's going to be gone, and I won't be able to breathe anymore.

"I've always figured..." My fingers find their way to a bit of Ravi's T-shirt, bunching the soft fabric against his side. "I guess I decided your father had chosen me because he truly believed I was the best person to keep you safe. I've clung to that idea until my fingertips bled. Then one night you climbed into my bed and told me you wanted me to be your first. The really sick part? I wanted it, too."

Ravi blinks. His lips part. "Liam..."

Every breath I take burns my lungs. "I've spent every night since then hating myself for being tempted, hating myself for trying to do the right thing. Meanwhile, it turns out maybe you don't love me the way you claimed back then, since all I keep hearing is how badly you want to leave town."

Does he understand what I'm saying? Is he hearing me? I don't know. Because when I stop talking all I can focus on is the way his lips are parted. The way his thighs are squeezing around my knee. I'm not sure how my leg got between his, I only know I don't want him to stop.

"Liam, I decided to leave because I realized you were never going to see me as more than your ward. At least, that's how it seemed. Has something changed?"

Nothing. Everything. I only know I can't let him go.

"What's wrong?" I say instead when his knees squeeze mine again. "You're acting awfully horny."

"I haven't been, uh..." As he cuts his gaze over to the bodyguard, his cheeks darken. "It feels weird getting myself off with Channing in the next room."

"You haven't been getting yourself off because of that guy? You don't want to have an orgasm with a wall between you and another stranger but you're willing to let one buy you, fuck you, and do God knows what else?"

"Different." His whispers are breathy, and so soft even I have to strain to hear. "I don't expect you to understand."

"Try, baby. Help me understand. It's tearing me up thinking about you giving yourself up to some stranger." I hadn't meant to admit that out loud, but what's done is done. "If it's about the money, I'll give it to you. I'll give you anything."

"But you won't," Ravi insists.

Even while his eyes are glazed over and he's grinding himself on my leg, he's got to argue with me.

"Tell me the truth, Liam. Could you ever love me back? If I went to Daniel right this minute and begged him to tear up my contract, would you take me home and make me yours the way I wanted you to that night I climbed into your bed? Would you honestly be able to see me as more than someone you've been obligated to take care of? Because I might have been young, but I knew what I wanted then, and I know what I want now."

His words wrap around my chest like a steel band. Ice water pours over my head. Sucking in an abrupt breath, I jerk myself away, putting space between his body and mine. "Ravi... I don't..."

The truth is, I want to. I also can't.

Denying him feels like suffocating. Like fucking torture. What I want to tell him is "yes, dammit, cancel the fucking auction and I will do anything you ask," but if I say that, then what? What happens when Ravi grows up a little more and realizes who I really am? When he regrets the old man he's shackled himself to?

Ravi is pure sunlight. He's idealistic and hopeful. He won't eat meat because it pains him to harm another living thing. He ran into a fucking drug warehouse to try and save a bunch of total strangers. What would it do to him, tying himself to a man who's made his living on death?

My silence goes on for too long, and as the seconds pass Ravi's expression turns serious. Then wounded. Then stony.

"Yeah, that's what I thought." His softly spoken words are a death knell in the midst of the cacophony of students rushing to class. "You're willing to give me anything to call off the auction except the thing I want most. Which means I can't stay. Which means I need the money so I can go."

"Ravi..."

He pulls himself to his full height, his glare intense enough to melt my face. His eyes narrow. Almost looks like he's putting on some kind of persona.

"Go fuck yourself, Daddy. I don't want to see you again."

With his words, Ravi may as well have sliced me open. Shoved my own knife into my gut and twisted for all he's worth.

I'm sure I'm dying as I watch him walk away.

CHAPTER SIXTEEN

LIAM

I DODGE ZED'S fist as it comes at me, using it as an opening to catch my friend in the ribs.

Zed winces and shakes it off as we circle each other.

"Okay, let's have it. Bev said your head's too far up your ass to see straight. Something to do with Ravi."

Closing my eyes with a grunt, I slide my wrist across my face to clear the sweat.

And like every time I close my eyes lately, I'm assaulted by images of my hand on his flesh. I hear the crack of my palm across his ass. The sounds of him shouting his orgasm to everyone in the zip code.

The harder I try not to want him, the more I do. I think that's the worst part.

And then *go fuck yourself, Daddy.*

"I'm fine," I insist.

Zed launches a kick my way. I'm a beat too late blocking

it, taking the edge of his foot on my chin before I reach up and grab it with both hands.

"Are you sure about that, buddy?" He gasps for breath and tries to pull his foot away, but I hold tight. This is what he gets for suggesting I'm not on top of my game.

Even though I'm not. Not even a little bit.

"Look, we can all tell you're twitchy as fuck. You have to know a meltdown can't fly around here. Bev said you'd been fighting with 'that kid who lives with you,' but I thought Ravi had moved."

Ravi climbing through his window half-dressed. Ravi draped over my lap while my hand reddens his light brown skin. Ravi's teeth sinking into his lip.

Go fuck yourself, Daddy.

Argh. With a shout, I flip my oldest friend onto his back. He hits the ancient mat with a satisfying thud.

"It's complicated," I say as he tries to push himself off the floor.

"Do us all a favor and uncomplicate it, will you? This business is plenty stressful without the team getting nervous because their leader is losing his grip. You need to take a few days off or something?"

More like a year. On the other hand, having to come into work is probably the only thing keeping me sane. Adhering to my schedule is the only reason I didn't challenge the meathead bodyguard Daniel Corvus put on Ravi and then drag the kid home by his hair like the caveman I am.

"I'm fine. Talk to me about the search and rescue in Mexico."

Zed staggers to his feet, breath heavy. Maybe I'm not the only one struggling today. We've been going for about half an hour, which is typically nothing for us.

"Yeah, about that. Sal called in while you were running some errand the other day."

The errand was ambushing Ravi outside of his morning class.

"And?"

He takes a swig from his water bottle. "It's not good news."

"Shit." I slam my fists together. Which is as unsatisfying as it is painful. "Why is this the first I'm hearing about it?"

My friend puts his hands to his hips. "Because you're a loose fucking cannon lately and nobody wants to come anywhere near you."

A harsh breath punches its way out of my lungs. "What happened?"

"The guys were a little too late. They found where the prisoners had been kept, but the kidnappers were long gone. Tourists. Some local teenagers. Bodies in a shallow grave."

I drop my head back onto my shoulders. A strangled "Fuuuuuck!" works its way out of my throat. "Fucking pieces of shit."

Across the room from where we're sparring is an old heavy bag hanging from the ceiling. I storm over to it, beating the thing and shouting until my body burns and my voice is hoarse. "Fucking piece of shit motherfuckers."

One of the uglier things we deal with in this business is kidnapping for profit. These gangs pull people off the street, often young people, demand a ransom, and then when the family pays they kill them anyway. It's not uncommon for our company to get hired to go in and find the person taken, especially if it's a tourist whose family has the cash. Sometimes we find them in time. Sometimes we don't. When the kidnappers know to keep moving and they've got the home turf advantage, the odds are against us.

We all know this shit happens. Knowing it doesn't help. Especially now.

Teenagers in a shallow grave. Fuck. I swallow bile, unable to keep Ravi's face out of my mind. The wrong buyer gets him from this auction, and something like that could happen to him. Or something worse.

The water in my water bottle is warm and barely eases my burning throat. "How's Sal holding up?"

Sal came to work for us because his sister was one of the many people lost to this kind of racket. When the police weren't able to do anything, his mother took up the mantle of vigilante, hunting the men responsible and having them killed or arrested. The gang, in return, murdered his parents. An entire family lost due to greed.

"He's seeing the company therapist as required in these situations. Tell you one thing, he's handling it better than whatever the hell this is." Zed motions up and down in my general direction. "Sal's not the only one who would benefit from a few visits with Doc Lambert."

Fuck him. I don't have time for that shit. "You ready to go again, or are you done for the day?"

Zed laughs. "You implying I'm weak, motherfucker?"

No, I'm trying to distract you from the fact that I am.

"You know better than to ask me something like that," my friend growls.

We return to the mat. Zed takes up a stance and charges me again. When we fight there aren't too many rules. We try not to do permanent damage, but since an escaping drug dealer won't adhere to rules, neither do we.

Which is why, when he manages to get me on my back, I sink my teeth into his arm.

"You actual piece of shit." He growls.

My laugh is a little maniacal as I flip him again. And clock him in the jaw. That's going to swell later.

"Who's the piece of shit?"

His answer is a battle cry as he bucks his hips hard enough to throw me off. I'd be impressed if I had time to be, but he doesn't waste a second before barreling toward me again. Before he can make contact, I slip to the side. And when he's recovering from the first punch, I throw another punch, and then another.

He doubles over with a grunt. Blindly, he gropes around for the water bottle he left on the edge of the mat, using it to swish around his mouth.

When he spits it out, there's blood.

And two teeth.

"Hell, man. Didn't mean to do that."

Still hunched over, he responds by putting up his middle finger. "Sure. Whatever, fucker. My fault for leaving my mouth guard in my locker. Now before I call the dentist to see if I can have these put back in, do you wanna tell me again how you're perfectly chill and nothing at all is wrong?"

Willing my heart rate to settle down, I bring my hands up, interlacing them behind my head. This man is my best friend. We've been through the worst kind of shit together. I'd tell him anything, but I don't know how to tell him this.

I'm still barely willing to admit it to myself.

"Look, we all know you want to fuck the kid. I think I speak for everyone when I say just get it the hell over with so you can go back to being a regular asshole we barely tolerate and not the extra-extra asshole you've been lately, okay?"

Everything inside me goes cold. "What did you fucking say?"

My offense is a smokescreen, desperately covering the guilt that curdles my blood. The shame. The utter panic.

Everyone knows. Everyone *has known.* Do they all think I'm a fucking predator? Is that what I am? In the end maybe I'm no better than the sick old fuckers paying to watch Ravi dance while they smoke cigars.

"Jesus, Liam. You can't think it's not obvious. Well. Maybe it wasn't at first to the rest of the crew, but you forget how well I know you."

"I haven't forgotten." When I say Zed and I have been through everything together, I mean everything.

In spite of that, I've never wanted to strangle him more for calling me on my shit. But Zed and I don't pull punches with each other. We never have.

"Then maybe you thought that knock I took to the head off the Gulf of Aden caused permanent brain damage. You must have, since you seemed to think I wouldn't notice how a little more than a year and a half ago you switched from mostly women to mostly men at our group sessions. Then you slowly stopped having them at all. And how you've been pent up as fuck ever since this auction shit hit the wire."

"Did Bev tell you? That Ravi's the one..." Getting auctioned off like a used car. Like cattle. Like foreclosed real estate. I can't even say it out loud.

"She did, but she didn't have to. You think I can't read? I have access to the same reports you do. And she was right to tell me."

"I'd hoped for some discretion considering—"

"Considering he has you twisted up like Mama Elisabetta's garlic knots? She was right to come to me. You should have done it first."

My throat's dry and tight, like I swallowed sandpaper. Another guzzle from my own water bottle helps me stall on my answer but does nothing to ease the pain.

"You're right. I think...I might be losing it a little," I admit on a shaky exhale.

"Because you want to fuck the kid."

"He's not a kid!" My water bottle sails across the room before I even process what I've done.

Zed grimaces with his two front teeth missing, undeterred. "The hero doth protest way too fucking much. You're the one who calls him that. Man, then."

"He isn't—" When I realize I'm about to contradict myself, I stop. "He's nineteen, man. I'm almost forty. Comparatively, he's a kid."

"A kid you'd like to fuck."

"Don't make me clean out the rest of your goddamn mouth. I'm not supposed to want to fuck a kid I helped raise. We hunt down pieces of shit like me."

"We hunt down child molesters and traffickers. People who groom someone below the age of consent into doing things they shouldn't do or otherwise wouldn't agree to. This is not that."

Exhaustion pulls me to the floor, knees bent up as my ass hits the mat. "He says he knows about the get-togethers."

His eyebrows shoot up. "Get-togethers?"

"You know, the group sessions. The ones where we—"

"I know exactly what the hell we do at those get-togethers, Liam. How does he know?"

Tell me how you know. Were you spying on me?

"Back before I started keeping closer tabs on him, apparently he looked into the garage one night when I thought he was gone. Ended up getting an eyeful. He says that's how he got the idea for the auction. He wants to..." Ugh. "...try things."

"So you're—what?—feeling responsible that he saw us tag-teaming some co-ed and then said, 'Hold my root beer float'? Come on."

"Some could argue that's grooming behavior."

"Fuck's sake, brother. You didn't even know he was watching. As far as you've told me, the first time anything iffy happened was when he crawled into bed with you on the night of his eighteenth birthday. When he was a legal adult, immature though he may have been. And you kicked him out of your room, if I recall the story correctly. So aside from the fact that you've been a grumpy piece of shit since, I don't see the issue."

"You don't think I'm shitting all over my high school best friend's memory by lusting after his son?"

Zed's chest shakes with his laughter. "Stan Novak was a shallow man who stroked his own ego by fucking younger and younger women behind his wife's back. He's dead because he finally stuck his dick in someone unstable enough to commit murder when he wouldn't leave his wife. That's the man's legacy, and that's not on you. Is the age thing a little weird? Yes. Also, I could give you a list of wealthy geezers whose wives were practically child brides, but we don't have that kind of time. Nobody bats an eye at that shit."

He's right. I know he's right. I can't decide if it makes things better or worse.

“Ravi was almost sixteen when he came to live with you,” Zed points out. “Whatever else you think about it, it’s not illegal at this point. How come you never adopted him, huh? Maybe deep down you knew this was brewing. It’s a little fucked up and weird, man, but you’re not his actual parent.”

You’re not my parent. But you could be my Daddy if you wanted.

The energy drains from my body, the logo on the mat blurring beneath me. My recent lack of sleep might finally be catching up with me.

I hit my wrapped fist on the mat. “I can’t stand that he’s making me feel this way. I can’t stand that he’s planning to auction his ass off to the highest bidder who will do fuck knows what to him just so he can get away from me.”

“What about stopping the auction?”

“Brennan Doyle’s organizing the whole thing in cooperation with Daniel Corvus, who’s got Ravi holed up in a hotel with security like a member of the damn royal family. The only way we stop the train involves starting a turf war with two well-armed and well-funded criminals.”

“Or...” Zed’s expression tells me he already knows the alternative.

I try to wipe away the sweat stinging my eyes. “Or by bidding on him, but Corvus got too much fucking glee out of telling me Ravi agreed to group participation. He’s expecting all the rich assholes to pool their money. Hell, he’s probably encouraging it. We’ve done well for ourselves, but not that well.”

Snarling, I rip my hand wraps off too fast, drawing blood when the wet nylon slices into my skin.

Zed's voice is quiet when he says, "Liam, you have the money. We both do."

"No." I know what he's suggesting, but no. "I'm not using that blood money. I fucking told you I'm never touching that shit."

Years ago, a military op went wrong and took out most of our small group. Not to mention a bloodcurdling number of innocent women and children. As the only survivors of the mission, the government paid Zed and me a lot of damn money to keep the story quiet. The money has been sitting in an account, untouched, earning interest for over a decade.

"I'm not going to spend money our friends died for." I almost choke on the words. "That those children died for."

The day that money landed in my account I could barely live with myself. I barely can now.

Zed regards me, taking a slow, deep breath. "I get it. Haven't touched mine either. But, Liam, if you're really afraid for him? I would think if you were ever in your life going to use that settlement for anything, it would be something like this. Tell me the truth here. Are you afraid for his life, or is this plain old jealousy?"

Mentally, I review all the rescues our team has made. The kids who were trafficked, hooked on drugs, returned home but never the same again. Some who were cleaned up and returned to their parents only to disappear again. Some of them didn't even survive the twenty-four hours Ravi would be with whoever wins him at auction.

The thought makes me sick inside. My recent nightmares are full of all the members of the old money cabal in Belle Argo, tying him to a table while they put their cigars out on him and plug his holes while he screams. Makes me want to kill them all slowly.

"Both," I admit. My gut roils as I add, "But I'm honestly terrified, Zed. If it was only jealously, I might be able to survive, but it's not. He also told me he doesn't want to see me again, so what the fuck do I do?"

Each time I recall Ravi's dismissal, I could swear I'm bleeding out. It's painful to even go home lately. Too much empty silence ringing in my ears.

"Well." My friend straightens up, shrugging his shoulders as if this isn't actually life or death we're talking about. "Not to pour gas on the bonfire, but you're probably right to be afraid. We're also not exactly strangers to rescuing people who don't necessarily want to be rescued. Guess you're going to have to decide how bad you want to save him."

CHAPTER SEVENTEEN

RAVI

"GUYS, I'm not so sure about this."

I'm standing on a weird fabric-covered platform while a stooped, ancient man named Cornelius is crawling around me on his knees, double-checking the hem of my pants or something. His head is between my legs. There's itchy fabric rubbing my thighs. People are staring at me.

I don't think I've been more uncomfortable in my life, and I've done some really questionable things.

I've scaled a barbed-wire fence to rescue a calf stuck in a ditch. Had to get a tetanus shot.

I've overdosed.

I've walked in on PJ and Mr. Monroe—

Actually, I prefer not to think about that one.

The point is, I never had to do any of that in a tuxedo that costs more than my car. Every bit of money Daniel Corvus decides to spend on this auction is wet cement in my stomach.

Over to the side of where I'm standing, there's a sitting area where a bunch of my fellow escorts are seated. They all look fancy while they drink champagne and kick back on brocade-covered chairs and couches. You know a store charges a lot for their stuff when they're willing to give away champagne for free. Which I guess is why everyone decided to tag along? Well, when I mentioned it on the group chat, Alexis said she'd always wanted an excuse to try on dresses at this place, and things took off from there.

"You getting cold feet, Rav?" PJ asks.

Only every five minutes. When I first decided to do this, I was certain. Now my idiot heart keeps coming back to *help me understand, baby.*

Did Liam even realize he called me baby? Was it more manipulation? Another way to control the silly kid with a silly crush?

"It's too late for me to have cold feet. I'm just not sure about this tuxedo. Do I look stupid? I've literally never worn one in my life."

Is it a bad sign that "I Knew You Were Trouble" is playing on the store's sound system? It feels like a sign that's not good.

"You wear suits when you go on a dinner date with a guy, right?" Simon puts in. He's perched on his boyfriend Sebastian's lap, in a window seat. On the street outside, a couple of kids who look high school aged are laughing and using the curb to do skateboard tricks. They seem so carefree.

What's that like? I don't remember.

"This is stuffier, though, with the vest and the bow tie and everything." I force my attention back to my reflection in the mirror, where Cornelius has me all trussed up. This is my second fitting in as many weeks, but he's been measuring and pinning for what feels like forever.

"It all feels like overkill." I jiggle my legs a little. "And I'm not good at standing still for this long. It's honestly getting painful."

"Do you want to look handsome in your tuxedo, or do you want to look like a little boy who got a hand-me-down from his older brother?" Cornelius mutters from around a mouthful of pins.

"Uh, I don't have a brother?" The tailor shoots a dirty look from between my legs. "But, okay. I do see your point. And, uh, I guess I would like to look handsome?" Not sure I've ever been handsome. Not that anyone's said. I get adorable a lot. Way too much.

With the wealthy escorting clientele in Belle Argo, I've learned "adorable" is code for "I've assessed you thoroughly and determined that it would take no effort at all to squash you under my thumb."

So, if this tailor can pull off handsome, then I suppose I'll take it.

"He might get more bids if he looks like a little boy," Adam points out. His dark shoulder-length hair is up in a bun again today.

"Uh..." Is he joking? Because I can't tell, and now I kind of wish I could disappear.

Literally everyone in the group turns to Adam, making hissing sounds and shut-up gestures. PJ seems to be threatening to slit his throat.

I distinctly remember Eve and Alexis spending an entire brunch one week trying to convince him that man buns were "out," but considering the way Cornelius's two female assistants have been eyeing Adam? Not so sure man buns are out, honestly.

"Am I really the only one thinking it?" Adam asks.

"You're the only one dumb enough to say it out loud, and that's coming from me," Dean says. He's got his long legs awkwardly folded on a love seat that's too low to the ground. Mostly he's watching his daughter, who's across the store, staring in awe at a rack of sparkly dresses.

Michael, on the seat next to Dean, gives him a sharp jab in the ribs. Dean glares daggers back before returning his attention to his daughter.

"Listen," Troy says with an unusually serious face, "if you really don't want to do this, we could all talk to Brennan for you. Surely you could come up with the money some other way."

Troy doesn't seem to realize he's idly tugging at a strand of Adam's hair that's escaped the bun. Neither of them do.

"Yeah, we can help you find a way out of this," PJ insists. "Brennan is reasonable. There's got to be some kind of deal we can make."

Sebastian, who rarely talks to all of us, clears his throat. "I'm sure Simon and I could work something out."

My throat feels super tight. "That's... Wow. Thank you. But I'm not going to take money from you guys. Really, I think this is the right thing to do. I can't keep living in Belle Argo with a guy who hates me and thinks protecting me means controlling me. I've thought about other options over and over, but this is the best and fastest way to reach my goal."

"Honey, we're just worried about you," Eve says. She's currently wearing a giant princess dress. There's a tiara in her braided hair. This place also does custom wedding gowns. Dean's daughter looks at her with a wide-open mouth as if Eve is actual royalty.

"I really do appreciate that." I'm sort of at a loss here. I wasn't expecting to get so emotional. Until they all came streaming into the store, I wasn't even expecting anyone else to be here.

"Okay, I've got everything I need," Cornelius says as he levers himself off the floor. "You can take that off when you're ready."

Thank God. If I had to stand still any longer, I'm pretty sure I would've jumped out of my skin.

"Uh, Rav." Prince, our newest member, tugs at his lip ring. He looks as out of place as I feel, the way he's covered in tattoos and perched in a fancy chair with a flute of champagne. "I think what everyone's trying to say is there's a chance you're going to get bought by some shithead on a power trip who gets off on breaking you into little pieces. Not that I can exactly see the future, but I've got a real bad feeling that this thing isn't going to go the way you expect."

There's something in my throat. Something so large it's almost choking me, and I can't get any words out. I clear my throat until I can breathe again, going over to where I've left my backpack on the floor by the floor-to-ceiling mirror.

"That reminds me..." I pull out a stack of papers and start handing them around. I count, making sure I've got enough copies for everyone here. A couple of the guys aren't, but it'll be all over the group chat, I assume. "Since most of you are here, I should do this now. These are for you guys. In the unlikely event that anything does happen to me. Channing was nice enough to take me to a lawyer's office yesterday." I gesture to my perpetually bored security guard, lounging in the back corner of the room.

Michael scans through the short document. He's the only one actually reading. Everyone else still looks confused.

Until Michael drops his glass. "This is a will."

Eve gasps. Adam's mouth drops open. Simon's face twists into anger. He stands and drops the paper in his boyfriend's lap before walking out of the room. Dean, he still looks confused.

Every muscle in my neck pulls tight. I try to massage them with my fingers, but it's no use.

PJ shoots up, face red. "Ravi, what the hell is this shit?"

The air leaves my lungs. I'm the one who did this, but it's suddenly very heavy.

My eyes are burning. "I know you guys think I'm ignoring the possibility of something bad happening to me, but I'm not. I've decided the benefit outweighs the risks, which I'm honestly hoping are really low. Kind of like when I decided to do tandem skydiving for my birthday even though a kid in my class had broken his leg that way. Anyway, uhm, this is for just in case, you know? You guys are the closest thing I have to family."

"Rav, you shouldn't be doing this," Dean says slowly.

"Yeah." Alexis nods. "It's so thoughtful, but it's too much. And if you really think something this bad might happen then what the fuck are you even doing?" She's leaning an elbow on Troy's shoulder, wearing, I don't know, cocktail attire? A tiny black dress. It looks amazing on her.

Then she nudges Troy, who straightens up and adds, "Yeah, Rav. This is fucked."

"Like I said, it's just in case. I have car insurance too, but I've never been in an accident. Look." I point to them all. "I don't know how high the auction's going to go, so I've done it in percentages. Half to animal rescues, food banks, a women's shelter, and a farm animal sanctuary in Beacon Hill. The rest is up to you guys. Most likely everything's going to be fine and this is overkill. If it isn't, though, who else would I want to give the rest of it to?"

Except for Prince, most of us fell in with Brennan because we needed money. And even Prince doesn't exactly seem to be independently wealthy.

Eve's the one who moves next, gathering her massive skirt up in her fists and running over to throw her arms around me. She's sniffling, and a wet drop hits my neck. It's all I can do to hold it together when the rest follow, resulting in a massive group huddle that causes Cornelius to yell at us all about being careful with the dresses before he gives up and stalks out of the room in a huff.

Alexis is the one who squishes my cheeks in both hands. The way she stands back to regard me with my face in her hands reminds me a little of my mom. "You're the absolute sweetest, Ravi. I don't know what else to say. This is terrifying."

Honestly, why is it still so hard to breathe right now?

I don't remember the last time anyone hugged me like this. Not for any reason other than to be kind. I'd like to say thank you, but my throat won't work. Honestly, my legs are wet noodles right now.

"Nothing to say," I manage. "Just as long as none of you murder me after the auction to get the money."

"You fucking asshole," PJ murmurs.

After a few awkward laughs, the huddle slowly breaks apart. Troy and the girls go to change out of their fancy borrowed clothes. On my way to do the same thing, PJ hooks an arm around my shoulders. "Hey, fuck you for this. Anyone hurts you, I'll kill them myself."

If anyone hurts me, I think Liam will kill them before PJ has the chance. It's sweet though, him saying that.

"We should all go out to dinner or something," PJ says with a resigned-sounding sigh. "Might be one of the last times we all get to hang out, considering..."

Considering I plan to leave town as soon as the money hits my bank account? Yeah. Throat still clogged with emotion, I can only nod.

But a few minutes later, when Channing and I are on the way to a nearby parking garage, I hear a high-pitched squeal, and then another.

"Do you hear that?" I can tell he already has, though, because his head is twitching side to side, searching for the source. I spot a tiny black ball of fuzz near the opposite curb, where a scrawny kitten is mewling its head off. It tries to stand but keeps falling down again.

There's a car heading right for it.

Someone yells my name behind me as I dart into the street. The shiny Lexus coming our way lays on its horn, and its tires screech as I bend down to scoop the kitten up. When I stand, there's a bumper two inches from my leg.

Whew.

There's a lot of yelling and tsking and "you shouldn't have done that" as I'm joined by the rest of the group once another stream of cars has passed. The guy in the Lexus puts his middle finger through the sunroof as he leaves.

"Oh, shit." Simon comes over. I guess he's not too mad at me to help a kitten. "It's bleeding."

At first I don't see it, but then I realize why it wasn't able to move earlier. There's something wrong with its back leg. "We can't leave it here."

Simon stoops down for a closer look, a crease forming in

the middle of his forehead. “We can take it to a vet, but I can already tell you the rescues are overloaded. Toe Beans has so many of these little guys they’re doing a BOGO on the adoption fee. I’d love to take it—” His boyfriend makes a loud and super obvious throat clear. “But we’re kind of at capacity right now.”

“Yeah, us too,” PJ agrees.

“Our place doesn’t allow pets,” Eve says sadly.

The rest respond with something similar; they can’t have pets at their place, or they don’t have time for one. Prince simply states, “I fucking hate cats.”

“A kitten, Daddy!” Dean’s daughter shrieks. Behind me, I can hear him explaining quietly why the kitten can’t go home with them either.

Hmm.

The small bundle in my hand is in rough shape. Something crusty around its eyes, the bit of blood on its leg. It’s a fighter, though, hissing and puffed up even though it can’t get away from me. It’s making these little squealing noises. A demand to be fed? For me to put him down? I don’t know.

It’s hurt, but it’s still fighting. Still making demands. I guess I know what that’s like.

The Belle Argo Premiere probably doesn’t allow pets either, but I can’t bring myself to drop the cat at an overcrowded shelter. I know what it’s like to have your parents leave you behind in an ugly world you weren’t prepared for. I’m sure as hell not leaving it here.

When I hold it up close to my face for a better look, it hisses but then changes course, sticking its tiny head out to boop its nose against mine. Well, clearly this kitten is a genius because it’s already found my kryptonite. That decides it.

Thinking back to the way Mr. Monroe's brother was all nice to me before, I'm hoping they'll be willing to make an exception at the hotel for this little guy. Or at least look the other way.

"Hey, guys? How about instead of going out to eat, we all order some pizzas and have them in my hotel suite, huh? Or maybe we could all hit the pool again?"

A few of the guys have come by to swim with me while I've been staying at the Premiere. Gotta admit, it feels awfully fancy getting to order drinks by the pool. Even if I'm only ordering sodas. Even if it's more of a gilded cage situation.

Thankfully, everyone agrees. Holding my new bundle, I turn to an absolutely furious-looking Channing. Bet he tattles to Daniel Corvus about me. Not that I care. Where are they going to get another virgin to auction off?

I tuck the kitten against my chest like it's already mine. "We're going to need to stop at a pet store."

CHAPTER EIGHTEEN

LIAM

"I'M ONLY SAYING, why should I have to clean up after myself? That's what the housekeeping staff is for."

The cluster of dudebros in front of me are all laughing as if they're above everyone else around them. As if acting like little shits has no consequences. Which, statistically, is disgustingly true.

They've all had too much to drink. Something tells me they're no better sober. What they are to me at the moment is useful cover. With all their yapping and their high fives, they've practically created a repellent forcefield around themselves such that even their waiter doesn't want to look this way. They're not even tipping well.

Right now, I'm all but invisible.

Across the hotel pool, Ravi sits on the edge drinking some kind of cola. His so-called friends appear to have invited themselves over for the fifth afternoon in a row to take advantage of the hotel amenities. Or to take advantage of Ravi. Haven't yet decided how parasitic they all are.

Not that I can judge too much. When I agreed with Zed that a few days off from work would do me good, following my former ward around certainly wasn't what he had in mind.

At the moment, two of Ravi's buddies are at risk of getting their fingers cut off. The long-haired one, Adam Luchera, crouches down beside Ravi, chattering into his ear while munching a slice of pizza. My background check turned up a possible tie to the Luchera crime family out of South Florida, so I don't know what the fuck he's doing here in Belle Argo, go-go dancing for chump change.

The other, Troy Ackerman, whose short hair is wet and spiked from swimming, is treading water while he grabs onto one of Ravi's legs for support. The little shit is one knee touch away from finding himself at the bottom of the pool, disemboweled by the drain.

My info says Adam and Troy live together, and that Adam has a girlfriend who works at a fancy stationery store downtown, but for all that, the two behave like they're fucking and they want Ravi to be the filling in their sandwich. They're a couple of filthy mongrels, all but humping his leg.

And what is Ravi's piece of shit "bodyguard" doing about any of it? Jack fucking shit. He's obviously there more to make sure Ravi makes it to the ball on time. If it were me. I'd have cracked at least a kneecap by now.

"I don't see why that's a big deal," one of the privileged pieces of trash in front of me says before signaling his already harassed waiter for more drinks.

At the nearby water slides, a tall white guy holds a little

girl with light brown skin in his lap while going down a twisty one. Dean Ness and his daughter, Ella. Mother deceased, according to my records. Childbirth complications. Dean played basketball for a D1 school in Georgia before moving to Belle Argo to become a sex worker of all fucking things. At the bottom of the slide is Michael Greene, the little girl's uncle. Records indicate that the two live in the same building, one floor apart. Dean's obvious devotion to his daughter is almost enough for me to forgive the way he tried to devour Ravi's face at Mercer Oak's party.

Almost.

"Man, those bitches were easy. Ripe for the picking. All it takes is a little something extra in their drink..."

Without taking my eyes off Ravi, who's got his head tipped back, talking to Sebastian Pierce of all fucking people, I pull my phone from my pocket and snap a quick picture of the table in front of me. Then I shoot it off to Bev with instructions to look into these assholes. I also sink back in my seat a little. Sebastian and his boyfriend are both here, and if they see me, I'm burned.

And then what? Pretend I simply happened to be in the neighborhood? That won't work.

"Tell you what, though, that last party at his place before the bank foreclosed? Off the fucking chain, man. Literally chains. Like a human buffet," one of the dudes says.

"Shut the fuck up," one of them hisses.

Paul Jeffries, a redheaded punk with a sketchy juvenile paper trail, is at a table a few feet over from Ravi, eating pizza with his much older college teacher boyfriend. Interestingly, one of the hotel managers is the brother of Mr. Jeffries's too-old boyfriend. The man in question, Westlake Monroe, hustles out from a door behind the pool bar, speaking quickly into a walkie-talkie. He gives a pointed scowl to Mr. Jeffries, a halfhearted wave to his brother, and then proceeds to transform into a polite hotel employee while addressing first Ravi and then his guard.

A chameleon. The worst kind of human, if you ask me. I'd rather deal with a straight-up psychopath who makes no bones about who and what they are than a slimy-ass weasel who changes allegiances as quickly as blinking.

"Heyo, Brunch Daddy! Come get in the water with us. It feels so gooood in here." Adam and Troy, the two punks all but hanging off Ravi, are calling out to the manager, who seems to be ignoring them. Pointedly.

After getting no love from the hotel manager, they turn their attention back to Ravi. "Hey, Rav, look over there!" Troy points over Ravi's shoulder.

The second Ravi turns to look, both Adam and Troy work in tandem, Adam hooking his hands under Ravi's arms and Troy pulling his legs, dunking him into the pool with a splash. I push to my feet, and so does Ravi's guard. A few seconds later I relax some when he reappears above the surface of the water, sputtering and laughing.

Laughing. That's twice now I've seen him laugh in the last couple of weeks. When did I last hear him laugh? Have *I* ever made him laugh? I don't think so.

Blood thunders in my ears as I observe the carefree way he's interacting with his friends, splashing everyone around him in retaliation. Has he ever been so carefree in my presence? Probably not, given I can't think of a time when I was that carefree either.

For one second Channing's gaze swings to me. He doesn't seem surprised to see me, which is oddly reassuring. Maybe the guy isn't completely useless after all. A knowing smile crosses his face before he returns to his seat by the bar, scanning the area in Ravi's immediate vicinity.

"...and let me tell you, that motherfucker's going down hard. It should be statistically impossible to make that many bad investments in a row but somehow he managed..."

Westlake, the hotel manager, comes hustling in my general direction, past the table of bros, clearly worked up about something.

He's barking into his radio. "Are you sure nobody's seen her? A person doesn't disappear into thin air in the middle of their shift like that. Are you sure she's not just having a cigarette by the staff entrance or some—"

"Hey, hotel dude. Come over and give us some service, baby," one of the bros calls out to Westlake.

If you ask me, the man's not conventionally attractive. Chin and cheekbones a little too sharp, eyes a little too deep. But he's well-built, with tousled hair, and those eyes appear to be cool blue and fringed by long lashes. I suppose I can see the draw.

My gaze swings back to Ravi. I like brown eyes better.

As the busy hotel manager passes the catcalling assholes, things get interesting. One of their hands shoots out to grab the manager's ass.

If they did that with the waiter, I missed it. Still, it would explain why nobody wants to serve them.

The manager jumps with a yelp and swings around to the four drunk men, who are probably each at least a decade younger. Early thirties, on the outside. Twenties, even. My quick check into Westlake Monroe told me he's my age, about a month older. For a second, though, he's a scared kid, his face smarting at the humiliation of getting grabbed by some over-sauced, moneyed-up Chads.

"Sir, if you can't behave appropriately, I'm going to have to have security escort you out."

He stalks away to a chorus of "Oh, security, huh?" and "It's hard to find good help these days," and even one "Do you know who I am?" For his part, Westlake seems more concerned with talking to whoever's on the other end of the two-way radio than the groping.

On the other side of the pool, Ravi's drying off with a towel. A few of his friends gather up pizza boxes while Dean wraps his daughter in a child-size robe. When they circle the perimeter of the pool and come my way, I do my best to remain invisible.

So far he hasn't noticed me watching him. I'm not sure why Channing hasn't said something, but there's no need to rock the boat.

Except the pieces of shit at the table in front of me are at it again. They must recognize someone in Ravi's group, because one of them calls out, "Hey, babe, how much for a quick trip up to my room?"

Dean gives the man an ugly look, scooping up his daughter and redirecting his path so there's a row of beach chairs between the two of them and the table of jackals. Ravi, though, who's walking ahead and focused on his conversation with Troy, doesn't see them until one has reached out to grab his arm.

"Hey, babe. I asked you a question. What, you're too good for us when you're not wearing your little shorts?"

Fuck. These guys know them.

Before Channing can react, I'm out of my chair, one hand clamped on the piece of shit's shoulder.

"You're going to need to take your hand off him right fucking now, or I will break every bone in your arm one at a time."

The guy gives me a hateful sneer. "What's it to you? He's just a fucking whor—"

I tighten my grip.

I'm rewarded with the quick release of Ravi's arm, and even a satisfying wince on the dudebro's part. But when my gaze travels up to Ravi's face, I'm met with a cascade of emotions. Confusion. Rage. Disgust. A hint of fear, before he wipes it all away. All the earlier laughter is gone.

I don't want him afraid of me, but I need him safe. I'm in the right here. I won't apologize. Doesn't stop my gut from twisting at the way he's looking at me. Who were those emotions directed at? Has he written me off or is he pretending?

How do I tell him that he may not be my responsibility anymore, but I don't know who I am if I'm not keeping tabs on him? I might hate myself for it, but not enough to stop.

"Ravi..."

I'm not sure what I was planning to say since I hadn't planned on him even knowing I was here. It doesn't matter anyway because he only lifts his chin into the air and walks away.

CHAPTER NINETEEN

RAVI

THE NIGHT of the auction I'm full of knots and butterflies. I've been nervous before. Devastated. Horrified. Freaked out. What I'm feeling as I stand backstage cuddling Mr. Cat (I'm not good at naming things, I know) is something new. My muscles are strung tight, waiting for something to go wrong. The whole situation's a little dizzying. I think I'm finally realizing I'm trapped. And I've done it to myself.

Still, I'm...resigned. The doors are locked. The train's leaving the station. No stopping it now.

"How you holding up?" Simon sidles up beside me.

I nearly hit the ceiling. "Holy sh—Simon. You almost made my heart explode out of my chest." After a closer look, I see he's wearing a nice suit and everything. "How did you get them to let you back here?"

Simon makes a "who cares?" gesture. "Sebastian invested in the club when it first opened. Comes with some perks."

"Oh. Nice."

I guess? I don't know.

Beyond the curtain they've put up to shield me from viewers until the auction starts, the smells of alcohol and cologne and the chatter and laughter of people who are going to be bidding on me are sending my stomach on a roller-coaster ride.

Well, I can't entirely blame the voices. When I woke up this morning, I had absolutely no appetite. Couldn't even manage to choke down a granola bar, which is so unlike me. Last night's pizza with the other escorts feels like a long time ago at this point.

It's not only the auction itself, but seeing Liam yesterday that's got me so messed up. The look on his face when he threatened that guy who grabbed me gives me shivers every time I think about it. And I've been thinking about it a lot. The last thing it should've done is cause me to have second (third, hundredth) thoughts about tonight, when it's too late to change anything.

Still. It was the first time I really could see how far he'd go to protect me. The threat he quietly whispered to the man who put his hand on me wasn't meant to be heard, but I did hear it. I wasn't as horrified as I probably should have been.

Maybe my reaction was wrong, but it only made me want him more.

"Here. Drink this." Simon nudges me, then hands over a glass of fizzy liquid. "It's ginger ale. You're looking a little green around the gills."

"Thanks."

After a sip, I close my eyes and soak in all the sounds around me. I can't make out any single voice well enough to know if they're talking about me, but I have to assume they are. Thinking back to the one time I went to an art auction with my pop as a kid, they had a little brochure with descriptions of all the pieces for sale.

Oh my God, they didn't make a brochure about me? Did they?

My breathing picks up. "I'm not used to having this kind of attention on me," I whisper.

"You went streaking through a drug dealer's production line not too long ago."

"That was different." Not that I don't see the comparison, but one of those things wasn't about me. I was distracting some bad guys with guns so some slightly less bad guys with guns could save people inside the warehouse.

Nobody was looking me up and down and deciding whether or not they wanted to spend time with me enough to pay for it.

"You know, it's funny. I thought this was a great idea when I first talked to Brennan about it. Didn't hurt that he was so enthusiastic, you know? I know he was only seeing dollar signs, but still. Now, I'm suddenly remembering how I had zero friends at my old school and how the kids made fun of me for crying when I was supposed to dissect a frog in biology, and that after I moved in with Liam, I had to eat lunch with the art teacher because on the first day of senior year I accidentally bumped into the captain of the football team, and then he had half the school out to get me. Liam's always telling me I'm too impulsive and I'm always all, 'fuck you, you're not my dad,' but suddenly I'm realizing he might have been right because this is a terrible idea."

Simon's hand lands between my shoulder blades. "Take a breath, man. Everything's going to be okay."

"Is it, though? Because it kind of feels like I'm going to die."

"You're panicking. Gotta breathe, babe." Simon takes an exaggerated breath, and I follow. Strangely, that does seem to help. "Look. The reasons you decided to do this in the first place—what were they?"

Simon's not yelling. He's not demanding anything. It's a kindness I didn't expect and didn't know I needed.

My brain takes me back to that first night I saw Liam with his friends and that girl they were sharing.

"Because I realized I was kinky when I saw Liam and a couple of friends all sharing this girl. I was so turned on I couldn't stand it, but I didn't want to be in their position. I wanted to be in hers. I developed a massive crush on him, which over the next few years turned into him being someone I couldn't see my future without, only he didn't feel the same way. Then he turned cold and mean once he realized what I wanted from him. Because I can't handle him constantly trying to control me and wanting something I can't have all the time. Because I can't stay here."

"Hold up. You're going awfully fast. Take another breath," Simon instructs.

I do, and then I continue. "Because I want to make my own decisions and live my own life without Liam locking me in my bedroom. And since I'm not good at meeting people, this seemed like a way to get money but also experiment with what I'm into rather than sit alone in my room while I fantasize and search up things like primal play. Win-win, right?"

"Let's call it that," Simon says noncommittally. "Is all of that still true?"

There's a moment of hesitation. When I think of the

things Liam said to me last time we talked, and then the way he threatened that man for touching me, everything's a bit blurry. When I really focus on it, though, nothing's actually changed. "Yeah. It's all still true."

"About the will. Are you really that worried about your safety? Because, seriously, Sebastian can help, and if we all of put enough pressure on Brennan—"

"Stop." I shake my head, which makes me dizzier.

Whatever Simon thinks, I can't back out now. This was the exact thing Daniel Corvus warned me about and I get the funny feeling he's as dangerous as Brennan. "I get why you guys are worried. I've acknowledged there's a chance of someone bidding on me with ugly intentions. Honestly, though, I think it'll be fine."

I hope. My mind goes to those emails I got, but Mr. Corvus assured me they had a way of making sure nobody who wished to do me harm would get into the auction. Maybe he was blowing smoke, but I believed him.

I really want to believe him.

"It's stupid," I say. "The trouble is, there's still this dumb high school kid with a dumb crush inside me who can't seem to let go of the possibility that someday Liam could change his mind. Fucking another guy and then leaving town is probably the most thorough way I could burn that bridge."

"They don't change their minds though, Rav. If a guy is stringing you along, it's because he can," Simon says. He's trying to be kind, but it burns anyway.

"You're right. I know you're right." The self-loathing on Liam's face after he let himself get too close outside my literature class told me all I needed to know.

"Showtime." Daniel Corvus sweeps in wearing a tux

that's even nicer than mine and takes hold of my shoulder. He points to Mr. Cat, huddled in my hands. "You can't take that thing out there."

I turn to Channing, who's been hovering in a shadowy corner. "Can you hold on to him for me? Just for, like, a couple of days. Until I'm done, you know?"

His gaze flicks over to Simon. "Why can't your friend take him?"

"His food and litter are all back at the hotel suite. You've got the key." I hand Mr. Cat over, and Channing looks into his hands as if the little guy's insulted him personally.

Mr. Cat lets out a quiet "meow" and headbutts Channing's chest. Channing sighs the most put-upon sigh I've ever heard, and I'm counting my mom when she had to fold laundry.

"Fine. You can pick him up here when you're...done," Channing says with no real enthusiasm. "If you're not back to get him soon, I'm eating him."

Ew. He's joking. Right? He must be. I cringe. "I'll be back to get him. I promise."

Mr. Corvus seems to find this entire thing funny. "Ravi, have you not been treated to Channing's delightful sense of humor before?" Then he gives Channing one heck of a glare.

Before I have a chance to even ask any more questions, Mr. Corvus says "Showtime" again, and the curtain is pulled away. I'm left squinting at a sea of faceless people. The stage I'm on has lights all around the bottom, and they're bright enough that everyone else is cast in shadow. I listen to Mr. Corvus read my bio: age, weight, and interests, then he moves on to what I will and will not allow on my twenty-four-hour date. He comes up with so many different ways to call me a virgin I'm almost impressed.

Though there's something super icky to me about being called "untouched."

It's weird, though, the way I can feel everyone's eyes, but I can't see them. Like I'm being watched by a room full of ghosts.

"I'll start the bidding at one million. Who's in?"

Holy… I suck my breath in so fast I almost choke on it. A million? I kind of assumed they'd start small and work up. One million is… Well, it's not small.

"One million," a man with a gravelly voice puts up his hand.

"One point five," says a woman in a glittery dress. I can't really see her, but I can see how it catches the light.

I blink against the dazzling sparkles, with my brain swimming even more now. I'm pretty sure I told Mr. Corvus I'm gay, but I'm suddenly not sure. What if I didn't? What if a woman pays all that money for a date with me and she wants me to do things I can't do?

My heart's racing hard. The nervous thumping was steady but a little fast when this all started—now I think this is what getting chased by a bear must be like. Only I'm just standing here. Waiting for my future to be decided.

What the hell was I thinking?

"I think I might faint," I murmur.

If Daniel Corvus can even hear me, he's not answering. Things are going so fast I can barely keep track of what's happening.

There's an older man who stands when he puts in his bid of—holy shit—two point five million, and he looks so much like my late grandfather on my dad's side I find myself praying hard that he's not the one who wins. His bid was a lot, though. He might.

I can't have sex with someone who looks like my dziadek. I can't.

"Three and three-quarters." Comes from the back of the room. I can't tell who even says it. Squinting into the dimly lit room beyond me, I can see there are a lot more people than I expected.

The lady in the mirror dress raises her bid to five million, and my stomach twists. *I'm not worth this much. They're going to be disappointed.*

Honestly, I thought Channing was fucking with me when he said I'd get more than two million. Like the wolf shifter novel reference, right? Jokes. *It was supposed to be a joke.*

Except this is no joke. For some reason there's a lot of saliva in my mouth. Mr. Corvus is gripping me by one shoulder, guiding me to turn this way and that, his words blending into a strange, echoing mishmash.

"Ten million."

My head snaps up. That's not right. That can't be right. Who could possibly want me that much? I can't even picture how much money that is.

There's this loud...rushing sound in my ears. I must have misheard.

When I try to follow the source of the bid, I could swear I see Liam. It makes my heart hurt.

I know I'm the one who said I didn't want to see him again, but I do. I want the way he used to smile at me before I told him I loved him. I want the gleam in his eye when he threatened to break someone's bones for touching me.

Somewhere in the distance, I hear Mr. Corvus say "Sold." But when I look up to see who won me, everything slides into darkness.

CHAPTER TWENTY

RAVI

WHEN I WAKE UP, I'm in the passenger seat of Liam's truck. Wearing a tuxedo. My shoes and socks are missing.

If it weren't for the last part, I might think I'd dreamed everything else.

"What happened?" I sit up straight, but my head's still fuzzy.

"You passed out. Right on the stage. Of all the ways I thought that auction might blow up, that wasn't one of them. I'm taking you home."

My pulse spikes. "We have to go back. Whoever won me is going to be pissed."

"I promise you, Ravi, whoever won you is damn pissed," Liam says through clenched teeth. It's very late, and there's not much light on this road, but I know all of Liam's sounds, especially his angry sounds.

"Liam, I'm serious. Take me back. I made a promise. If I

don't follow through on it now, I'll be in worse trouble than anything you could possibly do to me."

"I doubt that, but we'll find out." His low laugh makes the back of my neck bunch up.

"Liam, I don't know what you're talking about, but you need to *take me back*. I can't deal with your shitty, messed-up power plays right now."

Liam's house is on the edge of Belle Argo, so close to the border that if you go past the fire hydrant at the edge of his property, you're in the unincorporated area that sits between Belle Argo and Beacon Hill. His closest neighbors are undeveloped land, a nature preserve, and a five-acre fruit tree farm.

Which is why the longer the silence between us lingers, the more I worry. Usually Liam doesn't scare me too much. He pisses me off. But the last night I spent in his house, the one when he spanked me until I got off, that was a side of him I hadn't seen before. At least, I hadn't seen it directed at me.

And now? Now, the car is silent except for the road noise and the grinding of his teeth. Whatever he decides to do next, there won't be anyone around to hear me scream.

We pull through his fenced-in property and down the long driveway. The car is off and cooling before he speaks again.

"You're not going back."

"Liam, I have to."

Moonlight cuts through the window, and I can see his fingers tighten on the steering wheel. For a painful amount of time, he doesn't answer.

"You're not going back, Ravi."

I open my mouth to argue again.

"You're not going back, because I'm the one who bought you."

Wait. My pulse is all skittery again. "That's not right."

His laugh is as dry as the month of March in Florida. "I guarantee you it's exactly right. If you don't believe me, ask my bank account. You can probably hear it crying all the way from the bank headquarters in Texas."

"But..." No. This is not happening. "I could have sworn I heard someone bid..." It hurts to swallow. "Ten million dollars."

"Yeah, kid, it's a lot of fucking money."

If I thought I'd seen Liam angry in the past, I hadn't truly. Not like this.

"So what are you going to—" When I realize I don't really want the answer, I bite down on the question.

A hissing noise escapes through Liam's teeth. "You wanted to do this, so we're going to fucking do this. Get inside and get upstairs. Now."

The command in his tone makes me scramble, shoves me up the steps to the front door, makes me punch in the door code with shaky fingers twice before I get it right, and then up to the second floor. At which point I realize I'm not sure what else he wants me to do.

At the base of the stairs, he glares up at me with hateful eyes. "My room. Get your clothes off."

Is he serious? Is he fucking serious? "Are you fucking serious?"

I'm not sure if I want to scream or cry or fall to my knees in gratitude.

"Do I look like I'm fucking around here, Ravi?"

No. Liam has never looked less like he was fucking around in his life, and I've seen him torture a man to death.

For a second I can't move. All of my nerves are vibrating.

"Ravi." My name is a warning.

I dart into the room I haven't set foot in since my eighteenth birthday. Someone had illegally set off some fireworks in a nearby field, and it had reminded me too much of my parents getting shot. I'd been two doors down when they died, thinking I'd heard fireworks that were really gunshots.

It was the last time I turned to Liam for comfort.

I'm so frantic I can hardly breathe as I enter Liam's private space, pulling my tie and my jacket off haphazardly. This must be some sort of horny fever dream, right? Liam Masters, the man who's been awful to me for over a year because I had the audacity to let him know I wanted him, is now ordering me to...

"Take everything off, Ravi."

"I'm working on it, Liam."

"In this room I'm 'Sir' to you."

Oh boy. Why does that sound ridiculous and also hot as hell?

It doesn't help me that I've been hard since the second he told me to take my clothes off. Really, I can count on one hand the number of times Liam has sent me upstairs to my room since I've been living here. He was never much of a disciplinarian. Until he found out I was working for Brennan. Until I gave him a reason.

Thank fuck, because I think I would have been hard all the time.

"W-why am I doing this?"

"Sir. Why am I doing this, Sir." His expression is expectant.

"Why am I doing this, Liam, sir?"

"Always such a fucking brat," he murmurs. "You're doing this because you insisted on this goddamn auction. This is what you wanted."

"What?" Is this what I wanted? Now that I'm here, I realize I never actually considered this scenario.

"It was the only way to make sure you didn't go home with some psychopath who wanted to murder you," Liam growls.

"I really don't think—"

"Right now I don't give a shit what you think, kid. Since you've been intent on acting like an unruly asshole for weeks now, it's time I punished you like one. Get your clothes off and get on the bed."

I'm stripped down to my socks and about to climb onto the king mattress when he stops me. "Don't you dare leave that pile there. Pick everything up and fold it neatly. Put it on the chair." He gestures to the little reading nook by his window.

There's this searing sensation under my skin—embarrassment at having to bend over in front of him and pick up each piece of clothing before standing there and neatly folding it all while his sharp gaze never leaves me.

It's more than that, though. It's the chill of the air conditioning, pulling up bumps on my flesh and tightening my nipples. It's the heat of his gaze. It's the way I want him to consume me.

"Now you may get on the bed," he says when the last item is folded, and I've sort of awkwardly balled up the socks on top.

Oh, may I? Funny, considering it sounded like an order. I bite my lips to keep from asking out loud.

I'm honestly confused by how part of me feels like I won

the lottery and part of me thinks I hit my head and I'm still dreaming. Part of me still wants to tear him a new asshole for once again being a controlling, overprotective dick.

While I'm lying on my back on the bed deciding how I feel about all of that, something pulls tight around my ankles. And then my wrists. I lift my head to see he's tying me up. "Since when have you had restraints connected to your bed?"

There's an unhelpful thought in my head that maybe these have been here a while. Maybe he used them with someone else. I don't like that at all.

"Did I say you could talk?"

I bite my lips harder. Let's be honest here, if he expects me to be silent, this isn't going to last long.

A stinging slap lands on the top of my thigh. "Ow! What the hell is that?"

"A silicone paddle. I have one made of buckskin that's gentler, but I know how you feel about animal products."

I can't decide if he's being judgmental or considerate.

"Here's the thing, kid. In the last month you've done nothing but try my patience." Slap. "Scare the shit out of me. Repeatedly." Slap-slap. "And defy my orders."

Three slaps.

"Now you've got me spending money I never intended to touch to bail you out of that goddamn auction because you have no fucking clue how much trouble you could have put yourself in."

Slap-slap-slap-slap. The hits don't land in the same spot every time. He's moving up and down my thighs. I don't know enough to know if that's a good thing or not. Only that it spreads the pain all up and down my legs.

"Nobody asked you to," I say through gritted teeth.

"No? Nobody did?" He leans over me, nose to nose. His eyes are so dark. If I thought before that they looked like the ocean, today they look the way the sea probably does when it's getting churned by a hurricane. "You're right, baby boy. You didn't ask me to. You fucking begged me."

Then he turns and leaves the room.

What the hell is happening right now?

My body's strangely warm and, like, kind of shaking. I'm vulnerable and spread out with my cock jutting obscenely toward the ceiling. The worst part is the way my mind is spinning, trying to figure out what's actually going on. I mean, I sort of know what's happening, but...but seriously, what's actually going on here?

Liam said he wanted to punish me. Is this the punishment? Hitting me with a paddle and then leaving me here to think?

Liam returns, though, positioning himself at the foot of the bed. There's only so much I can see from where I am, but it looks like he has some sort of rod in his hand? Actually, it's sort of vaguely dick shaped. So maybe a vibrator? Or, like, a wand?

I've done a lot of research on sex toys and concluded that there are more styles than people on the planet. I even found a company that makes custom fantasy dildos to look like dragon cocks or tentacles or whatever. It's honestly mind-boggling.

I've been thinking about saving up for one. Guess I can afford the dragon cock now. If I ever get out of here.

"Your safe word is red, kid."

I know I'm right about the toy when the buzzing starts. Liam drags this vibrating toy, or whatever it is, over my inner thigh and underneath my balls, dipping a little lower toward my crease before going higher again. Gently, he slides it up and down my hard shaft until my hips are bucking, trying to fuck up against the vibrating thing.

It doesn't take long before I can feel my orgasm coming, so much faster and more intense than when I jerk myself off.

All of a sudden, the vibration stops. A pained whine leaves my throat.

"W-what the hell? I was so close. Sir."

"This is my time, Ravi. Remember? Whoever wins you at auction gets you for twenty-four hours. Yours to do whatever they want with. What I've decided is I'm going to make you sorry for all the hell you've put me through."

Before I can answer, he's turned the vibrator on again. Once again, right before I'm about to come, he pulls it away. My body tries to follow him, fruitlessly fucking the missing toy.

He leans over me, grinning as he turns it off.

Me, I'm thrashing on the bed in frustration. Gasping, nostrils flared, heart racing, and so, so confused.

The mattress dips with his weight. "I figure I may as well sit down," he says. "We're going to be here a while."

Oh. That doesn't sound good.

"How long, sir?"

He doesn't answer, but it's a long time. For what feels like hours he brings me to the edge and then cuts me off. Sometimes he puts the vibration on my dick, sometimes on my balls, and sometimes on my nipples.

A few times he brushes the head of it over my hole, and it's enough that I almost think maybe I'm going to manage to get fucked or at least get off before he can stop me.

But no. Every single time he seems to know exactly when I'm near the edge, and every time he stops. His expression is infuriatingly smug as he sits back and waits for me to calm down again.

"If you can't take it anymore, you can say red," he reminds me a couple of times. "Just know that at the end of this, we're done here. You take your money, you get out of my house, and you don't come back."

It's a punch right through my chest. He can't mean that. I don't want him to. Or maybe I do. No, I don't, but I should.

Tears sting my eyes. Considering that was my plan all along, his command shouldn't hurt so much. "Why?"

"You wanted to get used for money. You wanted to leave. So I'm going to give you what you've been asking for. Let's see if you can actually handle it."

Oh, to hell with him. He doesn't think I can take it. He wants me to cave. He'd get so much satisfaction if I used my safe word, I bet. Well, screw that. Screw him. I'm not going anywhere. Not until he kicks me out.

"I can handle it." Then an awful, terrible, wonderful thought pops into my head. "Daddy," I add.

I must have really gotten to him, because he doesn't even give me a hard time for not calling him sir. My satisfaction is short-lived, because for the next God knows how long, he really tries hard to get me to tap out.

My muscles burn as he teases me mercilessly. My toes curl so hard I cry out in pain when my foot cramps. After a while, all the frustration has tears streaming down my face.

I'm begging. Pleading. So much nonsense is coming out of my mouth I might have promised him my firstborn or a pile of magic beans. I don't even know.

My neck and face are wet, the tears collecting behind my ears and running behind my head. It's awful and beautiful. I desperately want it to end.

Also, I never want it to end.

Once he's finally said "Okay, kid, you can come," the barest light of dawn is coming through the window.

I nearly pass out. Nearly. Even though I'm lying down, the room is spinning.

Everything hurts. Everything. After however many hours of tensing my muscles and thrashing and crying, I'm so sore I can hardly move. There's also this surreal, floaty feeling. A buzzing sound in my ears.

Oh. No. That's the buzz of Liam's phone.

His words return to me as he picks it up to send a reply. *I'm going to give you what you've been asking for.*

Did I get what I wanted? At first, I thought so.

When he started, I didn't understand how he was punishing me when it felt so good. I get it now. He's wrung every drop of defiance out of me. At least for the time being.

As I'm lying there sweaty and sticky and wrung out, he removes the restraints from my hands and feet. His footsteps echo as he walks out of the room.

"That was Zed. I need to go into work. Stay here until I get back." Then he walks away with not even one backward glance.

"You're just going to leave? After all that?" I can't cover up the hurt in my voice, but I hate it.

The moment of softness on his face must be my imagination. In the next second he's gone, boots thundering down the stairs.

Now that I think of it, the entire night he hardly looked at me. Never even touched me.

Not with his own hands.

Asshole.

CHAPTER TWENTY-ONE

LIAM

BY THE TIME I burst through the doors of Masters and Loft at a little after six, I'm running on rage and fumes.

"Okay, tell me who we need to kill."

Zed is sitting at the receptionist desk out front with his feet propped on the desktop. We haven't had an actual receptionist in, well, ever. Not that it's seemed to hurt business. Bev goes through the voicemails every morning with only a minimal amount of annoyance.

Really, though, we should hire a new receptionist.

"Okay, first things first." He slides a cup of coffee my way. "You look like shit."

"I don't need coffee," I insist before taking a gulp that burns my throat. It does nothing to cauterize the guilt leaking from every pore. I'm pulled tight as a competition crossbow after what happened with Ravi last night.

All night. All. Fucking. Night.

What in the hell was I thinking?

Seeing him tied up and begging for hours punished me at least as much as it punished him. Nearly drove me out of my damn skull. I could have buried myself in that sweet body while he was immobile and helpless.

If I had, there'd have been no turning back. As it is, I'm barely rational.

"How did the auction go?" My friend is regarding me with concern but also a clear certainty.

"You already know, don't you?"

"Bev managed to convince Daniel Corvus that it would be in everyone's best interest to share the client list from the auction last night—who got in, and more importantly, who didn't. She figured whoever's after Ravi might be unhinged enough to have been a red flag for Daniel as well, and they wouldn't have gotten in. Of course, this is under the agreement that the information would be kept in-house. And yes, we also got the list of who did get in, which included who won. So." His eyebrows bounce up and down. "How did it go?"

Dropping into a chair, I thrust one hand into my hair and pull slightly, hoping the pain will help wake me up. "I'm not sure how to answer."

"Did you fuck him?"

No, I gave him pleasure until it became pain and then left him. "Not...exactly."

Zed knows damn well there are plenty of ways to play that don't involve penetrative sex. Still, he looks at me as if he can't fathom what I mean. "What did you do?"

"Dragged him to my bedroom, tied him up, and edged him for..." I check my watch. "Four and a half...maybe closer to five hours. I don't remember exactly what time we started."

"No wonder you look like shit. Did you at least talk after? Get things out in the open?"

When I don't answer, the curiosity on his face morphs into judgment. Judgment I'm not used to seeing from my best friend.

"Liam, you didn't."

"I untied him before I left."

"So you gave him what was most likely his first real sexual experience ever and then left him there by himself? Who are you right now?"

I'm not sure I know. Couldn't even look at my own face in the rearview on the way here. "You sent a text. You said you had important information." The squeeze of my hand on the to-go cup causes scalding coffee to slosh over my hand. "Fuck!"

"Okay, so"—Zed rubs his hand over his forehead—"are you honestly telling me right now that if I hadn't sent a message saying we had information, you would have stuck around and had an honest conversation with him? The guy you knocked my fucking teeth out over? Got to the dentist in time, by the way, thanks for asking."

Again, I don't answer. I don't have anything good to say.

"Jesus Christ. Okay." He drags his feet off the desk, his boots landing with a heavy thud on the floor. "I'm not going to give you shit about this because I suspect you're already doing it to yourself, but I hope you know you have one hell of a mess to clean up. It's not like you to be a coward."

"I've got twenty-four hours with him." I try to rub the grit out of my tired eyes. "I'll talk to him when I get home. After we deal with this."

After I make sure he's safe. Though I'm not sure what I'll say to him then, either. Every time I blink, all I can see is the dreamy, breathless way he looked at me when he finally came, the shining look of something a little too close to love in his eyes, and then the suspicion that came after.

You're just going to leave?

All the things I've done and lived through would drive most men to drink. Yet my final undoing will most likely be the love of the kid I was supposed to take care of.

Zed is right. I'm a fucking coward.

"All I'm saying is, I've seen him recently, and Ravi is looking pretty damn grown up, my friend. If you cast him aside, I might have to move in to ease his broken heart."

"Don't make me remove those fucking teeth again," I snap. Jesus. Zed and I may have shared someone before. I'm sure it would be hot to see my best friend fucking the kid if that was something he wanted. But easing his broken heart?

Surely fucking not.

My friend's expression is too knowing as he slides the open laptop on the desk over toward me. "All right, asshole. This is who we're looking at. Dylan Beck was barred from the action because he couldn't prove his ability to pay. He's a real estate developer here in town. Or used to be?"

He shrugs as if he somehow answered his own question.

"Anyway. He owned or co-owned several hotels and resorts in this state, including the Belle Argo Premiere, until he fell on hard times and was forced to sell his share to his business partner. He made some bad crypto investments, and there's a rumor he's had some Mafia run-ins. Promised too many favors to the wrong people to get his business done and appears to have overextended himself. Also..."

He pulls up a file—a picture of a kid about Ravi's age, lying in a hospital bed with his face covered in bandages. "This unfortunate young man used to be an escort here in

Belle Argo. This is what he looked like after a date with Beck. Nothing ever stuck because the proof was insufficient, and the kid ran home to Ohio without pressing charges. But he's the kind of guy who uses his money to throw his weight around and doesn't seem to have any qualms about asking bad men to give him more of it, which means he's dirtier than my mother's garden clogs."

Then he shows me a picture of our suspect. I recognize him. He was at the party where I saw Ravi grinding on his "friend." When I left, he was standing near the door. Staring. At Ravi.

Most of the men in the room were staring at him. He has a magnetic way of drawing attention, especially when he had his legs wrapped around his very tall friend.

Thinking back on it now, though, the gleam in Beck's eye was a little too hungry. I was distracted by my anger at Ravi for sneaking out and didn't process much else. I should've fucking clocked the danger.

"Okay. Good. This is good." Certainty settles in my gut. We'll have to question him first to be sure, but I've gotten good at listening to my hunches. And my partner's.

I'm already itching to make this guy bleed. "Let's grab him, then. Hang him up in the warehouse and find out what he knows."

This guy thinks he can beat young men to a pulp? Already I can feel his face caving under my fist.

"We will definitely do that." Zed's face falls. "As soon as we find him."

"Where the fuck is he?" I stand from my chair before forcing myself to sit again. "I know, I know. You already told me you don't know. What's the situation?"

"We suspect he's lying low. Bev's been chasing down his

real estate holdings. After a deep dive into the guy's financial records, she found a connection to a shell company with the name TMI. Ring a bell?"

"It does. Something to do with the trafficking ring we've been trying to dismantle."

"Exactly. Those kids who were taken from posh parties a few months back, some were transported on private planes. The planes belonged to a shell company called TMI. TMI also has a few industrial buildings, vehicles, and other assorted assets. Plenty of whispers that the guy likes them young, fewer on where he might be now. I've already got a couple of the guys out searching the warehouses, since those seem the most likely options."

"Fuck. Give me part of the list." This is a fucking nightmare. I need to find this guy. I need to make sure he never threatens Ravi or anyone else again.

Zed holds up a finger. "Before we go tearing through every boathouse, farmhouse, and outhouse, Bev was able to get us access to the guy's house. Said it's about to go up for sale in a foreclosure auction, and the agent let it slip there are some wild rumors about the place."

"What the hell does that mean?"

"Exclusive parties. The kind people testify in court about." Zed tosses his keys up into the air, catching them with a grin. "I'm about to go take a look."

I chug the rest of the coffee and push to my feet. "I'm coming with you."

Zed's eyes narrow. "You sure you're in the right headspace for this?"

Absolutely not.

"I'm coming with you," I say again.

CHAPTER TWENTY-TWO

LIAM

ZED WHISTLES. "This place is the stuff of nightmares."

The downstairs front of the house—the mansion, rather—seems fine. There's a side exit that leads out to a wide tiered patio, the kind people use for entertaining. The kitchen looks like the sort any wealthy asshole would be proud to show off to his wealthy asshole friends. Imported marble counters and lots of shiny steel. All of the upstairs bedrooms connect to private bathrooms with jetted tubs and private balconies.

The rear of the first floor, however, is a different story.

Through the butler's pantry—and who the fuck even has a butler these days—is a hidden sliding door. And through that sliding door?

"People were definitely held here." Zed points to a mattress against one wall, dirty and stained. It's sickening to even think what it was used for.

For a moment, my feet are frozen to the floor. I can

barely touch the thought that the guy who owned this house was in the same room with Ravi without wanting to gag.

There's a row of eyebolts along one wall, the paint peeling and the tiles chipped. Nobody was paying any attention to maintaining this room the way they were to the rest of the house.

"Photography equipment." I point to the other end of the large room. One wall is covered by one of those drape things photographers use as a background. On the ground is a tripod nobody bothered to take with them for some reason.

"Jesus," Zed mutters. "That's sick. Probably a real good thing Ravi didn't take this guy up on his offer."

"No shit."

Jesus. Thinking of what Dylan Beck could have done to him wrings my insides out. This bastard could have snuffed out the kid's bright light.

You're going to do the same thing if you're not careful. Leaving him on your bed with not even a backward glance. You're such a bastard.

Well, I never denied being a bastard. At least I don't hold people against their will.

Then I remember spanking Ravi to orgasm on his bed and then locking him in his room. Fine. Maybe I deserve to be sent to hell with the rest of them. But if I'm going to hell, I'm taking the guy who chained people to a wall in his hidden back room with me.

That's when a memory hits me. "Shit. Chains."

Zed looks up from where he's inspecting a doorway. "Yeah, I figure that's what the bolts were for."

"No." I rub my forehead. "I mean, yes. Also..." Dammit,

I'm going to have to come clean about stalking my damn ward. "The thing is, when I took this past week off? I wasn't exactly relaxing at home."

"I'd be surprised if you know how to relax."

"That's not the point." Looking up in despair more than thought, I notice the tiny intrusive eye of a camera mounted in one corner of the ceiling, aimed roughly at where the mattress and the row of bolts were placed.

Chills erupt on the back of my neck.

"Well, I suppose that's not too surprising." I point to the camera.

Zed pulls out his phone. "I'll get Bev on it. You were saying something about chains, though. Or...your time off."

Right. Fuck. "I was following Ravi." The confession rushes out, hot and guilty.

"You were..." Zed's gaze swings slowly in my direction. "I'm certain I misheard you, because it sounded like you said you've been following a nineteen-year-old college student with no criminal history."

My petulantly muttered "He'll be twenty in November" only buys me more of Zed's exasperation.

I know. I heard it when I said it.

"I'm honestly worried, man. This level of recklessness is unlike you. What if he'd seen you and decided to report you to the police?"

I lift one shoulder in a halfhearted shrug. "We have a few friends on the force. Besides, he did see me, and nobody's shown up on my doorstep yet."

"Nobody's shown up on your—" Zed breaks off with a humorless laugh. "That's fucking perfect. Okay. Moving on from all of that, because fucking *uh-oh*, man. What does following the beautiful twink you refuse to admit you want to fuck have to do with this horror house we're standing in right now?"

"That was a mouthful, Zed."

"Well, I like to keep my mouth full as often as possible, Liam. Stop fucking around and answer the question."

"Fine. When I was casually observing him on the Premiere's pool deck the other day, a group of obnoxious twenty or thirty-somethings mentioned parties at a house that had recently gone into foreclosure. They mentioned people. On chains." I gesture to the eyebolts on the wall. "Like the sort of thing that might be used to secure people to those hooks, perhaps. I remember sending Bev a picture of the guys because their conversation seemed fishy, but they were being vague enough that the meaning of it wasn't obvious."

Zed's upper lip lifts into a sneer. "Sounds like those guys you saw were party guests. Or customers." He pulls his phone from his pocket. "I'll touch base with Bev. See if she's had time to look into those guys yet. Oh, and by the way? You make an appointment to see the therapist or I'm going to zip tie your ass and drag you in there myself."

"Right." I turn and wander through the only doorway in here that doesn't lead back to the butler's pantry. Because the room needs to be checked out, and not at all because I'm avoiding my friend's judgmental stare.

What I see when I enter the room stops me cold. It's a shower room, most likely originally intended to be used by people on their way into or out of the swimming pool. The exterior door has been walled off, however, and though someone made a cursory effort to hose this place out at one point, there is very clearly dried blood on the tile.

Zed pokes his head in. "Fuck."

"Think they killed people in here?" I gesture to the dried blood on the tile.

"Or tortured them." He sighs. "We're going to need to report this to law enforcement. Not that they'll probably do anything."

"I think I saw an article in the *Belle Argo Times* about some detective getting arrested for their involvement in this whole thing." I gesture around the room, but we both know I'm referring to more.

"Must be the detective some of our witnesses mentioned. Maybe things are changing at Belle Argo PD."

Zed proceeds to scrape a sample of the dried blood into a small, zippered baggie for us to test before the police come in. While he's making the call to local law enforcement, my own phone rings.

It's Ravi.

"Kid?"

"Okay. Don't be mad, but I kind of decided to go out and find some breakfast. And, well, I think someone's following me."

This house. This call. I've been barely holding on to my sanity, and that was before *I think someone's following me.*

The words wrap tight around my throat.

What the fuck? I gesture to Zed, yanking the keys from his back pocket as I race for the door. "What do you mean you think someone's following you?"

"Well, it's pretty early on a Sunday morning for people to be out, and this car came up behind me almost as soon as I left your property. It's kind of nice, actually. Red? I'm not good with the brands though. Anyway, I drove around in a weird pattern for a while, and it's still behind me."

Once again, Ravi isn't taking danger seriously. If he was, he wouldn't sound like he's reporting the weather.

My race to the exit feels like moving through quicksand. Even at top speed, it's too slow. Way too fucking slow.

"Where the fuck are you now?" I'm in the car and starting it up when Zed jumps in.

"Downtown. I was on my way to get a breakfast burrito."

He was on his way to—"Of course you fucking were," I grumble.

Ignoring Zed's questioning look, I say, "Keep your speed reasonable. Not too slow, but I don't want you leading this guy on a car chase. Keep me on the phone. Zed and I are on our way. Whatever you do, stay in the car. Try to not get fucking kidnapped before we find you."

I'm tearing out of there like a rabid dog who's slipped its leash.

"You got it, Daddy."

Daddy. I choke on the word. I'm going to kill that little shit when we find him.

CHAPTER TWENTY-THREE

Ravi

I COULDN'T DECIDE if I wanted to be there when Liam came back. I'm still not sure.

The part of me that wants him to approve of me keeps pointing out that I owe him the full twenty-four hours. Really, though, the bigger question is will he return before the time is up or did what happened between us somehow push him over the edge?

So, once I heard the crunch of Liam's truck pulling down the long gravel drive, I didn't waste much time. In spite of being so sore and jiggly I felt like I'd done one of those boot-camp workouts Dean loves so much, I couldn't turn off my brain. No way was I going to get any sleep.

What I know for sure is, I'm starving. And there's literally nothing in the fridge. Not even a loaf of bread that I can use to make sandwiches. Apparently while I was gone Liam has been living off salsa and tortilla chips and that nasty green juice of his.

Since I need to get food anyway, I text Channing to ask him if I can pick up my cat. For a moment, I pretend I wasn't just low-key held hostage by a pissed-off mercenary. Just going to run some errands. Normal guy shit.

Surprisingly, Channing's up, and his answer comes immediately.

Channing: Right fucking now. Little shit's trying my patience. He's put so many holes in my shirt I could use it to strain spaghetti. I'll be at the club all day.

Ravi: I need to make a stop on the way, but I'll be there as soon as I can. Be patient with him; he's just a baby.

Channing: No promises.

He's joking. Right? Who honestly hates kittens?

Still, I should go get Mr. Cat.

I'm surprised to find the keys to my car in the kitchen drawer where Liam always keeps them. He's been so controlling lately I would have thought he'd hidden them somewhere. Maybe even the car itself. But no, it's sitting around the side of the house, next to the garage.

When I pass the door I've looked in the window of so many times, I try not to wonder if he's had any of his little group get-togethers recently. There's a sticky, blurry feeling inside me I can't get a handle on when I consider the prospect. Watching him do those things to other people got me off, but I don't like the way him doing things with other people means he's not doing them with me.

Yes. He should definitely be doing them with me.

There's a certain satisfaction in me about what happened last night. Yes, it hurt, and okay, it was also sort of humiliating. For all of those hours Liam edged me, even though looking at me seemed physically painful to him, I also knew I had his full attention.

For a little while I was his and he was mine. The way I've always wanted.

The drive downtown is quick, all things considered. In the middle of a weekday it might take over half an hour, but this morning it's quiet and there's no traffic.

Which is how I notice the red sedan in my rearview.

Plus, it's awfully shiny.

I try to tell myself it's a coincidence that it's making all the same turns as me. It's hanging back enough that I could be wrong. I also can't get a license plate or anything because there are no front plates in Florida.

So I try, once I get into downtown, to make a few random turns. Instead of heading directly to the parking garage down the block from Gil's, I drive down the street where most of the bars are; one that almost nobody would have a reason to travel early on a Sunday morning. For a second I think I've lost the person, but then they appear again.

"Dammit."

My brain feels sluggish, almost as if it were scrambled by the most intense orgasm ever. Even so, there's a prickle of awareness that I need to do something here. As quickly as I think of it, I discard the idea of driving home. If Liam were there I might, but the last thing I need is to be on two and a half acres of land in the middle of nowhere when some sketchy car is following me around.

Not wanting another lecture from Liam, I pick up the phone to dial Brennan. He's the only other person I can think of who would know what to do in this situation.

"You've reached Brennan Doyle" is quickly followed by an automated voice saying "This customer's mailbox is full."

After circling the block Gil's is on, the car hangs back

again. I'm not dumb enough to think it's finally stopped following me, but I do think they've figured out that I know they're following me.

It's probably better to call Liam than to get killed. Probably.

My hands wrap tighter around the steering wheel, but it doesn't change how shaky I feel. Is it fear, or the comedown from my orgasm blackout?

The answer doesn't change the fact that right now I'm completely alone. And out of my depth.

Sighing in defeat, I grab my phone from the cupholder and hit the voice command button. "Call Demanding Asshole."

He answers on the first ring. "Kid?"

The nickname makes me want to growl at him. It also kind of gives me the shivers, because he called me that when he had me naked and tied to his bed.

"Okay. Don't be mad, but I kind of decided to go out and find some breakfast. And, well, I think someone's following me."

Footsteps echo on his end of the call. "What do you mean you think someone's following you?"

"Well, it's pretty early on a Sunday morning for people to be out, and this car came up behind me almost as soon as I left your property. It's kind of nice, actually. Red? I'm not good with the brands though. Anyway, I drove around in a weird pattern for a while, and it's still behind me."

"Where the fuck are you now?"

"Downtown. I was on my way to get a breakfast burrito." My stomach rumbles when I say the words.

He grumbles something I can't make out before adding, "Keep your speed reasonable. Not too slow, but I don't want you leading this guy on a car chase. Keep me on the phone. Zed and I are on our way. Whatever you do, stay in the car. Try to not get fucking kidnapped before we find you."

I roll my shoulders and take a deep breath. "You got it, Daddy."

It sounds a little like he's being strangled on the other end. In spite of the fact that there's a potential murderer or whatever following me, I still enjoy rattling him so much.

Wherever Liam has been, he gets to me surprisingly fast. I've only had to circle the block a few more times before a black SUV pulls up close behind the red car. I'm pretty sure I've seen it parked in Liam's driveway before. The vehicle swerves around the red car and then makes a sudden ninety-degree turn, blocking the street.

Then Liam's out, aiming a gun at the red car. Dammit, he's going to get arrested. I glance around, thankful the street is otherwise empty for now.

"Shit." My focus is all on my rearview, and I kind of didn't realize I'd been drifting toward the curb. I pull into an empty spot in front of a flower shop, only a couple of blocks down from Gil's. There's no chance I'm in the space properly, but I need to get to Liam.

"You can't shoot someone in the middle of downtown," I yell.

But Liam's already approaching the car, knocking on the window with the butt of the gun. When the window rolls down, it's a scared-looking teenager holding his hands up by his shoulders.

I know this guy, I think. "Wait. Liam. Put the gun down."

Liam glances my way but keeps his gun trained on the car window.

My phone rings in my back pocket. I ignore it as I draw

closer, because the kid in the driver's seat is definitely familiar. By kid I mean he's maybe a year or two younger than me, so not really a kid. Liam must be rubbing off on me.

Okay, I feel like that sentence would be funny in a different scenario.

"Liam, I'm serious," I say as I approach. "Stop. I know him. He was staying with Simon for a while. One of the other escorts."

"You do know that escorts are criminals, Ravi."

I want to roll my eyes at him so badly right now. "He's not one. He was crashing on Simon and Sebastian's couch for some reason." I look at the wide-eyed driver. "Right?"

"R-right. Jacob." His gaze bounces between me and Liam and occasionally over to Zed. "I'm sorry. I didn't know who I was following. I swear I wasn't going to hurt anyone. There was a weird AppTasker request to follow someone around and say where they went. Th-that's all. I knew it was sketch, but also I kind of really needed the money."

My phone goes off again. When I pull it out, it's Brennan.

"You needed something, little man?"

Why does everyone have to call me little? I know I'm not big. I *don't* need it pointed out all the time.

"It's fine now," I tell Brennan. "Someone was following me, but it's just this kid who used to live next door to Simon and Sebastian."

"Jacob?" Brennan's tone wakes me up. Brennan's always seemed fairly unthreatening to me in spite of his reputation, but the way Brennan says that name sounds like a bullet seeking a target.

"Uhm. Yeah. That's him. Liam's talking to him now."

"You tell that hostile asshole you live with he does not touch that kid. I'll take his hand."

So many questions. So many.

"Okay, that's..." The sort of thing Liam would say. How did I end up here, in the middle of the street like a damsel in a weird gang soap opera? "You know what? I'm going to let you tell him yourself."

So I hand over the phone while Liam keeps the gun in his right hand. He responds in a series of grunts to whatever Brennan's saying before growling a clipped "You'd fucking better" and returning the gun to its holster.

He hands the phone back to me and then nods to Zed. "We need to move the car." To Jacob, he adds, "Your guardian felon has asked that I keep an eye on you until he gets here. Which is fine, because I have some questions."

"He's not my—"

"I give zero fucks, Jacob."

Why does the kid who's younger than me get called by his name when to Liam I'm always "kid"?

My stomach chooses that moment to rumble again. Loudly.

Liam glances over at me and then points down the street to Gil's. "Go get your damn burrito. As soon as Brennan gets here, we'll go home."

Then he grabs my chin and leans in, whispering for only me to hear. "You didn't stay where you were supposed to. I owe you another punishment, kid."

CHAPTER TWENTY-FOUR

LIAM

BY THE TIME we get back to my house, Ravi's face is unusually red. I think he's even on the verge of tears.

I'm used to my word being final. I've faced down gangs and suicide bombers and armed war generals, but here I am about to be brought low by a nineteen-year-old twink.

"He's all I have, Liam. Please."

He's pissed because I won't let him go get his damn cat. Furious, in fact. On the inside, I'm already desperate to give him what he wants. Anything to wipe that look from his face. But if I cave now, I know I'll regret it.

"There's no way that guy was serious about eating the cat. He can wait."

"I know, but, Liam, if he's impatient, he could let it go or give it away or, I don't know, get mad and throw it across the room. I went to school with a kid whose father did that to their dog when he was drunk, and he had permanent neurological damage. You've seen things like that happen. I know you have."

Whatever issues I had with Corvus's oversized employee, he was not hot-headed. That much I'm sure of, or we'd be on the way to the damn club. Right now, I have half a day left with Ravi, and I intend to use it.

"He'll be fine for a few more hours. I gave you my answer."

Waiting isn't going to kill him. It really isn't. The way he falls silent, I know he knows I'm right. He may not like it, but he knows. Self-loathing swells in my chest all the same.

I pull up in front of the house. "Get inside," I order.

He trudges up the front steps with his shoulders hunched. The defeat on his face is enough to make my insides squirm, and that's before he opens his mouth again. "Liam, please. I'll do anything. He's the only thing in my life that loves me. Doesn't that matter at all?"

I don't expect the way that makes my heart sink.

There are a lot of ways I could answer. Reminding him he's got friends. Reminding him a kitten probably doesn't love him so much as see him as a safe and reliable source of food.

Telling him I'm right fucking here and I love him? That would open a can of worms I can never close.

Even though I do.

"You're due a punishment for leaving without permission. You're still on my time. If you take it like a good boy, we'll go and get your cat."

A crease divides the center of his forehead. "It won't take all night again, will it?"

Is that really his only concern? Jesus.

"It won't."

"Fine." He raises his chin, marching inside as if he's on a mission. I suppose he is. "Naked on your bed again? Should I go ahead and starfish so you can tie me down?"

The ground moves under my feet, threatening to pitch me into the stairs. Goddammit, this kid's going to be the death of me. "If you think you can behave yourself, I don't need to tie you down."

His amber eyes flash. "I don't know, Daddy. I'm not so good at behaving."

Fucking kill me now.

"Go."

For a few seconds I indulge in the sight of him marching up the stairs, his pert ass bouncing under a loose pair of shorts he must have thrown on before heading out. Then I detour into my playroom to gather a few things, including the last remaining shred of my sanity.

When I walk into the bedroom, he's on his hands and knees. The full moon of his ass hits me right in the face. His uncut cock is hard already, hanging heavily between his legs.

"You don't have to stay in that position," I tell him. "We could be here a while."

He flips onto his back. "You said it wouldn't be all night."

"That's right, I did. Given that it's still pretty early in the morning, that would be a long-ass time. But I don't intend to make this easy on you, and you're going to want to be in a more comfortable position."

"You also said you'd tie me up if I couldn't promise to behave."

Now I have a dilemma. He's leading me, and I generally

can't stand subs who try to top from the bottom. I also really fucking love seeing Ravi tied to my bed.

Holding his defiant gaze, I slip the loops over his wrists and tighten them slightly. "I'll leave your legs free this time. You'll probably need to move them around."

The best place for this would be in my garage. There's a padded bench made for exactly this sort of thing. I could drape him over it and have easy access. It's effortless to picture him in there, surrounded by my toy collection and the scent of polished wood. Taking him in there, though, is crossing a threshold neither of us is quite ready for. Not yet.

Each boundary I've set with Ravi has wound up being one I eventually smashed through or jumped right over. A voice in my head tells me I might as well give in. Sounds an awful lot like my old buddy Merrick, but he died the night I "earned" Ravi's auction money.

Still, there's a certain sort of person I have in my workroom, and Ravi's not one of them. They're temporary. Faceless. I don't want Ravi to be faceless or temporary to anyone.

Not even me.

"You might want to put your legs flat on the bed for now," I tell him. "You'll be doing a lot of squirming in a minute. Rest now, while you can."

When he wants to, Ravi complies so fucking beautifully.

"Good. Remind me of your safe word, kid."

It's a little sick, the way calling him kid when he's naked and spread out for me gets me so fucking hard.

Especially when I've never been more aware that he's nothing of the sort.

"I don't need a safe word. I'm not going to use it, Sir." He presses his lips together at the end of the sentence, as if he refuses to say anything more.

"The sooner you tell me, the sooner we can start."

"Fine. Red. My safe word is red."

"You remember the rules."

"If I use it we're done here. I already said I wasn't going to."

This isn't me being an asshole. At least, it's not meant to be. I've got a list of reasons longer than my left leg that this entire situation is the worst idea I've ever had. Even so, I keep circling around Ravi like he's a planet and I'm just a moon, helplessly stuck in his orbit. The last thing I need is to find out we're incompatible in bed. Plenty of past partners couldn't handle me.

"I don't know a single person who's never safed-out of a scene, kid. You might."

"Maybe *you* might." The brat has the nerve to stick out his fucking tongue.

The stubborn jut of his chin keeps me from responding, even though he could have a point. For all the years I've been doing this sort of thing, I am way out in deep water right now. If he asked me to kill for him, that would be easier than whatever I'm getting into right now.

"All right. We'll start off easy."

I pour some lube into my hand and reach for his cock. He's uncut, so it's not that I really need it, at least not yet. It's that I want the slip and slide of my skin on his.

It isn't long before he's bucking his hips, thrusting staccato into my hand, seeking relief.

When we did this before, it took every drop of restraint I had not to look at him. I knew if I let myself really fall into his gravity, I'd never climb out.

What's changed? Everything, and also nothing.

Nothing except I'm tired of fighting.

The muscle he's worked so hard for in the gym is typically hidden under loose clothing, but now his abs flex with each thrust and his arms strain against the ties. I was right about the squirming.

"Come whenever you want to, kid."

There's confusion written all over his face. After hours of not being allowed to get off before, he's wondering if this is a trap.

It's absolutely a trap.

My cock is a steel bar in my pants, but I'm ignoring it for now. Right now, this is about him.

I brace one slippery hand on his upper thigh as he fucks my fist. He growls in frustration at being held down from all his thrashing, but on my end it's immensely satisfying to feel his leg flex and strain against my hand while he tries desperately to get himself off.

When his release comes, it's on a strained moan, nothing as loud or showy as the way he came after I edged him for hours. It's the part of his wet lips and the bunching and releasing of his muscles I find so gratifying. That, and the fact that his eyes never leave mine.

"I'm struggling...to see how this is a punishment." His chest rises and falls with each heavy pant of his breath.

"Don't worry." I pour more lube on my fingers, coating them liberally. "You'll figure it out soon."

Then I proceed to coax him back to life, which only takes a few minutes. Oh, to be young again. "There are few things I miss about being a teenager," I murmur, "but this is a definite bonus."

"I'm not that young. My birthday's in a few months." He nearly moans the assertion. "And getting boners all the time is hardly convenient."

My heart stutters when he mentions his birthday. I'm an absolute ass.

His parents getting killed so close to his birthday meant I'd chosen not to do much to celebrate. I didn't want him to have that cloud hanging over the day he was born. I realize now it was a mistake.

Ravi deserves to be celebrated.

Next time I'll do something big. If he stays.

I bat the thought away. "Hmm. Well, at the moment your boners are awfully convenient for me."

Then I slide my slicked finger into his hole.

The crook of my finger makes his eyes fly open and a surprised gasp leaves his mouth. The sound is like candy on my tongue.

"W-what are you doing?"

"Don't tell me you haven't figured out about your prostate. I found the dildo under your pillow when I was searching your room."

"Ooooh, there are so many things wrong with that sentence. You should not—ahhh—you shouldn't be searching my room." The way he whimpers takes the teeth out of his admonishment.

"My house, my rules, baby," I say as I work him with my fingers. My strokes are gentle but steady. This is only the second wave. I'm pretty confident I can get at least a couple more out of him, but I have to start off easy.

For all his whimpering, he pulls his legs up. He's digging his heels into the bed, canting his hips to get a better angle. Using my hand like that toy under his pillow.

"There's nothing sexier than the way you're writhing on my finger right now."

Maybe it's the lighting or wishful thinking, but I could swear his face goes up in flames.

I slide a second finger into him. Because I can, and because he's going to need it in a little while when I bring my toys out.

"Oh, God. Liam. It's... Oh, fuck. F-feels so good. So, so, soooo..." He's a constant, relentless ball of motion. He always has been, but it's the first time I don't really mind. "This feels way better than a dildo."

"Skin is always better than plastic," I agree. Especially his skin.

Slowly and steadily, I finger him, loving the way his warm, tight hole greedily sucks me in. I'm brushing his prostate with each pass. The forceful way his inner muscles squeeze, I swear he's going to break my fingers.

I'm slow but steady as I work him over. One hand stroking his cock, one working his ass until once again he's burbling cum.

Not much this time. It's to be expected.

"God, I didn't even know I could do that." His eyes are glassy, and his tone is filled with wonder.

"That's the point of all of this, right? To learn new things?"

There's a beat where the rise and fall of his chest freezes. It's clear he heard the bitterness in my voice.

I can't help it. There's a swirl of acid in my stomach. An ashy taste in my mouth when I think of him sharing these experiences with someone else.

Maybe all I am to him is an experiment. The idea that he would have done this or something like it with any asshole who paid for the pleasure kills me.

Well, fuck that and fuck them. I paid, and the pleasure is mine.

"I'll give you a minute." He doesn't realize it yet, but I won't be giving him too long. By the time we're done here, he won't be as satisfied and glowy as he looks right now.

While he catches his breath, I go to the bathroom and run water over a washcloth to get him cleaned up. This is a technique I use sometimes in interrogation. Giving the person a break, a moment of kindness, lulls them into a false sense of security.

Besides, I need to get the vibrator.

It's thicker than the one I used on him previously, which was more of a vibrating wand. This one is meant to fill him up. It's also got a much more powerful motor. The three fresh C batteries inside are about to come in handy.

He's got his eyes closed when I return, but his fingers are twitching, so I know he's awake.

"Ready for more?"

"More?" He breathes the word. Confusion crosses his face.

"More," I agree. It's the only warning he gets before I slide the lubed dildo inside him, slow but steady.

"Oh, Jesus, that's big." He's startled. Breathy. But his eager groan tells me he likes being filled.

"It is," I say with a smile.

Then I turn it to the lowest setting.

"Oh. Ohhhh. Ho. Ow."

"Yeah, I'd imagine you're a bit tender right now." If he's not seeing how it's a punishment yet, he's about to.

I plant one knee between his spread legs, using it to hold the dildo in place. Then I take his cock in my still-slippery hands and start to jack him off again.

"Liam, I don't know if I can come again." There it is. The nerves in his voice. The uncertainty.

"You're damn well going to try. Unless you'd like to use your safe word."

He clamps his lips tight. It looks like he's actually biting down on them. He's adamant as he shakes his head.

Right now I fucking love how stubborn he is. All those moments of defiance are coming home to roost. My chest could burst open with the satisfaction.

This next one takes some doing. I fuck him slowly with the dildo, then faster, aiming deliberately to nudge his prostate a little, but the vibration does most of the work. I'm fairly gentle as these things go, but the struggle between pleasure and pain is all over him. The ties on his wrists are going to leave bruises the way he's thrashing.

I like that a little too much.

After a few minutes he's keening, and he's crying a little, but then he comes again after a few minutes more. Things are coming out of his mouth, but it's nothing I can understand. I'm not sure he even understands. It's all a jumble of sentence fragments and sounds.

"Oh God," he whimpers after a few minutes of catching his breath. "Th-that was it, right? Was that it? Because I don't think I can handle any more."

"Are you sure?"

"I'm sure. So sure. I'm, like, really, really sure."

The military taught me a lot. The most valuable lesson? "You have no idea what you're capable of yet."

"Sir. Daddy. Nooo."

The dildo is still inside him. A shiver runs through me when I reach down and turn it on again, this time cranking the intensity up to a higher setting.

"Liam, no," he says tiredly.

"Are you using your safe word?"

"I really don't think I can..."

I turn the vibrations higher.

"No. No, I really can't."

"Are you using your safe word?"

He's either shaking his head or simply thrashing due to overstimulation. Or both.

"Daddy. Please. *Please.*" He's crying. He's begging. What he hasn't done is say "red."

"You can handle more than you think you can."

I turn it up again.

"Liam, it hurts," he whines. He bites his lip so hard it bleeds a little. "Oh, God. It feels good but it hurts."

"You can take it, kid."

Then I put my hands on his legs and press him to the bed while I take him into my mouth.

"Liam. Oh God. I don't even—I don't understand. It hurts. It hurts so fucking much. It feels so fucking good. Your mouth. God, you have no idea how many times I dreamed about—I can't... I don't... Oh, fuck. Aaah!"

This time, when he comes, the hoarse scream he belts out with his entire chest is so. Fucking. Good.

His legs are trembling. He's come so many times, his body repeatedly tensing and releasing that his muscles twitch and jump involuntarily.

At last I allow myself the relief of unzipping my pants and pulling out my cock. While Ravi catches his breath, I stroke myself quickly and efficient, shooting far too quickly over his stomach and chest.

He regards the spatter through half-lidded eyes, sliding a finger through my cum and bringing it to his mouth. He murmurs something about going to get Mr. Cat, but by the time I finish cleaning him up, he's asleep, lashes fanned across the apples of his cheeks.

My cum is gone from his skin, but the red marks and bruises are harder to erase. They'll mark him as mine long after our twenty-four hours have ended.

Lord help me, I'm fucked.

CHAPTER TWENTY-FIVE

RAVI

WHEN I WAKE UP, I'm achy and confused. There's bright afternoon sun coming in through a window that's not mine. I'm in Liam's bed.

Liam, who's asleep next to me, with what feels like a possessive hand on my sternum. A light snore and the fluttering of his lids make him look more human.

He never did take off all his clothes, but at some point he took off his shirt and his ever-present tactical pants.

It's not the only time I've seen him this way, but it's one of few. After the night I climbed into this very bed and told him I was in love with him, he never let me crawl into his bed again. Never again flipped pancakes in his boxers on Sunday morning. Things just weren't the same.

Part of me wants to reach out and touch him like this. To slide my finger along his stubbled jaw and his puffy, pouty lower lip. I want to run my hands through his messy hair.

I want to sit and stare at him, as unhinged as that probably sounds. He's never soft like this when he's awake.

My bladder is screaming at me, so I force myself out of bed to answer the call. Since I don't know what's going to happen when Liam wakes up, I go ahead and slip on my clothes.

"Oof." The way my muscles ache, you'd think I'd done a hard workout yesterday and not had a ton of orgasms in a twenty-four-hour window.

The twenty-four-hour window that's going to be up before too much longer. The thought makes my chest tight.

I'm still pissed at Liam for the way he treated me before, and for the way he's been monumentally controlling. The way he's switched from not wanting me to something else so fast has given me whiplash.

But. But...

The idea that I've finally achieved what I need to leave him doesn't feel the way it was supposed to. I was supposed to feel free. Relieved.

I have money now. I can go anywhere I want. Never again in my life will I have to rely on someone else to take care of me, especially someone who doesn't want to. This is the part where I pack my bags, right?

Shouldn't I feel accomplished? Gratified? Proud?

For sure I should at least feel sexually satisfied.

Instead, it's as if someone has reached inside and hollowed me out.

I'm so lost in my thoughts while I'm washing my hands that I don't realize at first that Liam's right behind me.

He's practically glowing with the afternoon light hitting his hair. Larger than life as usual, but maybe a little more accessible.

Sometimes he jokes about being old—I always figured it was to remind me I was too young for him—but he's tan and sculpted, with abs that would make literally any male model jealous. The tattoo on his arm flexes as he reaches forward to turn off the sink faucet, which is when I realize I've been rinsing my hands for at least a minute.

"Sorry." I clear my throat. "Guess I was distracted."

He almost sort of smiles. "How are you feeling? Hungry?"

"I want to get Mr. Cat. You promised."

He nods. "You need to eat and take a shower. The hot water will help with the soreness. How about while you're cleaning up I'll go get food, and I'll pick up the kitten for you?"

"No."

It's funny how after all of this time he still doesn't expect me to push back against him. The way he's looking at me, you'd think I had morphed into my extraterrestrial form.

"He's my cat, Liam. I want to get him."

He sighs deeply, as if I've asked for something completely outlandish. "Never fucking though I'd be jealous of a cat," he mutters. Then he grabs the waistband of his shorts and shoves them to the floor. "Fine. Shower first. It'll save time if we go together."

It's all I can do to keep my eyeballs inside of my head. I've seen Liam Masters a thousand different ways over the years, but never like this. Never peeling off his boxer briefs while nudging me into the shower.

If only I could go back and tell eighteen-year-old me not to lose hope.

Because Liam Masters is naked. Completely naked. Like,

head-to-toe skin. It's not only the lightly furred trail that leads from his abs to his dick, but also the dick itself, which is kind of hard but not all the way, nestled in a tightly packed and neatly trimmed nest of curls.

"You're going gray?" This is going to bite me in the ass later, but I can't help myself. Nor can I hold back the giggles coming out of my mouth.

Another sigh. "Yeah, yeah. It's very funny. I seem to be going gray from the bottom up." He gives me a look. "I am almost forty, kid. You really want in on all of this?"

I've noticed he has a few gray strands in his hair. They're more liberally sprinkled in his stubble, which is maybe why he usually shaves. This is the first time I've seen him all the way naked.

Reaching up, I comb my fingers through the strands on his head. "You look hot, Daddy. I like it," I tell him.

Since I first realized I wanted him, I haven't been able to see anything else.

He gives me a sour look and then turns on the shower. "Of course you do."

"You know it's never bothered me. Your age. I don't know why it bothers you so much."

"Gosh, I don't know. Maybe it's knowing when I was first overseas killing people and trying not to get blown up myself, you weren't even eating solid food yet. Or knowing I failed my best friend because he gave me his only child for safekeeping and I...defiled him."

I don't think I've ever seen Liam blush before. I like that, too.

It's impossible to hold back the grin spreading across my face. Still, I have to ask: "Are you going to flip out again?

Start being shitty to me because you feel guilty for wanting me back?"

Until he reaches over to pull my lip from between my teeth, I don't even realize I'm chewing on it again.

"No, kid. I'm done fighting how much I want you. You have no idea how exhausting it's been denying how I feel. I honestly think it created a mental health crisis."

That sounds good. Or, not good, but...I'm glad he wants me. I'm glad he's not fighting.

He tugs the hem of my shirt and pulls it off over my head. Then with my shorts already on the floor, my briefs follow. Lastly, he gets on his knees, pulling off one sock and then the other. I don't know what makes me think he'll groan about the hard tile or have trouble getting up off his knees, but he doesn't.

That pesky ball of hope is glowing bright in my chest again, filling in the emptiness I felt when I thought of leaving. It gets brighter and stronger with every move Liam makes. It feels too early, though, too fragile, this new thing between us.

What if I ask him about staying and everything shatters? I don't think I can handle it if he rejects me again.

"Come here." He pulls me under the spray, grabbing a scrubber and some bodywash; the kind that has that spicy, earthy, manly smell I can never quite identify. Slowly and carefully, he washes my hair, scrubs me all over (firm but also gentle), and then rinses me off.

All along I'm sneaking glances at his body, at his cock, which is thick and red at its bulbous end, even redder when it's thoroughly hard. After a while, so is mine. But he doesn't mention it, so I don't either.

Honestly, I never thought I'd see the day when I don't want to come again, but I could use a break.

I'm expecting him to turn off the water when instead he turns me to face away from him. Both hands come down on my shoulders, massaging firmly.

I can't hold back my satisfied groan. "Oh God, that feels so good."

"You'll be sore for a little while. After everything. This will help. You'll want to drink plenty of water today. Take a walk or go for an easy jog. You won't feel like it, but movement creates blood flow, which is healing. Remember that, Rav."

"Okay, Daddy."

He's silent for a while. I get the feeling he's gearing up for something. In spite of the relaxing massage, I'm braced for what comes next. I'm braced for him to break my heart again.

"Tell me how you're feeling."

Oh. "Well. Sore, like you said. Inside and out. A little tired still. Otherwise, okay."

"Good. I meant emotionally, though."

"Emotionally?"

"What we did was a lot. It was new. This sort of thing can bring up emotions, especially at first. I need to know I haven't ruined you, here."

"I—" *I love you.* How do I tell him that's the main thing I'm feeling? Even more than ever?

The thought of it makes my heart try to beat its way out of my chest.

Soon. I'll tell him soon.

"I don't regret it, if that's what you mean," I tell him. "I guess I'm a little confused. You were so angry with me before. After the auction, and after you picked me up downtown. Now all of a sudden you're being nice."

"That's how it works, kid. You went against my wishes, and I punished you. I'm ready to move past it if you are. As far as I'm concerned, we're good."

I turn in his arms, looking up at him. At the way the water from the shower is clinging to his eyelashes and lips. "Are we really good, Liam? After everything?"

This is about so much more than the last twenty-four hours.

His expression softens. When his arms slide around me, warming the chilled skin that isn't under the water, I want to grab hold and not let go.

"I won't apologize for wanting to keep you safe. But I see now that I didn't know how to handle the way your feelings had changed toward me. Or the way I realized mine had changed toward you. At the same time I was trying to protect you, I was also pushing you away. I'm done with that. I don't have it in me to pretend anymore."

Does that mean what I think it means? "I'm going to need more words."

His chest caves with the force of his rough grunt. Then, he leans down to kiss me. Really kiss me. For the first time, Liam Masters is kissing me the way you kiss someone you need like water, and I'll do anything to keep him from being thirsty.

His tongue in my mouth is the stuff of all my high school fantasies. I'll never wonder again what it means in one of my books when someone feels a kiss all the way to their toes. Mine are bunching against the tile.

“More,” I demand when he begins to pull away.

He laughs a little, but then he complies. His tongue is wet and warm, sliding against mine. Ohhh. Boy. I could do this all day.

Except. Except if I’m staying, we need to have a conversation. We need to establish some ground rules. I put my hands to his shoulders, pushing away some.

“You need to remember I’m not one of your subordinates, Liam, and I’m not your ward anymore. I get to make my own decisions.”

“Being with someone means taking their feelings into account when you make decisions. You’re an impulsive dopamine seeker who puts himself in harm’s way for fun. That affects me.”

“Not for fun. I did what I did to help people.”

“You can’t ask me to cover my eyes and not notice when you’re about to do something ill-advised. I’m always going to want you to be safe. You can’t expect me to be someone I’m not.”

I guess that’s fair. “How about I promise not to ignore you in the future when you express your concerns?”

He clenches his jaw. “It’s a start.”

“Well, I assume we can keep discussing these things in the future if we need to. Keep negotiating.” I need that assurance that if I stay I won’t regret it later.

“I’m pretty sure that’s what relationships are about.”

“Pretty sure?”

He looks away and then back again. “I...don’t exactly have a ton of experience with them.”

“In forty years?”

He shrugs. “Started dating the neighbor girl, Tara Porter,

before I went off to boot camp. She cheated on me while I was away. After a few more failed attempts, I decided dating wasn't my cup of tea."

"And now?"

"Maybe tea's not so bad."

CHAPTER TWENTY-SIX

LIAM

"I HOPE HE'S OKAY," Ravi says as we pull up to the club. It's late afternoon, so they're probably not open for business yet. "He's probably confused by the fact that I've been gone."

"He's a cat, Ravi. I doubt he's got any idea. As far as he knows, he was starving on the street, and some guy picked him up and fed him, and now some other guy is feeding him."

For all Ravi's insistence that he's a grown-ass adult, the way he pouts and crosses his arms is reminiscent of a petulant toddler.

"It's going to be fine" I try as we approach the door.

Nothing.

In spite of the relatively early hour, there's a bouncer outside. Not the one I saw before, and this one isn't in a tux. He's wearing jeans and a golf shirt, looking oddly like the handsome werewolf guy from that vampire show everyone used to fan themselves over.

"Fuck no," the guy says when he sees me.

I plant my feet wide. "On whose order? I do have a membership here." If he's barring me entry on sight, does that mean he was specifically ordered not to let me in? Or is this simply because they're closed?

"You've caused enough fucking trouble here."

So it is me.

It doesn't matter, because Ravi comes barreling in from behind me, striding right up to the bouncer before I can stop him. "Hi, Fred. You remember me, right?"

The piece-of-shit sentry's smile is a little too fond. "Course I do, little guy. Glad to see you made it back in one piece."

Every cell in my body bristles at the implication that I would have harmed Ravi in any way. Even knowing that's the exact thing I was afraid of someone else doing, the accusation rankles.

"Did you get to see my kitten? Channing's been watching him for me."

"Oh yeah." The guy laughs. "We've all seen. He's fucking pissed. Don't worry, though. He's been feeding it and everything. Even gave it a bath when it got food all over its face. Real messy eater, that one."

Ravi's beaming brighter than the Florida sun right now, and I could swear the bouncer is giving me some smug fucking side-eye. Some kind of "Hey, look, I made him smile" or some bullshit. Fucker.

My usual patience is nowhere to be found right now. If I'm honest, it's been thin on the ground since the day Ravi came into my life. Thinner since the day my cock started pointing his way like a divining rod. Now, when the bouncer seems to be issuing some sort of challenge?

Fuck this guy.

My hand goes to my gun. "How about you let us the fuck in so he can get his cat back, yeah?"

My other hand goes to the pocket with my cell phone. Still haven't ruled out calling law enforcement. This place is shady as fuck.

When Fred's face turns to stone again, Ravi has the audacity to reach up and tug on the guy's sleeve. "Please, Fred? I've really missed him."

There's a prickly sensation at the back of my neck when the man steps back to push the door, allowing us entry. I'm not sure how I feel about Ravi aiming those liquid eyes of his at someone who isn't me. My teeth could turn coal to diamonds right now. If I knew he was mine, I don't think I'd have this itching inside me, but that talk we had in the shower didn't cover everything.

He hasn't agreed to belong to me. He hasn't said the words. Until he does, I don't think I'll be settled.

You haven't actually asked, have you?

Now isn't the time. Soon.

Low voices filter to us when we enter the main part of the club. A seating area that was previously situated around a spanking bench has been altered, the bench replaced with a mahogany card table.

Seated around it, drinking what looks like scotch and smoking cigars, are three of the sketchiest men in the Belle Argo area besides possibly myself.

Brennan Doyle is to my left, Daniel Corvus to the right. Straight across is a man I only know by reputation. Nathaniel Cavallari. The latter has popped up in case files, but I've never met him in person. Dealing cards is a mousy young thing with her tits spilling over her bustier, a baby face, and hard eyes. She's as likely to offer me a drink as throw a chair at me, I'm betting.

Cavallari looks up at me, his gold-flecked eyes assessing. "Mr. Masters, how are you?"

"How the hell do you know who I am?"

Brennan flicks a couple of cards over to the scantily clad young dealer. "Nathaniel here oversees the unincorporated area between Beacon Hill and Belle Argo," he says.

"Your house is practically on my territory," Cavallari says with a smile. "I know who all of my subjects are."

"I'm not one of your subjects, pal, and if you insist on thinking otherwise, we're going to have a problem."

Any reply the creepy-ass motherfucker might have made is drowned out by Ravi shouting, "Mr. Cat!" He's across the room in a heartbeat, making grabby hands in front of the guy who was following him around before the auction.

"I missed you so much," he says, baby-talking to the little black fuzzball. "Did Channing take the best care of you? I bet he did. Did you miss me too...?"

He's cuddling the cat to his chest as he follows Channing out of the room.

"Kid. Where the hell are you going?"

"Don't worry," the object of my psychosis calls over his shoulder. "I just need to get the rest of his stuff. You can have a nice chat with the guys. I'll be right back."

Jesus. I scan the three men at the table. Daniel Corvus, who has no history and a club filled with a number of employees who look like ex-cons. Brennan Doyle, who does have a history and a rap sheet longer than a CVS receipt. Nathaniel Cavallari, who tends to keep to himself, or so I thought, but who owns a suspicious amount of the land between this club and my house.

Channing's absence aside, there are three obvious sentries posted at each exit point in the room. Then there's the dealer, who appears to have a knife sheathed in the top of her thigh-high boot.

Nice chat, my ass.

"Rav seems like he's in a good mood. It's nice to see." Brennan fucking Doyle had better wipe that knowing look off his face before I remove it for him.

"His mood is none of your damn business." I'm fucking seething right now.

"Beg to differ," he mumbles with half his attention on his cards. "Whatever you think of me, Ravi's family, and I protect what's mine."

"He's not yours to protect. He's mine." Goddammit, I know I'm letting him goad me like a wet-behind-the-ears recruit. My fuse is too short for this shit.

Doyle's eyebrows hit his hairline. The other two are studying me over their cards. Cavallari looks like he's holding in a laugh. Fuck. I need to staple my own mouth shut.

My conscience prods at me for essentially calling dibs on the kid while he's out of the room. And Ravi's had one foot out the door this entire time. I'm not sure if I'm too late to call him back. I'm not sure if I should.

Still. Ravi is too good to belong to filth like Brennan Doyle. He's too good for filth like me.

Doyle lays his cards on the table, face down. Turning his attention back to me, he says, "I owe you one, by the way. For what you did for Jacob."

Are my eyes still in my head? Is my jaw still connected to

my face? Am I hallucinating? Because Brennan Doyle just told me he owed me. I draw in a deep breath and let it out, letting my clenched fists relax a little. Only a little.

"What the hell are you talking about?"

Brennan clicks his tongue and returns to his cards. "Don't try to tell me you weren't ready to turn that kid into pulp when he scared your precious little twink. Jacob's a good egg, though. Stuck in a shitty situation and he's made some not-so-wise decisions, is all. Had him staying with one of my guys for a while, but his stepfather gave him no choice but to return home. I get the feeling you know about being stuck in shitty situations, Masters. I know I do."

This day has been full of surprises. Finding out the lump of coal in Brennan Doyle's chest might beat after all? Frankly, I wish there was another chair nearby for me to sit down in.

"I spoke to your colleague," Daniel says loudly enough to broadcast the obvious change in topic. "She asked for names of anyone barred entry to the auction. The list of those we didn't let in was longer than those we did, but after doing my own digging, I believe I know who you're looking for."

What? "Who? And how?"

"The how is a bit complicated, but I'm missing a couple of employees since the night of. Both recently received sums of money that weren't easily explained, and one was caught propping a rear door shortly before your boy went on stage."

"He's not—" I bite down on the insistence that Ravi's not my boy. The insistence I've been making for the better part of two years is more habit than anything else.

I did just insist to Doyle that he's mine.

And he is. He's mine. I'll worry about the rest of it later.

"Why the hell didn't you tell us sooner about all of this?"

I'm trying to keep my cool, but I can't stop the twitch of my neck that makes something in me pop and crack.

Corvus's expression seems to convey "I'm telling you now." Along with a heavy dose of "Don't piss me off."

I clear my throat. "And?"

"The man you're looking for is Dylan Beck."

The guy we've already been looking into. I remember the hungry look on his face when I slipped into Mercer Oak's party while everyone, including the shit security, was busy watching Ravi scaling his fellow escort like a kitten in a tree.

I don't know whether to be pissed off or thrilled.

"We already suspected him. How do *you* know?"

"Aside from tracing the source of my former employees' recent windfall, he's got a loose but significant connection to the young party promoter who was implicated in the trafficking ring you've been investigating."

Tony. That little shit was alarmingly well connected. "The investigation is over." At least, it's supposed to be.

"Of course it is," Daniel says with a look that tells me he's not buying what I'm selling.

"Regardless, the man you mentioned is already on our short list, but the bigger issue is our missing staff. We value loyalty here, and they've broken it."

"I know that guy you're talking about, sort of." Brennan takes a hearty sip of his drink. Leave it to Brennan Doyle to chug a drink you're supposed to savor.

"One of my guys had a date with him awhile back," Doyle continues. "Kid landed in the hospital. Never trust a man who doesn't know not to break his toys." Another glug of liquid.

Then, out of nowhere, he snaps his fingers, as if he's having a lightbulb moment. "Jacob. The one who followed

Ravi. His stepfather developed a lot of the real estate around here, and I'm pretty sure the two were friends or business partners or whatever. Overheard the kid mention a while ago that stepdaddy owns a yacht called the *Sally Sue*."

What a stupid fucking name for a boat. I suppress a growl. "You're thinking he could be using the friend's boat."

"I'm thinking if you were stalking and threatening someone who's under the protection of one trained killer, one who learned by doing, and one with some kind of hairy-ass dog fraternity at his disposal—"

Corvus barks a laugh. Unexpected, given that Brennan just insulted the guy's staff by calling them dogs.

"—you'd want to hide your ass in a place that's not under your name or the name of one of your businesses," Doyle finishes. "Am I wrong?"

What does it say that for a second I want him to be? That I want Brennan Doyle to be the violent, brainless Neanderthal everyone makes him out to be? If this lead is legit, then I need to check it out now, and I don't want to. What I want is to take Ravi back home and finally sink inside of him.

It's a fucked-up thought. From a fucked-up guy. Times like these, I'm not sure I'm any better than men like Dylan Beck.

If Doyle's right, it's not something I can ignore. Beck threatened Ravi.

For a second I study Doyle's profile. The subtle lines at the corner of his eyes. The highlights in his hair that might actually be the start of him going gray. Brennan Doyle is older than I am, if I had to guess. You don't stay alive in this line of work without being smart. And ruthless.

"No," I admit. "You're not wrong."

Chattering voices from beyond the room tell me Ravi's on the way back.

The phone next to Brennan's left hand emits an alert. The sound of a cash register. He picks it up, scowls, and then drops his cards on the table with a wad of cash. "I need to take care of something. You people have fun."

Probably off to check on one of his dirty businesses. I scoff but otherwise keep my thoughts to myself. The intense glance he cuts my way tells me he heard the sound, but the way he storms out as if his ass is on fire says he's got bigger concerns than my judgment.

"I need to check this out," I tell Corvus. "Can I leave Ravi with you? I need to know he's safe until I can get back."

He waves his hand. "Take Channing. He'll help sniff out our traitors."

"You're not leaving me here." Ravi's standing a few feet away from me, kitten still cuddled against his chest, scowling. "This involves me, and I'm not a child who needs a babysitter. I'm going with you."

He might be right. Of course he's right. I've also never wanted to lock him in his bedroom more.

CHAPTER TWENTY-SEVEN

Ravi

If there's one thing I'm good at, it's staring down Liam Masters. I've had plenty of practice. I can out-stubborn him better than almost anyone, and we both know he didn't have time to argue with me. He hates it, though. His knuckles are white on the steering wheel as we speed down the access road to Belle Argo's private marina.

He calls his team from the car. I think I hear a woman's voice over the phone, which means it must be Bev. I haven't heard him mention another female employee, which probably sucks for her. Really, I should have a talk with him about his company's lack of gender inclusivity.

Then again, I'd expect working for Liam to suck regardless. For years, simply living under his roof and having him think he had the authority to give me commands was grating as hell. I can't imagine how bad it would be if he actually signed my paychecks.

Then again, he does pay my tuition. Or...did?

Did. I can pay it myself now.

Maybe that'll make things different between us. If I can pay my own way, it'll feel more equal. Maybe Liam won't need to be in charge of everything.

If I stay.

Okay. Liam's still going to be Liam. But maybe... Well, I hope when this is over we can come up with something that makes us both happy. Because I don't think leaving would. Make me happy, that is.

"Kid, I need you to stay in the car when we get there. Stay out of the way. I know you love to run headfirst into stupid shit, but this is one time when I'm telling you not to."

"Don't call me kid." My neck tightens at his use of the word now. "Kid" was an insult that turned into sort of a sexy endearment, but right now it's neither. He's trying to put me in my place. That's not happening.

His reaches across with one large hand, landing it on the top of my leg. "Ravi. Please."

Well, this is new. Turns out Liam saying "please" has more power over me than his commands.

"Fine. I'll stay away from the big guys with the big guns. Happy?"

He pulls a face but at least seems appeased. It's not as if I have a weapon right now.

"You could give me a gun."

"Fuck no. Nobody's running in there yet anyway," he says as he pulls into the small parking area outside the slip management office. "We're going to play this smart and wait for the team. They're on their way."

With the car stopped, he's checking his pockets and pulling out his gun when there's a loud bang. His black Mercedes tips to one side.

Everything inside me turns cold.

"Unless they shoot at us first." Liam turns to me with his jaw set. "Get down and stay out of sight." Then he pushes open the door and slides to the ground outside. From the back seat, Channing does the same. I'd like to argue that if they're both hiding behind the vehicle and I'm inside cowering on the floor, aren't there more layers of protection between them and the bullets? Shouldn't I be out there with them?

I can't just sit here. My brain wants to spin. My legs want to move. My lungs want to scream.

But I know Liam. I know how he thinks. He's hoping whoever's shooting at us hasn't seen me through the tinted windows and that I'm safer if I'm not out in the open.

For once, I decide to listen. My body's still sore and sluggish from earlier, and I don't have anything to defend myself. Before everything went to hell between us, Liam taught me some self-defense moves, but if anyone out there is Channing's size? I'm not sure how much I can do.

None of that logic helps, though, when the shooting picks up. While I try to cover my ears, to stay ducked below the level of the window, I'm also craning to try and see what's going on. Mr. Cat lets out a tiny mewl from his carrier, and I nudge it under the seat as far as possible to keep him safe.

There's some movement on a small yacht across the way, cutely named the *Sally Sue*. We had a roly-poly calico named Sally Sue when I was little.

What's not cute is the guy who jumps from the boat deck down to the dock, barely breaking his stride as he shoots. It's a semi-automatic handgun. I think Liam told me once the maximum number of bullets is, like, eighteen? At first I try to count, thinking it would help to know when the guy runs out. Except then he reaches into the pocket of some bag that's strapped to his chest and pulls something out. I can't see what it is, but when he throws it, it makes a ton of smoke.

Now I can't see a thing. All I can do is hope that Liam and Channing are okay.

And try not to think of my parents. Which...once the night they were killed pops into my head, it's impossible to rid myself of the memory. The pops and bangs I'd thought were fireworks.

"Fuck," I whisper to myself as I press my hands harder over my ears. I hate this. I hate feeling helpless like this. The way I'm shaking.

When my parents were killed, I was two doors down. A rare sleepover party I'd been invited to, probably mostly because we were neighbors. People in our neighborhood were always shooting off illegal fireworks, so we figured that was what we'd heard.

Knowing I'd been so close to them, and I hadn't realized...

Breathe, Ravi. Focus on the breath going in. Focus on the breath going out.

When I was a teenager, I'd get so impatient with my mom, so annoyed that she kept telling me to breathe whenever I was in pain or to breathe through anger, when what I wanted was to be able to *do* something. I really should have appreciated her help more when she was around.

My relief when the smoke clears is short-lived. Channing and Liam are racing for the boat. The guy who looked like he threw the smoke bomb is on the ground now, with blood pooling beneath him. There might be someone else still up there on the deck. I could swear there's movement near the cabin. Maybe it's only shadows shifting with the boat's rocking?

Whatever it is, I have a bad feeling.

I see the fire before I hear the boom. It's so surreal I can't make sense of it, because who the fuck sets off an explosive on a boat that probably cost more than Liam's house?

Liam, who just went on the boat. There's fire where he's supposed to be. In that first breath my feet are glued to the floor, everything slow and surreal and muffled. My brain's put itself on pause.

"No." Once it unfreezes, I'm out of the car and running. There's no thought in my head of what I'm going to do. How can I even help? All I know is the boat is leaning backward now, nose slightly upturned like the rich snob it is, and I have no idea where Liam went.

All I know is I have to get to him. I have to. And he'd better be alive. He'd better be, or I'll set every boat on fire.

It's confusing when all of a sudden I'm running but I'm not going anywhere.

"Stay fucking still, you little shit," someone growls in my ear.

I hadn't felt him grab me. I hadn't even realized he was there.

At least I can answer the question of who, though. Mid-struggle, I freeze at the sight of his face.

"You were at the party." It's the guy who tried to grab me before. The one who wanted to buy me for two million dollars.

"For a little guy, you've been a lot of fucking trouble," he grits out. He's trying to pull me backward, and I'm trying not to let him, but he outweighs me by a lot.

"You know what? Get in line." I nearly roll my eyes. "People have been telling me I'm annoying for years now. If I'm such a pain in your ass, why were you trying to buy time with me?"

"I don't want any time with you." His arm ratchets around me tighter. Even as his voice takes on a tone that's almost apologetic. "It's nothing against you. What we needed was an investment. Daniel Corvus was short-sighted to limit auctioning you off to the wealthy in Belle Argo when there are much deeper pockets elsewhere in the world. Some of those guys would absolutely salivate over a tiny, feisty thing like you."

A boulder sinks into my stomach. When Liam kept insisting on the danger of the auction and I kept blowing him off, all I'd been thinking of was what an enthusiastic or slightly sadistic buyer might want to do.

I figured I knew myself well enough to know that a guy handling me too roughly wouldn't be much different than going streaking through a warehouse full of guys with guns. It might not be sexy, but I could handle it. Maybe it would even be sort of exciting. If I was really lucky, I might get off on it. Honestly, the wills had been more of an I'll-never-need-this-but-I'll-do-it-anyway sort of thing.

Whatever Liam thinks of Brennan, I know he stakes his reputation on having quality employees. He draws a hard line on "mishandling the merchandise."

This is something else though. "Are you saying you wanted to resell me or something? Is that why you were trying to get me for cheap?" In spite of everything, I almost want to pat myself on the back for actually thinking someone paying two million for me would have been cheap. If the guys could see me now.

But as the puzzle pieces snap together, I struggle harder. Every calculation I made hinged on a certain set of assumptions. Never once did it occur to me that someone might want to do something other than bid on me and fuck me. Or...you know, fuck-adjacent.

"It wasn't an easy decision. You're so pretty and delicate. The trouble is, I'm in deep with some guys who make Brennan Doyle look like a toddler playing dress-up. If it weren't for that? Mmm. You're so soft. Flexible. Gorgeous. I'd love nothing more than to lose my cufflinks inside you."

Lose his—oh. OW.

I've done enough research on *that* to know it's not my thing.

"We're in real trouble now," he breathes. "The money we put into getting you was supposed to be returned to us by our overseas investors. I hope you'll understand. I can't lose that money now. Shit's been underwater for too long."

When he lets me go and takes a step back, I'm honestly confused. Is he letting me go?

Oddly, it's the sad look on his face that gets me before I even realize the gun he's got his gun pointed right at me.

"Ravi!"

Oh. Thank. God.

That's Liam's voice. Taking my eyes off the gun in front of me would be stupid, but I want to. The urge to spin around and see for myself that he's okay is nearly impossible to override. But then the guy glances over my shoulder, and I see him adjust his aim.

Then it hits me. He won't shoot me, right? He can't. He said he needs me. *To sell me.*

He'll shoot Liam, though. I know he will. So I take a

breath, I put my head down, and I run myself straight into him.

My head and shoulder hit with a painful thud. There's a boom that makes my ears ring as I make contact, landing on top of him. There's a flash of numbness and cold, adrenaline pumping through me, and for a moment I'm not sure if I've been shot and I can't feel it. But then I realize the guy I'm on is staring sightlessly at the evening sky.

There's a hole in his head. Liam did this. Liam shot him.

"I'm okay," I yell as I push off the body.

My hand slips in the growing pool of blood, making me gag. So, not exactly okay, but I'm not too hurt. He probably bruised me. My hands and arms are scraped from where I fell. But I'll be fine.

Better than this guy.

It hits me as I look down at the face of the man who wanted to sell me and ship me off to God knows where, as I take in his unseeing eyes and the blood and whatnot coming out of the bullet hole... I'm not dizzy. I'm not panicking. This is a bad guy—*a worse guy*—who wanted to hurt me. Who's probably hurt others. He deserved it.

The thought puffs my chest. Honestly, this is kind of empowering.

"Liam, are you okay?"

No answer. I get to my feet and look around, which is when I see a crumpled heap on the dock where Liam is supposed to be. Slumped over. Twisted. Wrong.

I try to shout again but my lungs don't work.

Liam, he's just...lying there. Not moving.

CHAPTER TWENTY-EIGHT

Ravi

"I can do this myself." Liam growls. He's trying not to act hurt, but he can't help it. His leg flinches under my hand.

"Stay still. The doctor said to change the bandages regularly." I press a gauze pad to a spot above his knee. "At least the bleeding's stopped," I add.

Sometimes you really need to look for the bright side, am I right?

"Shit." He's all manly and stoic when I press the gauze on and start taping, but he's also kind of pale, and there's a seemingly permanent crease between his eyebrows.

Not that I care. He's sitting up. He's alive.

"I'm so glad you're okay," I can't stop myself from saying. Honestly, I want to wrap myself around him right now.

When I saw him on the ground, when I saw the blood, I felt my chest caving in. When it was Liam's blood, I did get a little lightheaded.

The only thing that got me to breathe again was the moment when his hand finally twitched.

"It's lucky that guy was a lousy shot," I add. Trying to find that silver lining again.

"He was a lousy shot because you used your head on him like a battering ram. Going off half-cocked like you always do."

For a moment, I'm frozen. Not gonna lie, his words sting. I know Liam's in pain right now, so I'm trying to understand.

"He was going to shoot you."

"He did fucking shoot me, kid."

Asshole. "In the leg. Sorry for saving your life, you cranky old man."

My frustration gets to me, and I press the gauze a little harder than I should while I put the last piece of tape in place. His hiss makes me feel both guilty and satisfied.

"Ravi."

I'm about to get up when he reaches out to grab my wrist.

"Thank you," he says seriously.

My shoulders relax some. "You're welcome."

"We've got a problem, though."

I don't like the tone of his voice. Or the regret in his eyes.

"Do we, though? We're both alive. The guy who threatened me is dead. We're..." Dating? Having weird punishment sex? "Together. Anything else we can work out, right? I don't see the problem."

"You never do," he murmurs. More regret. No. Not okay.

"What's that supposed to mean?" For once I find my voice rising.

"What it means is, while I was at the hospital I had a

conversation with Daniel. There were others, you know? Other guys who demanded entry to the auction and were turned away. Quite a few."

"Liam, I know your line of work makes you cynical, but you can't possibly think every single one of them was planning to sell me to some gang leader in Brazil."

Channing found a burner phone on Dylan Beck's boat before it blew. There were text messages. With...plans.

"We don't know they won't, either. The guy was right. There are a lot of sickos out there wanting to do sick shit to a cute little thing like you. Wanting to break your spirit. And, Ravi, you've got a sensational spirit. I need it to stay that way."

Wow. That's...sweet? Wait. The way he says it, it doesn't sound like it's a good thing. The warmth spreading through my chest makes a sudden retreat.

"I've got you to protect me though, Liam. Don't I? It's what you kept saying you wanted, so fine. I was stubborn before. We can have a conversation about it. Come up with an arrangement that makes us both happy."

Maybe I bristled at it before, but I can see now that things are bigger than I thought. While I don't share Liam's level of concern, I'm not totally ignoring what's happened. Besides, if we're going to be together, we need to be a team.

His expression turns thoughtful. Sad. "I'd like to think so. But you've never once listened to me. And in the end I didn't protect you, did I? You protected yourself. You protected both of us. If you hadn't run at Beck the way you did, I might be dead, and you'd be on a boat or a train or who the fuck knows where. I don't like to admit it, but it's true."

My vision goes hazy. My eyes burn. This is such a rare moment of Liam being real about his feelings, and it's not the victory I thought it would be. Not when it sounds as if he's saying goodbye.

"Liam, don't. Don't give up now." I can see it in his eyes. The way they've gone cold. Defeated. Until this exact moment I would have thought Liam Masters had never been defeated in his life.

A tremor runs through my body. There's this dread creeping through me that feels a lot like what happened when I found out my parents had been shot. I'm not sure I want to hear what he's going to say next.

Then I realize I already know. This is the moment before the police officer took me by the arm and said, "Son, we need to have a talk."

This thing between us is dead. Maybe it was never real and I was too stupid to realize.

No. That's not it. Something changed between our shower together and now. Something I don't know how to fix, or shove, or stare my way out of.

"I think you were right before, about leaving town. You should. I want you to. It's better that way."

His words slice right through my sternum. I think things were better when I didn't have the answers for what was going on in Liam's head.

"You don't get to make that decision for me," I say with as much force as I can find inside myself. It's hard to find anything at all when it feels as if my world is sliding out from under my feet.

Why did I think I was finally getting what I wanted? I should have known better.

"Don't make this harder than it has to be," he says quietly. "This is why I resisted you for so long."

"This is why? Because you thought someone might shoot you while they were trying to kidnap me?"

"Something I couldn't protect you from, yes." He nods and swallows and licks his lips in a way that makes me think he isn't telling me the pure, unvarnished truth. He'll never admit it though, maybe not even to himself.

I remember Liam telling me that when he was in the military, he had to take a polygraph more than once. Apparently they asked questions meant to trap him in lies. When I asked him how to beat it, he told me there were different ways, but the best trick was to convince yourself your lies were true.

That's probably what he's doing right now.

I try again, even as cold dread slithers through me. "Liam, it's over. What happened today can't possibly happen again."

"It's not only that. Like I told you before—I've never really been in a relationship. You're half my age. You're a kid. We were never going to work, and I didn't want you hurt. I still don't. It's time for you to go, though. It just is."

You don't want me hurt. And yet here you are, killing me.

"So, we can learn to be in a relationship together." I cringe at the hint of desperation in my voice. "And stop saying how young I am. My friend Dean was already a dad at my age. I. Am. Not. A. Child."

Liam's sigh is so loud. "I'd bet any amount of money he was in over his head, baby. And so are you. You just don't know it yet."

He's got an answer for everything, doesn't he? "So, just like that, you get to decide? What if I want to stay?"

My friends are here. My favorite restaurant is here. *Liam* is here.

Either he's suddenly really interested in the lamp on the bedside table, or he can't look at me. Whichever it is, I'm not seeing the emotion I hoped to see in his eyes. They're hard. Firm. Icy, for such a tropical color. I also know from experience that Liam doesn't believe in agonizing over things.

You don't worry about making the right decision, he told me once. *Make the best decision you can with the information you have, and then you don't go back.*

"You keep reminding me you're an adult." Maybe it's wishful thinking that his voice has gotten thick and emotional. "You want to stay in Belle Argo? I can't stop you. But you need to take that mangy little Halloween icon that's squatting in your bedroom and find somewhere else to live."

Oh. "I see." Except I don't. But I also kind of do. Honestly, I feel pretty stupid right now. All along Liam's been telling me who he is, and I didn't listen. Stubborn, like he said.

My eyes burn as I swallow against the need to scream. It takes a few tries before I'm able to push down this ugly, angry thing trying to claw its way out of my throat.

"You're telling me," I manage in an almost whisper, "that the guy who dragged me back here from the hospital because I couldn't be trusted to look after myself is now saying I don't have a home anymore."

"You're a damn millionaire now. Multiple millions." He clears his throat. Swallows. "That money was a payoff from the government, you know. The money I used for the auction. Zed and I were the only survivors on a mission to take out the home of a known terrorist. Only we were given the wrong address. One house over. Ended up blowing up a bunch of women and children before the neighbor's goons started launching grenades at us. A fucking bloodbath. I swore I'd never use that money, but I'm glad it went to you. Now you've taken the sin away for me. You've got the freedom you've been wanting. Your home can be anywhere."

"I only ever wanted it to be with you."

"I'm not a good person, kid. The bad shit I've done extends far beyond the military."

If it weren't for the weird buzzing in my lips, I'd think I was dead. Everything else is dull and weirdly numb. I'm standing outside my own body, wanting to beg or scream or punch him in the fucking face. If only I could make my arms move.

"I know exactly what kind of guy you are. I've seen what you do." I think of the falling-apart warehouse. The knife. I overheard part of the conversation. The man had committed multiple sexual assaults but kept avoiding conviction.

"You help people, Liam," I insist. "You kill the worst guys. I know you do. I know who you are."

He closes his eyes and says nothing. I guess it's like he said. He's made up his mind.

For I don't know how long, I sit there. Frozen. Staring. If I move, everything might fall apart. By everything, I mean me. My skin is tight, and I can feel the cracks everywhere, and if I move...

Maybe Liam's right. Maybe I am too much of a child, because none of this makes sense to me. Or maybe Liam's the child, the way he's lying there on the bed with his eyes closed and his chest rising and falling as if he's pretending to be asleep.

"Turns out my war hero's a fucking coward." At least

when it comes to me. To hell with that. I deserve better. "Fine," I whisper. "You want me to go? I'll go. I'll pack up my stuff and I'll leave in the morning."

Somehow I force myself to leave the room. My hands shake as I pull the door closed behind me.

CHAPTER TWENTY-NINE

LIAM

When I wake up again, it's late. Or early. Which in itself is nothing new. My life has been a series of sleep deprivation trainings, from special ops training to going wheels-up at odd hours.

What is new is the way I'm feeling. My head's fuzzy from the painkillers the doctor gave me. I don't usually take them, but I was a weak punk when it came to rejecting Ravi. Once I realized it wasn't right for him to stay, I knew what I did was the only way to get him to go.

The empty chasm that opened inside me when I told him to leave, when he visibly held himself back from crying, is an ache inside me. A pulsing blackness that beats in time with the ache from the bullet graze above my knee. The wound will heal, but I'm not sure the inside of me will.

He was right to call me a coward.

I blame the meds for why it takes me a minute to realize I can't move. There's a sound by my head. When I push my hand backward to reach for the gun I keep strapped behind the headboard, I can't.

Something tightens around my wrist. My fuzzy brain finally clocks the threat, and my eyes fly open wide.

"Oh, good. You're awake."

"Ravi?"

He doesn't acknowledge me. He doesn't need to. I know it's him. I can smell his bodywash, and after this past weekend, the touch of his fingers on my skin is something I'll never be able to erase.

"I didn't think you usually slept so soundly," he says. "I was worried. Didn't really want to do this while you were sleeping." He comes around to the foot of the bed, standing there between my spread feet. I can't move those either.

Not that I've never been restrained. I spent some time with a Dom who firmly believed one had to submit before dominating. Still, I'd forgotten how crazy not being able to move makes me until this moment.

Even as I'm itching to fight my restraints, there's a phantom hand on my chest urging me to be still. Telling me there's danger present.

Ravi's never been particularly menacing outside of my attraction to him, but standing here now when all I can see in the nearly dark room is his silhouette and the glow of his eyes? To me, Ravi's always been sweet and bright. Like eating a popsicle in the sunshine.

I thought I knew all of him, but this is a different Ravi. This is someone new, someone I haven't met before. This is Ravi as a predator.

And he scares the shit out of me.

"Ravi, what the hell is going on?"

Why the fuck am I tied up?

Unease creeps into my chest. Something terrible squirms around inside that aching chasm, and it knows what's about to happen. My brain hasn't quite caught up yet.

"You were wrong," he finally says.

"Tell me what I was wrong about." Because in spite of the ache, I'm still convinced that what I did for Ravi was the right thing. *I know*. Not for me, but for him.

"Remember when you tied me down and edged me until I had knots in muscles I hadn't even heard of before?"

Do I remember him naked and spread out before me, writhing and begging with tears running down his face? If I live to be a hundred, I'll never be able to think of it without getting hard. It's the worst kind of comfort, right now. He's carving me into pieces while singing me a lullaby.

"Yeah, kid." My voice scratches and cracks. "It rings a bell."

"You left me. Before you left me, though, you said something like, 'You got what you wanted.' Remember?"

My lungs lurch involuntarily. I tug at the ties around my wrists and ankles, knowing they're strong enough that it would be hard to get out without help. I'm the one who purchased them, after all. I'm the one who attached them to my sturdy steel bed frame.

"I remember."

"But I didn't though, Liam." The bed dips as he climbs onto it, creeping on all fours between my legs. "I didn't get what I wanted at all. You know what I wanted?"

I'm going to regret this. I already do. "Tell me."

"You. You were always what I wanted. Well." His laugh is dry and harsh and so unlike Ravi's it stings my skin. "Mostly at first I wanted my parents back."

His grief makes me wonder if I might drown. "I know. I'm sorry."

He scoffs at me. Fucking scoffs. "Later, though, when I finally made peace with them being gone? It was you. You were my first crush. My first obsession. My first love. I wanted you to want me back so badly. You know, I saved myself for you, thinking you'd make it so good for me. Then I realized you were never going to love me back the way I wanted, so I just wanted it gone. My virginity, my loving you."

Fuck. Fuck. I can't see blood, can't smell it, but I know it's there, leaking out of me from every goddamn pore.

"Ravi, I'm sor—"

"Save it."

Those two words slice right through me. My mouth closes up before I've even processed the command.

Or maybe I can't process it because I've realized Ravi is moving again, slinking forward like a panther in the dark. He's climbing on top of me. Straddling my hips.

He's completely, utterly, one hundred percent naked.

"Ravi, what the hell is happening right now?"

It's a useless question. The fingers tugging at my loose sweats, hooking under the edge of my boxer briefs, are pretty damn self-explanatory.

"I haven't gotten anything I've wanted, Liam," he says matter-of-factly as he drags my pants and boxers off my body. He's careful over the wound above my knee, and then he must realize his logic error because he stops.

The sweats are loose, and the fabric of my boxers is stretchy, but there's no way to remove them completely without untying me.

"I guess those will have to stay right there," he murmurs. Not sure he's even talking to me.

"What's happening? What are you doing?" I want to hear him say the words.

"It's like I said. If you couldn't love me, then I wanted to lose my virginity, and I wanted to leave you behind. So. It was a virgin auction, Liam. Technically speaking, I'm kind of still a virgin." He sounds exasperated, as if I'm an unruly child he's having to patiently explain the rules to.

"Virginity is a construct."

"Fine," he snaps. "I wanted to get fucked, okay? I wanted to *try* things, Liam. So I intend to get what I really wanted before I leave."

Of all the words he's said so far, the last three are the hardest to hear.

"You intend to, do you?" I manage.

My answer is the snick of a bottle, and then there's the telltale slipperiness of lube drizzling over my dick.

"It's the kind that gets warm when you rub it in," he explains. "Simon gave me lube and condoms before the auction. He wanted to make sure I was prepared."

Prepared. For some other man to fuck him. Bile rises in my throat.

Then he demonstrates the warming lube to me, sliding his grip up and down my shaft. A better man wouldn't buck into his hips. Wouldn't revel in the slide of his fingers.

I'm not a good man.

"Oh. I almost forgot. Your safe word is red," Ravi adds.

Fuck. My. Goddamn. Life.

His silhouette rises onto its knees. Then he moves to straddle me. The hand that was jacking my cock leaves me aching and needy as it slides behind his back and works its way down.

He's using his lubed-up fingers to prep himself. Even in the dark, I know that's what he's doing. I've seen that hole up close. I've seen my own fingers pushing inside. My hands jerk again, itching to reach for him. Again, I'm stopped by the force of the restraints.

Holy ever-loving motherfuck.

Part of me is furious. How dare the little shit do this to me? Part of me is pissed that I'm not the one pushing into his warm hole, spreading him open.

My hips give another kick. The stoicism I've worked hard to cultivate is nowhere in sight. Especially when a cloth chafes my dick, wiping off the lube.

Even knowing what's coming, the telltale rip of foil makes my pulse shoot sky high. So does the cool sensation of a condom at the tip of my cock, the squeeze of Ravi's fingers as he rolls it down. Goddammit, I wish I could see better right now.

His knees press into my hips as he rises up again, positioning himself over me. His hand is on me again, his slippery fingers braced on my stomach. There's some wiggling and squirming as he tries, I assume, to get himself into the right spot.

Then I feel it. The tip of my cock presses at his opening. It's all I can do not to buck my hips again.

"I've been practicing," he whispers. "You're bigger than my dildo, but that's okay. I think I can take you. I know I can."

This is going to end badly. You need to stop him.

I've never been more certain of anything. This is an absolute train wreck.

He's angry. So am I. Whatever this is right now, it's toxic. Nothing good can come out of it. There's also an ugly, selfish voice whispering in my ear that this is actually perfect. He's giving me what we've both always wanted, and I don't have to feel like shit about fucking him if he's got me tied down.

So, when he says "Remind me of your safe word, Liam" I don't try to buck him off. I don't tell him to stop like I know I should.

I say, "My safe word is red, kid."

Then an unholy sound rips out of me as he begins to sink down, squeezing my tip in the most delicious, amazing, constricting heat.

He's using me. I'm merchandise. An upgraded fucking dildo.

I don't think I've ever wanted anything more.

"I'm going to fuck you now, Daddy," he whispers.

CHAPTER THIRTY

Ravi

At first, I didn't think this was going to work. I only sort of planned it out.

Lying in my bed after packing up the few things I actually wanted to take with me, I couldn't sleep. Couldn't relax. Couldn't reframe things in a positive light the way my mom and my therapist always tried to get me to do.

There's no silver lining to finally getting everything you want and having it ripped away just as fast.

As I stared at the popcorn ceiling, all I could feel was this ugliness boiling in my blood. Watching Mr. Cat curled up by my pillow, the need to hurt Liam the way he was hurting me crowded my insides. To use him the way he'd used me.

So, I guess that's what I'm doing. Liam would say I'm being impulsive again, but it's working out better than I expected.

"You're so big," I whisper as I slide down the length of

Liam's monster cock. "I've never been so full." I'm breathless with the effort of taking him.

This isn't the moment I wanted it to be. Him on top. Sweetness. Love is what I wanted. But I'll take this, if it's all I get.

I've experimented with a few things. Things I later found out I shouldn't have tried to put in my ass, and I guess I'm lucky I was able to get them out.

Would Liam have been even angrier than when I overdosed if he'd had to pick me up from the hospital because I had a cucumber lodged inside of me?

God. Don't think about that now.

Anyway. Liam's cock is something I don't ever want to get out of me. It's so intense. And so, so good.

He groans and pulls at the ties I attached to his wrists. Does he want to touch me, or is he trying to get away?

"If you use your safe word, I'll stop," I remind him the way he reminded me. I don't bother with the second part, the part where he told me if I safed-out, then everything would stop, and I would have to leave.

I'm leaving anyway. Like he wants me to.

Through the pale sliver of moonlight on his face, I can tell that his lips are pressed into a thin line, his jaw set and stubborn the way it always is. Why is that so freaking hot?

My ass meets his pelvis, my balls resting lightly on his stomach, and I can't hold back my satisfied groan. It hurts, but it's a good hurt. Intense.

This is exactly what I wanted.

I bounce a little, feeling the satisfying ache that fills me every time I try to get him a little bit deeper. A quiet sort of growling groan comes out of his throat.

"Is this what you wanted too, Daddy? Did you want to

fuck me, but you were too afraid? Or are you too stubborn to use your safe word?"

He answers me with a defiant glare. The hope inside me still wants him to want me back. This new, angry darkness in me feels somewhat gratified at the idea of taking the thing he refused to give me even when he had me at his mercy.

I'd stop if he asked, but he won't. I know he won't, like I wouldn't. Because I wanted everything from him, even if I couldn't say so.

"Now who's the one tied down and helpless?"

Still no answer.

I lift up, slowly at first. Carefully, because I've seen porn where the top pulls out too far and can't get back inside, and I've never liked the way it seems to kill the momentum. This train needs to keep rolling because this is probably my only chance.

"Ravi..."

He doesn't finish. Is he saying my name because he's turned on? Is it a protest?

"See, if we had a normal relationship, I'd know what you wanted," I say. "I'd know exactly how to make you feel good. Since you're being all stubborn and lying there looking like you've got your lips glued together, I'm going to have to guess. Or I'm going to have to do what feels good to me and hope you like it too."

I like that option better.

Guessing only ever leaves me confused.

So after a few tests, some slow slides where I figure out how much to pull off him and how fast to sink down, I find a rhythm that works. An angle that hits my prostate just right.

"Oh, fuck, Liam. Daddy, you feel so fucking good." My

words aren't enough, but they're all I have right now. "This is exactly what I hoped for, you know? For my first time to be with someone like you. For it to be sexy and memorable." I lean forward to kiss him when I sink down again. "Some of the guys have some real first-time horror stories, you know? Simon said his first didn't even know to bring lube. At least now I know, whatever happens in the future, I'll always have this."

That seems to piss him off. He punches his hips upward, but I keep my legs clamped right against him. Like that time at summer camp when I learned to ride a horse.

Save a horse, ride a man, right? I saw that on a T-shirt once.

"You feel as good as I thought you would," I tell him. "No." I grind down on him again. "You feel even better. I used to fuck myself down the hall in my bedroom and pretend that dildo was you, but it's like you said—plastic and silicone can't hold a candle to the real thing."

His chest and abs ripple, expanding and contracting in quick staccato motions. His nostrils flare. He's fucking me harder now, thrusting his hips up as much as he can with the limited range of motion. It's hard and fast, though, almost as angry as I feel, and so aggressive I need to brace my hands on his chest to keep myself steady.

It hurts. He's stretching me too fast. His hip bones bruise me with every jab. It's so, so good.

"Is this what you wanted, kid?" He fucks up harder. It's no longer me sliding up and down. It's like Liam's one of those fuck machines, and I'm holding on for the ride.

What a ride it is.

"Not exactly." There's a buzz inside me; the one that tells me my orgasm is building. I squeeze my muscles around him, strangling him, wanting to hurt him and urge him on at the same time. “What I wanted was for you to want to keep me, Liam. But if this is all I get, then this is what I'll take. I'll make sure you remember me every time you jerk off for the rest of your life.”

“I can't,” he rasps. “I can't.”

“I know,” I say sadly.

I'm not even lying. Whether I like it or not, I understand better now. When he told me about those innocent people his team killed, the guilt was all over his face. Even if it wasn't my fault, I still carry guilt about not being there when my parents were killed. His guilt won't let him be with me. Maybe mine is why I've clung to Liam, even knowing he'll never let himself be happy.

With one hand braced on his stomach, I slide the other up and down my dick, pinching the foreskin a little because an orgasm always feels better to me when there's some hurt, and pushing my hips down. I fill myself with him, with the overwhelming ache of him, as much as I possibly can before it's all over.

No matter what, it's going to be too soon, especially after that night when he edged me for so long. By the time his hips stutter and he comes with a strangled groan, I'm too impatient for my own release. I've got places to be.

Places that aren't here.

When Liam forced me to have orgasm after orgasm, it reached a point where the orgasms were honestly more pain than pleasure. Where my oversensitive body didn't seem to know if what it was feeling was good or bad, but it was pretty sure it had been duped in spite of the cum leaking out of me.

This orgasm hurts more than all the others.

A primal yell that bursts out of me as I shoot all over my hand, all over his stomach. There's moisture leaking from my eyes and running down my cheeks, but I ignore all of that.

I don't want to wipe my tears away. I earned them.

When the final aftershocks have passed, I lift myself up. Sort of like he did to me before, I wipe the cum from my hand right onto his chest. Then I release him from the restraints quickly, because I'm not sure what he'll do once he's free.

I can't read his face, which causes a little spark of fear. Like I used to feel when I thought there was a ghost in my parents' basement. My body shakes as I back away.

Which is also why I don't take the time to clean him up. Besides, it might do Liam good to sit here with my cum on his skin and think about what he's done. Since he likes punishments so much.

"Consider this your penance, Daddy," I say too fast.

I'm sort of on a schedule anyway. My phone, which I placed on the bed by Liam's leg, lights up in the dark. Probably Michael, letting me know he's almost here.

As I back away, Liam struggles to sit up. "Ravi..."

But there's nothing more. No protest. No asking me not to go. He doesn't even stand.

Maybe his knee hurts. Maybe he's too spent.

His eyes glitter in the dark. His jaw is slack. Feeling emboldened by the now-or-never-ness of the whole situation, I return, leaning down to press a kiss to those pouty, parted lips.

"I'm going to miss you, Daddy."

My clothes and everything else are waiting for me at the bottom of the stairs, including my backpack and Mr. Cat, in the carrier I got for him when Channing took me to the pet store.

He's mewling, the sounds soft and insistent. A protest.

"I know, Mr. Cat," I whisper to him. "I'm not happy about this either."

My phone lights up again.

Michael: I'm outside.

Ravi: BRT

One last reckless impulse has me wrenching open the kitchen junk drawer. I hastily scrawl a message on a sticky note before stepping out into the humid, dark morning.

Who's going to keep me from doing stupid things now, Daddy?

I'm proud that I only wait for a second to see if he follows before I close the door behind me.

CHAPTER THIRTY-ONE

Ravi

"So, where do you think you're going to go?" Michael glances at me from the driver's seat of his swanky Volvo, which I have to admit I love riding in even though it's got leather seats.

They're heated. Which is nice, because I'm feeling awfully chilly for a Florida fall morning.

"It's a good question," I say as I stare out the window. I'm not sure I've ever seen Belle Argo like this, with all the pretty buildings downtown as the sun paints the sky baby blue and tangerine as the town wakes up.

I hate how beautiful it looks when I'm bleeding inside, but it also feels like something sacred.

Not that I haven't been out at this hour before, coming home from a party that ran late or something. But I don't think I ever really took the time to appreciate it. The beauty of the lightening sky, the day laid out before me with absolutely no plans. It's almost as if I'm seeing Belle Argo for the first time.

My dad loved to paint sunsets. I know why. They're pretty. I'm realizing now, though, the sun rising is something really special.

After I've been silent for a while, Michael chuckles. "Still thinking it over?"

"I've been thinking about it for over a year. Closer to two, now." My birthday isn't too far off. Not that I'm looking forward to it.

Another year of being alone? Of not getting what I want? No, thank you.

"But it was all this huge ball of ifs, you know? It was if I can make Liam see me as an adult, and then it was if I can't have him, I'll leave. If I get enough money. Brennan sent me a text yesterday to confirm the wire transfer into my bank account. I keep staring at the number. I've never had that kind of money in my life. Never even imagined it. Now that I have it, I'm not sure what to do."

"Move some into high-yield savings," Michael says. "Multiple accounts so you don't exceed the amount each one is insured for. Keep what you need for a few months of cushion in your checking account. The rest in an index fund. That'd be my suggestion."

In spite of how raw I feel, my lips pull into a smile. "Thanks. Really."

He gives me an almost-smile. "I'm guessing you weren't talking about your financial plan, though."

"Not really, but what you said was helpful. Thanks."

"You know you can always call me, right?" Michael gives me a friendly pat on the shoulder. "It would be nice to hear your voice, Rav. We've all grown pretty fond of you."

That opens my tired eyes wider. They're burning again. "You have?"

Why is it that the first time I feel like someone cares about me is when I'm all set to go? It makes my stomach hurt.

Michael makes a sort of *pssht* sound. "Why the hell wouldn't we?"

I shrug. "Just never was really good at making friends. I was too annoying. Too much of a goody-goody. Too whatever. Then I'd think I'd made friends, only to have them turn on me or ghost me without telling me why."

"Maybe you haven't noticed, but every person in our little group is a little 'too whatever.'"

My smile stretches enough to make my lips hurt. "Fair point."

Maybe things were never meant to work out with Liam, but at least in the end I made some friends.

So why are you leaving?

Because I can't stay. I just can't. Not when Liam is so close. Already, it feels like there's a jagged shard of glass lodged in my chest. I feel like if I stay, I'll keep bleeding until I die. Slowly.

When we pull down the block from Gil's, where I left my car (why does it seem like ages ago?), I'm surprised to see an entire group of escorts clustered along the sidewalk.

"Is this..." I can't finish. My throat closes up.

"The entire brunch crowd. Except Dean. His daughter has a fever, but he said to wish you well on his behalf." There's a flash of something I can't read that passes across his face, but before I can ask, he smiles again. "Come on. Everyone wanted to say goodbye."

The tears in my eyes spill over. I can't even stop them.

When I get out of the car, I'm shaky. All the anger and adrenaline running through me when I did what I did with Liam has drained away, leaving me exhausted. Seeing everyone here... Well, I don't know what to do with that.

"Hey, Rav!" Troy holds up what looks like a to-go container. "We got you one of those burritos you like."

I peer into the window of Gil's, confused. "Are they even open?"

It's only a little after six. They don't open for breakfast for another couple of hours.

"They've got kitchen staff already," Adam pipes up. "They said they didn't have the time to serve us, but they let us get some stuff to go. After Troy and I sexed up the owner a little."

Simon rolls his eyes. "Was it really your sloppy fucking blow job skills that got us all breakfast, or was it maybe when I showed them my boyfriend's black Amex?"

Troy gives him the finger. Simon gives it right back.

My lips curve into a smile even as I'm drying my cheek with my hand.

PJ rushes forward and pulls me into an unexpected hug. "Can't believe you're actually fucking leaving us. You know how hard it is for me to make friends?"

"Uh..."

"Here." Prince, whom I still don't know all that well, nudges me with his elbow. "You'll need caffeine for the drive, wherever you're going."

"Where *are* you going?" Alexis asks.

She's wearing flannel pajama pants, with her long blonde hair pulled into a messy bun. Guess I'm not the only one who's cold. Then again, we're sort of edging toward fall, which means it's "only" about seventy degrees this morning. When I first moved here from Virginia, the temperature was oppressively hot. I'd walk outside and immediately feel as if I needed a shower. Now? The mornings are downright cool.

"Uh..." It seems to be the only word I know this morning.

An insistent meow from the back seat has me reaching through Michael's open window to pull out Mr. Cat's carrier.

"I don't know for sure," I say after I set the carrier down. "I was actually thinking maybe Canada?"

Everyone stares at me. Everyone. Michael, Christian, PJ, Alexis and Eve, Adam and Troy, Simon, and especially Prince, who looks more horrified than the rest of them.

"You know it's cold there, right?" Troy's eyebrows dip low with concern.

"Sure. I know. But I acclimated to Florida, so I'd adjust to being there, too. And I hear the people are friendly."

Who doesn't like friendly people?

"The people are friendly here, too." PJ points out.

Simon scoffs. "Not you."

PJ narrows his eyes. "Not you either, you little shit."

Simon pokes out his tongue.

"I'm nice," Troy points out.

"Sometimes you're a little too nice." Adam rolls his eyes.

Next thing I know, they're all arguing among themselves about who's nicer or who's a bigger asshole. I can't quite tell.

Michael whistles. "Settle down, kids," he says, a look of humor on his face. "We're here to say goodbye to Ravi. Show him our support."

The murmur of agreement that goes through the group makes my chest ache more.

"Still, though," Eve says. "If you don't have much of a plan for going, you could maybe stay? My roommate is moving out soon to live with a boy." She brushes her braids off her shoulder and shoots a glare at Alexis, who giggles and throws her hands over her face. "So I'll have an open room once she moves her shit."

"Seriously, Rav. Stay. You could crash on my couch," Michael offers.

Don't cry again. You can't see to drive if you cry.

"Thanks, guys. Really. I can't tell you how much I appreciate it."

Honestly, it's so tempting. The way they're all looking at me right now? Happy? Hopeful? It's *everything*.

It's on the tip of my tongue to say yes. Yes to the couch, yes to more brunches. Yes, I'll stay. But then I see Liam in my head, telling me he wants me to go. If I ran into him on the street tomorrow, I wouldn't be able to take it.

"At the risk of being super cringe right now, I love you guys. And I'm not saying I don't want to stay, because I actually really do. My heart hurts too much right now. Maybe once I've gotten some distance from Liam, it'll be different."

"Hey, we could help with that," Adam says solemnly. "They say getting under someone helps you get over someone, right? Troy and I love a good threesome. We'd treat you right."

Next to him, Troy nods his agreement.

Jesus, they're both completely serious.

Neither of them seem to notice the wide stares and a few fist bumps from the rest of the crowd. There's been a pool going on about if, or maybe when, the two would admit they're sleeping together. Or maybe it was if they're a couple? I don't know. I did put money in, but I guess I won't be around to win the prize. Even though they haven't said anything shocking, it still feels like a clue. Adam and Troy await my answer, seeming blissfully unaware of the commotion around them.

"Thanks, guys. Seriously." They're trying to help. "Don't take this the wrong way, but you're not really my type."

"Oh, that makes sense." Troy rubs his chin. "I've seen that Liam guy you're into. Daddy energy."

"Wait, when did you see him?"

Troy snaps his fingers. "You've got pictures on your phone, remember?"

Oh. Right. I've basically been carrying a shrine to the man in my pocket for years. Feels silly now.

"Also, he was at that party. The one where you made out with Dean."

My sleepy eyes fly wide open. "What did you say?"

"That's right," Adam agrees. "Didn't stay long, but he was staring at you like he wanted to either eat you or murder you."

That was the night Liam and I fought when I came home. The night he spanked me. Oh God.

What if he'd let me know he was there? What if I hadn't kissed Dean? What if Liam had come over and dragged me out of there in front of everyone? Would things be different now?

I glance down at my watch, which I didn't leave even though I probably should have. It's mine, after all, and if Liam really doesn't want me, then it doesn't matter if he can track me. It's not as if he's going to follow.

The conversation moves on to other things, and we end up sitting on the sidewalk for a couple of hours until Gil himself comes out to glare at us threateningly with a broom in his hand. Everybody hugs me goodbye. PJ twice, which kind of surprises me. He always sort of acted like he was reluctantly accepting my friendship.

Michael lets me go with a sort of confusing comment about being the master of my own destiny. Maybe he's right. It's time I stop chasing someone I wish would want me and decide what I want all on my own. Guess I'll have plenty of time in the car to think about what that might mean.

When I settle into the car with my cat, my to-go coffee, and half a leftover burrito, things are only sort of blurry. I'm almost proud of myself that I make it as far as the Florida-Georgia line before I really let myself get emotional.

It's thinking about Liam getting shot that does it, of all things. Walking out of his house hurt so much, but I thought the pain would lessen the farther I got from town. Only, it hurts more now. Like that shard of glass in my chest is pushing deeper.

With every mile the ache seems to intensify. As if the old connection between us is getting stretched to its breaking point.

Is he okay? Does he need help changing his bandages? Is he in too much pain? Then I can't help thinking about that moment in the shower when I really thought we were on the verge of having everything. Fuck that sack of garbage, Dylan Beck, for aiming a gun at him. After telling me he was pissed he hadn't been able to sell me.

What we needed was an investment.

Wait. Wait. *Wait.*

We. He said 'we' needed an investment.

"There was somebody else."

Dylan Beck was working with someone. Or for someone.

"Well, now I feel stupid. It didn't hit me before, Mr. Cat. Better late than never though, right?"

Mr. Cat lets out a meow from the back seat.

Michael's right. I do need to be the master of my own destiny.

I take a swig of my coffee and pull off at the next exit.

CHAPTER THIRTY-TWO

Liam

I CAN'T TELL if the blood running down my arm is mine or that of the man I just killed.

"Jesus Christ, Liam. Was this really necessary?"

My friend, my business partner, nudges a toe at Harold Ruben, who lies sightless on the forest floor. What's left of him, anyway.

My pulse hasn't yet returned to its typical steady beat. It's rushing and erratic in my chest and in my ears like it has been for days. Since Ravi left.

The threat at my feet may have been neutralized, but my nervous system hasn't gotten the memo. Likely because the threat wasn't really the trafficking drug dealer.

The threat is coming from inside the house.

It's me. I'm the problem.

"It was necessary that he be stopped, Zed."

I'm given a look of extreme skepticism. "Yeah, and I

stopped his two security guys with bullets. No mutilation or dismembering required."

"You know what he did." I point at Ruben with my knife. In the course of searching property records for another case, Bev stumbled upon the interesting fact that when the uptick of kids going missing happened in Belle Argo, eighty percent of the venues were short-term vacation rental homes. Most of which were owned by the same guy. While our search of those homes turned up a suspicious lack of security cameras, a more thorough sweep of the properties turned up hidden cameras in the bedrooms, bathrooms, and showers. Oh, and a cache of some new street drug inside a toilet tank.

It didn't stop there. Harold Ruben was a bad, bad guy. His own son and stepdaughter mysteriously disappeared on a trip to Argentina after the stepdaughter made assault accusations against him. A neighbor with whom he'd had a dispute was conveniently killed in a home invasion. A business rival's niece was found taking it at both ends at an East End rave, high as a kite on that same street drug we found in his rental property. Nothing touched this guy, but everywhere he went people ended up destroyed.

Well. He can't destroy anybody anymore.

I realize my business partner is silent, still staring at me with what appears to be concern.

"What?" The word shoots out of my mouth. I'm too exhausted for this shit. I don't even know how I'm still standing, and I sure as fuck don't have the patience for my oldest friend to stand there and judge me for doing what he knows damn well I've always done. What we both have always done.

"Nothing much," Zed murmurs. "Just wondering if my best friend's lost all his marbles or if he still has some left."

How the hell am I supposed to answer that? I open my mouth, but nothing comes out.

"Come on," he says with a sigh. He juts his chin in my direction. "We need to get back to the plane. You're bleeding."

How the fuck can he even tell? But I look down at myself, finally seeing what he's seeing. A dark patch on my abdomen, fresher looking than Ruben's blood, which is already beginning to oxidize and dry on my skin and clothes.

I make a circle in place, taking in the surrounding forest. My team tracked Ruben here to this private island in Chilean Patagonia, sometime during the night when I was tied to my own bed with Ravi's ass milking me like a stud horse.

Once I got past the paralysis of watching him walk out the door, the office was the first place I went. I couldn't stay in that bed, remembering. I grabbed on to the opportunity to hunt this piece of shit down with all ten of my greedy, desperate fingers.

When I blink to try and clear the memory of Ravi riding me, it only gets blood and sweat in my eyes. "Aside from the house and the airstrip, this island is five hundred acres of forest. We can probably get away with leaving these guys for the wildlife and they'll be gone before anyone can find them."

Zed huffs. "Fuck, you really are feeling reckless today." He tosses me a foldable shovel. "Start digging, numbnuts."

So, for the next few hours, we dig. Deep enough that the bodies couldn't be immediately found, even if someone were to show up in this desolate place. We relieve them all of any phones, accessories, and weapons we can find, then unceremoniously dump them in.

We're nearly done covering the grave when I'm caught with a wave of dizziness. My legs, which still aren't in the best shape, threaten to buckle. I throw a hand out, catching myself on a nearby tree.

"Woah. Shit." Zed grips my shoulder. "You're losing blood faster than I realized."

Maybe. Or maybe it's the fact that I haven't eaten or slept in at least twenty-four hours. Or...all of the above.

After we've trudged the handful of miles back to the plane, my vision is tunneling. My feet are so heavy I'm stumbling on tree roots. By the time our pilot, Deon, has gotten us into the air, all I want is a shot of whiskey and a bed.

"Hang on there, hot shit." Zed slaps me when I turn onto my side in the seat. "Gotta lay you down so I can fix you up."

"Fuck." It's a small plane, made for the times when our team needs to get in and out of hard-to-reach places. The craft is designed more for maneuverability than it is for luxury or comfort. The seats recline, at least enough so that those of us who are used to sleeping literally anywhere can rest. There's no bed.

My friend hauls me out of the chair and dumps me somewhat unceremoniously into the aisle. Pain shoots through me—from my spent muscles, the stab wound in my gut, and the chasm that opened when Ravi left. My pain is a living thing taking over my body. It has its own heartbeat.

"Ow. Fucker."

"Don't go blaming me for this. You're the one who went off on a torture spree because your boy toy left the state."

"He's not my boy toy." He's not my anything. Not anymore.

"Let me guess. You pushed him away? Don't bother answering. It's exactly what you'd fucking do."

My only answer is a strained grunt when he pinches the wound on my stomach together. Then another when he hits my skin with a blast of cold.

"The lidocaine is more than you deserve," he grumbles. "After being such a dumb shit."

"He's not for me," I say. I've repeated those same four words over and over these last couple of days. When I'm really struggling, I pair them with: "He's safer without me."

"Is he?" Zed jabs a needle into my flesh. The numbing agent hasn't really even had time to take effect. "Or maybe." Another jab. "That's the lie you tell yourself, because Liam Masters is nothing if not a martyr." Jab. "And you think the only way to redeem yourself is to make yourself alone and fucking miserable."

What I know is that I had one job, and that job was keeping Ravi safe. I failed.

I'm silent, biting my lips together against the pain of the sutures. Every one of us knows how to do them. It's part of our training. Some of us are better at it than others. Zed is not the best at them even when he's in a good mood.

"Your bedside manner could use some work," I argue.

"Fuck you and your bedside manner. You don't deserve that shit right now. Look, it's one thing to go down in a blaze of glory if that's what finally makes you feel better. Frankly, I'd rather you didn't, since I don't want to lose my best friend. But if you continue on this path of recklessness, you're going to put everyone around you in danger worse than anything you were afraid of happening when Ravi was around. And Ravi won't be any safer."

I sink into the hard surface of the tiny plane aisle, puzzling over his words. Usually I'm the one in charge. The one with the plan. Right now I don't even know how to admit to my friend that he's absolutely right.

"Everything fucking hurts."

"Of course it does. In the last few days you've gotten shot, stabbed, and concussed."

"That's not what I mean." Not entirely, anyway.

"I know that's not what you mean. Here. Done. We should get you to a hospital to check for internal damage, but it'll hold you for now." He stows the med kit and hauls me up, dumping me into a chair.

My head swims. When I close my eyes, all I can see is Ravi's shadow beside my bed. Ravi rising and falling on my cock. Ravi walking out the door.

"He fucked me," I murmur. "Then he just left."

It's shameful how pathetic I sound. But I'm too spent to care.

"You fucking told him to, dumbass."

He's right. I did.

"He didn't stay and fight." Even as I say it, I know it's bullshit. Ravi's been fighting for us for nearly two years. "It doesn't matter anyway. He's too young to know what he wants. The kid's pre-med for fuck's sake, even though anyone with half a brain can see he hates it."

Another painful jab from my friend. "You're not going to want to hear this, but I'm going to go ahead and throw it out there that maybe if you hadn't rejected him so thoroughly and so repeatedly, maybe if you'd given him some damn support as his guardian *or* as his lover—either one—he might not have felt like he needed to be the thing his dead parents wanted him to be. I sure as fuck don't get why he'd want your cranky ass, but I've seen the way he looks at you. I'd bet my car, my house, and my own dick that all that kid's ever wanted was to know you approved of him."

That's saying a lot, coming from Zed. He's awfully proud of the monster between his legs.

My face burns. "I do approve of him. That's why I let him go."

Ravi's capable of so much. What if I'd held him back?

Nausea swirls in my gut as our plane climbs higher into the sky. For all the times I've flown, I'm never entirely comfortable until we're on the ground again.

But I do my best to settle into my seat, gripping the armrests, because it's part of the job. Maybe being uncomfortable was always going to be a part of loving Ravi, too. It sure as hell is now.

"What happens in a few years when he gets all the kinky curiosity he's been feeding out of his system and the novelty of being with an old man wears off?"

"Jesus fucking Christ, Liam." Zed scoffs. "I've seen you drag children from burning buildings, slog through miles of rain and mud with fifty pounds strapped to your back, and face my mother across the Thanksgiving dinner table, which is something even I can't do sober. We've been through too much shit in our lives to not grab hold of the good stuff when we can. You're all, 'Oh, I can't keep him safe even though I'm a badass who assassinated two different warlords during my career.' For fuck's sake. Stop being such a coward."

Direct hit.

"Ravi called me a coward." I huff a humorless laugh.

They're both right. The deep-down truth is that aside from the man currently scowling at me, I've lost everyone I ever loved. Everyone I truly cared for. Sending Ravi away was a preemptive strike against losing again.

Except...Ravi's lost everyone he loved too.

"I'm a real piece of shit, aren't I? I sent away someone I loved rather than risk him ever looking at me like he didn't want me anymore." I'm not talking to anyone in particular. The picture is finally clear.

Zed answers anyway. "You sure are, partner. But I still love you."

I respond with my middle finger.

"Thanks, baby, that means a lot."

"Zed, if I weren't dying, I could beat the shit out of you right now."

We're getting ready to land when the phone I stuffed deep into a cargo pocket vibrates. I pull it out to reveal an unexpected notification.

Ravi has arrived at Shadow.

Adrenaline nearly shoots me out of my seat. "What the fuck?"

This doesn't even make sense. I'd assumed he would leave the watch so I couldn't track him. My phone's been off or out of range for most of the trip, so I'm only now realizing the tracker is still active.

"Why didn't he leave town?" I show the phone to Zed. "And what the fuck would he be doing there?"

"I don't know, but I suggest we find out." A smile spreads across his face. "You want him back, don't you, brother?"

More than anything.

I straighten in my seat. Is this intentional? Did he come back to find me? Or is this something else?

"He might not want to see me." Maybe Daniel Corvus

and his little sugar baby who needs sex "more than air" are having a grand old time with him right now.

My old buddy raises his eyebrows. "You going to let that stop you?"

Fuck no. Ravi's mine.

I'm going to get him back.

CHAPTER THIRTY-THREE

RAVI

I'M TAKING a big risk here. Either I'm about to get everything I want, or I'm about to piss off a large man with many implements of torture and zero patience.

Big risk, big reward, though. Hopefully.

"So, Daniel says you're new. I remember you from the auction." A man about Liam's age stands in the doorway of the private room. His hair is dark, darker than Liam's. Eyes, too. Hard and almost black at the center.

Flinty.

The man's stubble has a light smattering of gray, like Liam's. He looms in the doorway, utterly still. Unnervingly so. He's sizing me up; not in the angry way Liam used to, but more like an assessment. I wonder what he's seeing.

Coming here is meant to move my life forward. The farther I got from Belle Argo, the more I realized my fellow escorts had it right. This is where I belong. Add to that what Dylan Beck said to me before Liam shot him. It's been nagging me since I remembered. There was someone else involved. I need to tell him that much, if nothing else.

Yesterday I checked Liam's home and office with no luck. My watch is strapped to my wrist, so Liam hopefully knows where I am by now. If I'm wrong and me being here doesn't bring him out of the woodwork? Well, Daniel tells me this big guy here is "excellent at teaching newbies."

Baby steps, right?

"Yeah." I clear my throat. "The auction was..." The beginning of the end? My total undoing? "Quite a night."

"He also said we might be getting company." The guy (his name is Red. I don't know if that's a nickname. There's nothing red about him) glances around as if he's expecting to see anything other than me and the things that were already in here (a spanking bench, a bed, and a wall covered with various implements, one of which looks similar to something my mom used to cut pastry crust, so I'm going to have to look that one up when I get home).

"We might." I show him my watch, not that I expect him to understand. "My, uh..." What? Liam's not my boyfriend. Definitely not my guardian anymore. He's not my anything. "Liam. He might come looking for me. Otherwise it'll be the two of us."

His eyes narrow. "So, what is this? Some sort of revenge fuck situation? Are you trying to make him jealous? Get over him by getting under me?"

I swallow around my nerves. Sounds mercenary when he puts it that way. And not very like me. At least, not like the old me.

I don't feel very much like the old me anymore. I also don't think being here is going to get me over Liam. If he doesn't show today, then I'm going to learn. I'm going to wait. Then I'm going to show him what he's missing until he caves.

Standing straighter, I give Red a glare. "Sort of. I'm not sure about fucking, but...I'd like to do some experimenting. I found out I like getting spanked, tied up, and flogged. I'd like to see what else there is. Is that a problem?"

To my surprise, Red breaks into a grin. "Nah. Everyone here is using or getting used by someone. Good for you for claiming it. Let's go ahead and see you get naked."

My nerves have me wanting to strip in a hurry. Like ripping off a bandage. Just get it over with. But I'm stalling for time, still banking on the idea that if Liam knows I'm here, his overprotectiveness and jealousy will override everything else.

He'll come for me. He has to.

It's not over between us. It will never be over.

So, I force myself to go slowly. Shoes, then socks, then shirt, then pants, then briefs. Each item gets folded and neatly placed on the bed to my right.

The way Liam told me. Like a good boy.

"Nice." Red looks me up and down, and my body heats. No, he isn't Liam, but he's handsome. He's got the same kind of vibes. A little protective, a little murderous. A lot horny.

Adam and Troy would like him, I bet. Red seems like a guy who could wrangle two goofy but oddly mother-hen-like, threesome-seeking fuckboys.

I take a deep breath, heart pounding. I remove my watch and lay it on top of my clothes. *Come on, Liam.*

Now I know why my father told me never to gamble. This one might really leave me with nothing.

"Tell me where you want to do this."

My eyes cut to the pillory. Tempting, but I'd rather not be restrained by someone I don't know.

Someone who isn't Liam. Maybe I'll get there, but not today.

I think back to all those times when I watched Liam in the garage. Him and his friends gathered around a naked body. Often on a table. Or a spanking bench.

"There," I say, pointing to the padded piece of furniture specially designed for easy access. "No spanking, actually. But teasing. Toys. I like edging." My face nearly catches fire, remembering the night of the auction.

Liam spanking me was the first real intimacy between us. My first orgasm with him. I want to hold on to the specialness of that for now. If this doesn't work out the way I want it to, maybe someday I'll be ready to let someone else do that to me. I definitely got off on it. I'm just not ready yet.

"Sounds good, cub. You make yourself comfortable; I'll lay out my tools."

"Okay. I'm ready." I think.

Whatever Red sees on my face makes him come over. "You're sure?"

One last time, I glance at the door. My heart sinks a little. I guess I was wrong. Liam's not coming.

I'm getting myself into position when there's a knock at the door. Red cracks it open to speak with someone on the other side. Then he swings it wide to reveal...

"Zed?"

He grins at me while I resist the urge to cover myself. I've seen him in various states of undress too, after all. He was the most consistent participant at Liam's garage parties. Not that he knew I was there.

Liam walks in behind him. Or rather, it's more like a sort-of hobble. He definitely doesn't look good.

"What happened?" I stand from my half-kneeling position, no longer caring that I'm completely naked.

Liam looks terrible. He was worse than when I saw him last, and that's saying something.

"Little trouble in the jungle," Zed says.

"Forest," Liam corrects.

Zed shrugs. "Forest. Jungle. Either way, trees and mayhem." His eyes flick up and down. "So, little Ravi, you sure grew up."

"Oh my God."

It's a little weird. But it's also funny, and I kind of needed the laugh.

I roll my eyes up to the ceiling. It's painted black like the rest of the room.

Liam's right inside the door, braced sort of haphazardly on a single crutch, staring.

"What are you doing here, kid?" He's not stern or angry or even stoic the way he's always been. The question is soft and almost sad.

My heart squeezes, and it hurts.

"What happened?" I ask again.

Ignoring my nudity, I cross my arms over my chest. I'm not answering his question until he answers mine.

"When you left, I decided to take point on an investigation. Mistakes were made."

"When you told me to leave, you mean?"

"That," he says softly. "Ravi, why are you here?" He glances at Red.

"Sort of was hoping you'd come." There may be others in the room, but the only one who matters is him.

"You took the watch on purpose."

"Well, it is my watch." I meet his gaze, feeling raw and vulnerable. "Also, yes, I hoped you'd come."

"You wanted me to find you."

"Duh." I roll my eyes. "I was all the way to Georgia when I realized how stupid this all is. Or I guess I realized before I left, but it took me that long to admit it and turn around. I decided this decision shouldn't be up to you since you have a history of making bad ones where our relationship is concerned. Hoped maybe if I came here, you'd get jealous and come find me."

"And if I hadn't?"

"That's what I'm here for." Red gives a friendly little wave.

Liam's chest rises and falls under his loose T-shirt. I recognize it as one he sometimes sleeps in, thin and threadbare. Not at all fitting with the dress code at Shadow. I'm glad Daniel let him in. "You're lucky I'm half-dead, or I'd kick the shit out of you."

"You look like you should be in a hospital," I say.

"I'll be fine. Zed stitched me up."

Oh. I'm not sure that's a good thing.

"Don't worry. I'm dragging him to get checked out once we're done here," Zed adds.

"Tell me what's happening here, kid," Liam says with a deep sigh.

"I told you I'd seen you in the garage. When you said you were having poker night."

Zed chuckles. "I mean, technically we were pok—"

"Shut the fuck up." Liam snaps. To me, he says, "That something you want? Different guys touching you at once?"

I lift one shoulder. "It looked fun. Hot."

Liam hobbles over to me, finally lifting his hand to touch me. He grasps my chin in his fingers. "I'm not staying here for this."

Oh. My shoulders sag.

"Not unless I know you're mine. It's not my place to share someone who doesn't belong to me."

Oh. *Oh*.

"That depends." I straighten my spine, head tipped to make eye contact. It's not easy to look authoritative when you're my size, especially when you're naked and, well, kind of hard. But I give it my best.

"Are *you* mine?"

"Look at me." Liam gestures to his battered self. "You really want all this? Bunch of body parts slapped together with duct tape?"

"I told you. It's what I've always wanted, Daddy. *But.*" I blow out a harsh puff of air. "I'm going to expect a lot of groveling from you after the things you said. That's how it goes in my books. The guy who's an asshole goes way out of his way to apologize and make things right. *That's* what I want."

Off to my left I can hear Red and Zed (ohmygod I *just* realized their names rhyme!) muttering things like "Holy shit" and "Jesus Christ."

Liam's eyes flash with heat. He takes a long, deep breath. "You want groveling? Fine. We do this, you're leaving here with me. No going back."

"You're the one who told me to go." I don't call him an idiot out loud, but I think we can all agree it's implied.

"Won't happen again. Promise. Now, stop being a brat and get back over on that bench so someone can fuck you." He inches backward with regret on his face. "Unfortunately,

Zed already warned me that if I ripped my stitches, he'd cut my balls off, so these guys are going to have to be my hands and cock, so to speak."

Now my heart is thumping for an entirely different reason. I can't even believe this is happening.

There's something I need to tell him first though. Before this situation gets going and I forget.

"Wait. Not yet. You need to know something."

Everyone freezes. Liam raises his eyebrows. "Tell me, kid."

"The other reason why I came back. I remembered Dylan Beck when he grabbed me, he said 'we.' As in 'we needed you.' He was in some sort of financial situation because of this Tony guy making him lose money or whatever, but it sounded like there was someone else involved."

Liam turns to Zed. "Guess we're not done yet."

Zed shakes his head. "Are we ever? Howsabout we fuck your hot twink lover and get you seen by a less handsome than me but definitely more qualified medical professional? Then we'll deal with the heavy stuff."

The heat of Liam's gaze hits me full force. "Is that okay with you, kid?"

"More than okay."

"Good. You say 'red' if you want to stop. Got it, kid?"

"Yes. I'll say 'red' if I want to stop, Daddy."

"That is so fucked up." Red chuckles from his spot against the wall. "I fucking love it."

Liam gives Red a look, but it doesn't wipe the humor from his face.

"No offense meant, man." Red holds up his hands. "Honestly, I'm envious. Wouldn't mind having a twisted little thing of my own to throw around the house."

Seeming to accept this, Liam eases onto the bed behind him. He tries to hide it, but I catch a wince when he sits.

Zed says "Let's do this" and pulls up the hem of his shirt.

"Wait," I say again.

Zed pauses with his shirt halfway over his head. I'd laugh if it wasn't so serious.

"Liam, if I go home with you, we need to negotiate some boundaries and rules. You're not allowed to lock me in my bedroom anymore."

Zed lowers his shirt, eyes wide.

Liam sighs. "You're right. I'm sorry. Anything else?"

"I sleep in your bed from now on."

"You'd better."

I make myself as tall as I possibly can. "If you leave me or try to kick me out again, I'll...I'll GPS *you* and stalk you like you did to me until you can't take it anymore. Tell me you understand."

Whoo. So much adrenaline right now.

Liam tips his head as if to ask "where is this coming from?" But he should know better. I guess he does because all he says is "Understood."

"The cat stays."

"Yeah, baby. I know how attached you get to fluffy things."

"Good. And also, stop getting shot."

He gestures to himself. "Not sure that's something I can promise, kid."

"Try. Please. For me?"

Liam nods. "For you I'll try. Anything else?"

"Plenty. But the rest can wait."

There's so much inside me right now. Buzzy adrenaline and nerves and excitement for what we're about to do. Not the scene, but everything to do with the two of us. All the possibilities. Possibilities that didn't seem to exist before.

The future. Liam and I finally get a future.

"Anything in particular you want them to do, kid?"

My eyes fall closed, pictures playing in my mind. "The first time I saw you in the garage, it was this girl with long, dark hair. You touched her all over, teased her until she was begging. You fingered her and fucked her, while someone else used her mouth."

All this time later, I can still hear him as he leaned over her body, calling her a good girl, telling her what they were going to do. I've jerked off to fantasies of being in her place so many times.

My legs are already shaky. Suddenly, I'm not sure I'll make it through this after all.

"Ah, I remember her." Zed's smile looks wistful and fond. "Solana. Nice girl."

Liam shakes his head. Then he turns to me and eases further back onto the bed. "Okay, kid. You ready now?"

"Ready." Any other worries I have, we can handle later.

"Red, yellow, or green?"

"Green. Very green. All sorts of green, Daddy."

"You got a real fucking brat on your hands, don't you, *Daddy*," Zed says without any hint of anger.

"But he's my brat," Liam says. "Aren't you, kid?"

Yes, I am. So I take a deep breath, and I let it out slowly, finally feeling able to say the thing I tried to say the night I turned eighteen.

"I love you, Daddy."

All I can see right now is Liam's smile.

CHAPTER THIRTY-FOUR

LIAM

NEVER GAVE a lot of thought to doing something like this with someone I loved.

Never gave a lot of thought to falling in love. Now that I can admit I have, this scene feels like the most natural thing in the world. I've always enjoyed sharing.

Besides, I've got plenty of groveling to do. Starting with giving Ravi anything he wants. Giving him his fantasy. Doesn't hurt that his fantasy is also mine.

It's one of the many reasons I figured I'd never be in a relationship. How many people are honestly okay with getting passed around among your friends?

I take in Ravi, his brown skin glowing under the room's soft lighting, trembling slightly as my friend runs a hand over his back. Looking back on it now, I don't know how I didn't see it sooner. He's exactly what I need.

"I love you too, kid."

Zed puts his hand to his hip. "What are your orders, Liam?"

Ravi shivers harder. It's on the warm side in this room, so I know he isn't cold.

He's shaking because he wants this, wants it from me, and from now on I refuse to shove Ravi's wants away like they're some kind of burden. I'm going to grab Ravi's love with both hands, like the gift it is.

"Still green, kid?"

"Green, Daddy."

Fuck it. Twisted or not, I'm not going to tell him to stop calling me that. I know he gets off on it too. Examining that shit is going to have to wait for another time. Possibly my next mandated session with our company therapist.

Right now, I have a scene to direct.

"Touch him," I tell the two men. "Slow and gentle. Tease him. Make him needy."

The big guy, Red, slides his finger slowly down Ravi's spine, while Zed goes for the face. Sliding his palm across Ravi's jaw, over his throat. Down to his chest, teasing his nipples.

"You okay with my friend putting his tongue in your mouth, kid?"

"Yes, Daddy."

"How about other places?"

One of the benefits to being an observer? I get to see the way every inch of Ravi's skin erupts in goose bumps.

"I've never tried that."

Fuck yes. All his firsts are mine. They always will be.

"Is that a yes or a no?"

"Yes."

Zed gives me wink and then gets down on his knees,

running his tongue across Ravi's lips. My friend palms my kid's throat while he pushes his tongue in, and the sight of it is making my cock throb harder than the stab wound on my stomach.

"Other end now, Zed. Make out with that asshole for me." Aching to be the one touching him, I dig my short nails into my palm.

Once I'm all healed up I'll be able to do it myself. Maybe before, if I can convince Ravi to sit on my face.

My buddy groans and pulls away, leaving Ravi's lips wet. I look to Red. "You got something you can fuck him with, right? Something big that vibrates. He likes a thick cock. Don't you, baby?"

"I like yours, Daddy." Little shit has the audacity to wink at me.

Brat.

All the same, my chest swells. Ravi still prefers my dick over a dildo. Damn right.

While Red goes to a table full of toys, Zed pries apart Ravi's cheeks. He starts out careful and slow, with tentative licks, then a heavy swipe from his taint upward.

The throbbing in my pants intensifies. I'm fighting the urge to pull myself out, to jerk off while I watch this show. But I really don't want to rip those stitches. Besides, making Ravi suck me off later when we get home sounds fun.

When we get home. That phrase suddenly feels very different.

"Get in there, partner. Fuck him with that tongue."

Ravi lets out a frustrated whine. "I don't know how long I can last if he keeps doing that."

"Suck it up, kid. You come before I say so and there'll be a punishment."

"Argh." He gnashes his teeth, his shaking hands braced on the bench. "How are you going to punish me? You're, like, one brisk wind away from an ICU bed."

"Don't worry, baby. I'll pay you back when I'm all healed." I pause to let things sink in. "With interest."

"Oh, fuck!" I can't tell if he's responding to me or to the fact that Red decided to buzz his balls with a big, veiny vibrating dildo.

I nod my approval when Red holds it up to show me. "It expands," he tells me proudly.

"Good. Baby, I'm going to have you suck my best friend while Red here fucks you with that giant vibrator. Then I'm going to let them both shoot their loads all over you. If you come before they're done, you'll have to answer for it later. Don't know what the punishment will be yet, but I'll have plenty of time to think about it while I'm in that ICU bed, you fucking brat. Maybe I'll force orgasms out of you until you're sore and begging me to stop again."

The way Ravi glares at me tells me he remembers that day clearly. I remember it too. Fondly.

As it is, I'm angry that I can't get in there with them. I want to be the one making him ache. Coming on him. Licking us all off his skin. We'll have to see about doing this again sometime. If he wants.

"Get to work, guys."

Zed returns to Ravi's head, feeding him his cock an inch at a time. He presses forward until Ravi gags before backing off and setting a steady rhythm. At the other end, Red fingers Ravi and then slides the lubed toy into him carefully.

Good. The guy seems nice enough; I'd hate to have to hurt him.

There's a jolt of Ravi's body and a strangled cry when it gets turned on.

"Do *not* bite my dick," Zed admonishes.

"You can bite his dick if you need to safe-out, kid. Since he's got your mouth full."

My friend shows me his middle finger. "Fucker," he says without any heat.

"Kidding, baby. Keep your hands on the bench. If you pick them up, I'll assume you need to stop."

He makes a noise of affirmation. I love that even though his mouth is on my best friend, he's looking out of the corner of his eye at me.

Zed's eyes fall closed, his head dropping back to his shoulders with a groan. "Oh, hell, he's good at this for a newbie."

Must not be suffering too much, then.

Ravi, on the other hand, seems to be alternating between fucking back against the toy in Red's hand and squirming to get away. Edging himself, trying to hold off until the other two have shot their loads like I told them to.

"Good boy," I say softly.

The way Ravi trembles at my words has me sitting up straighter.

Red's got his left hand sliding the toy in and out of Ravi's ass, the other working his cock. He's a big guy, bigger even than me, and I've had more than one person have difficulty taking me.

Ravi took me just fine, though. I think back to that morning in my room. We'll have to have a conversation about that night. About the things he said. We've got some ground to cover before we get on the same page, but I finally know we can get there.

I'm salivating over the thought of getting to properly fuck him. Ravi took my dick so well. Especially considering it was his first time.

This guy, though? Well, for more than one reason I'm glad we showed up when we did. Maybe Ravi wasn't going to let this guy put his dick in him. I don't know. What I do know is now I'm here, and now I'm in charge.

Zed is the first one to crack. Ravi's hollowed cheeks and sloppy tongue work tell me he's trying hard to get my friend to the finish line. Which he does. With a hoarse shout he pulls out of the kid's mouth in time to shoot all over his upper back.

A little later, Red does the same, blowing his load on the right cheek of Ravi's ass.

With a triumphant cry Ravi pushes up to a kneeling position and bats Red's hand away, reaching back to work the vibrator with one hand while he pumps his cock with the other.

My God, I don't know what's hotter. This, or him tying me down and riding me with revenge flashing in his eyes.

I'm so fucking proud of him. And I'm the luckiest son of a bitch, because that hundred and twenty pounds of horny defiance is all mine.

Some people would look at this and think it's all wrong. The kid who came to live with me when he was a teenager, now kneeling in front of me with a toy in his ass and the cum of two other guys on his skin.

They'd be right. It's obscene. Filthy. Immoral.

It's what I love. *He's* what I love. And I love it even more knowing he's getting off on this so hard. Later, so will I.

"Can I come, Daddy?" Ravi asks with a frustrated moan.

"Make it count, kid."

He's got the most gorgeous O-face I've ever seen. Long eyelashes brushing over his cheeks. Lips parted, slick and sticky with Zed's juices.

My hands clench into fists until my knuckles turn pale. It's killing me not to be in there with him.

I force myself to scoot forward so I can get a closer look, right as he spills all over his own hand.

He's gasping as he comes down. I can see the effort of it all over him. It's in the crimson flush across his neck and his labored breathing. I make my way over to him, putting my hand against his chest so I can feel the beat of his heart.

With a swipe of my fingers, I scoop the cum from his hand and feed it into his mouth. "Taste yourself, kid. I want you to lick every drop from my fingers."

When I was learning enhanced torture techniques, I subjected myself to some of them to know what they were like. I got through it, but it was hell.

The worst torture I've ever experienced is Ravi Novak sliding his tongue between my fingers and not being able to fuck his face until I feed him my cum, too.

I'd cut my tongue out to be able to feed him forever.

When he finishes and licks his lips, it's almost the thing that makes me pass out.

"Was that—" He pulls in a shaky breath and opens his eyes to look at me. His lashes are damp, I realize. "Was that good for you, Daddy?"

Even though it's agony to fold my body forward, I lean down to brush a kiss across his lips. "I've never seen anything more gorgeous in my life."

Zed makes a fake gagging noise. I give him a look intended to shut him up, but he only laughs.

"You didn't come, Daddy." Ravi makes a pointed look at my pants.

Yeah, and right now my dick hurts worse than my stab wound. "You can make it up to me later. At home."

"We're going home?" His face is lit like a fucking ray of sunshine.

"After the hospital," Zed insists as he pulls his clothes on.

"After the hospital," I grumble.

"Good." Ravi nods. "Then I'll make it up to you at home."

Red hands me some cleaning wipes and I get to work cleaning the other two guys from Ravi's skin. Then I hand over his clothes.

"Oh." Ravi does this thing that used to drive me crazy, where he holds his hand up as if he's waiting to be called on in class. Now, it's kind of cute.

"We have to stop downstairs to get Mr. Cat."

"He's here? I figured he'd be wherever you've been staying."

"I didn't want to leave him alone in a strange place. Innes at coat check has been letting him hang out with her."

Kid's probably got the entire staff of this place wrapped around his finger.

"Come on then, baby. We can talk more in the car on the way to make sure I'm not dying. Not that we'll cover everything today. I suspect it's going to be a long conversation. Zed will take Mr. Cat home for you."

My friend makes a face. "Man, stop volunteering me for shit."

I ignore him, pulling Ravi against me. Yes, it hurts, and

no, I don't care. I'm too relieved to have him in my arms for anything else to matter.

Even all sleepy-eyed and fucked out, Ravi lifts his chin. "Yes. We definitely have a lot to talk about."

A possessive impulse comes over me. "Whatever happens, though, I'm not letting you leave again. You're mine now. You agreed."

His hands go to his hips. "You said you're mine too. So if you try to run off I'll start stalking you. You won't be able to get rid of me."

"So you've said, baby."

"You think I won't do it?"

Do I think the kid who used to spy on me through the window, who admitted to once following me to the East End and watching me torture a guy, won't make good on a promise to keep tabs on me?

"I know you will, baby."

I've never been happier to be threatened in my entire life.

CHAPTER THIRTY-FIVE

Ravi

It turns out one of the things I don't like is blindfolds. At least not while moving. The time Liam tied me up and fucked me while I wore one was interesting. Riding in a car with one on?

Pass.

"Can I take this off now?"

"Hold your horses," Liam grumbles. "One of these days, I swear I'm going to teach you patience."

"That time when you tied me to the bed and fucked me and we tried to see who could hold out the longest, it was not me who came first, Daddy," I remind him.

He mumbles something I can't make out over the sound of rain beating on the building roof. "Do you want to keep complaining, kid, or are you ready for your birthday present? I have the feeling that once you see it, you'll shut that bratty mouth."

"I'm ready." I give a little clap with my hands. "I hope

it's a gift card for the bookstore downtown. Or a gift card for Gil's. Oh...I could use some new sketchbooks."

My first day back on campus, I went and switched my major. From Biology to Art. Trust me, everyone's happier.

His sigh makes him sound totally beaten, but I can hear the smile in his voice when he says, "Those are all things you can get for yourself."

"But they're more fun when someone gives them to you as a gift."

"Right. Well." Liam clears his throat. "The thing is, it occurred to me that I've done a pretty shit job with your birthdays since you moved here. That first year, there was nothing I could do to cheer you up, so I thought maybe not making a big deal out of it would be better."

I reach around, grasping at thin air until he takes hold of my hand. "I understand why," I assure him.

He's right that I didn't want to celebrate that first year. He's also right that I've missed it more recently. Lately there's been this need to replace that memory with something better.

"Well, I think this will make sure your birthday is memorable for a different reason from now on." There's a sound of creaking metal as he leads me through a door. "Watch your step, baby. There's a metal strip going across the doorway."

There's a dripping sound nearby. And muffled noises, like grunting or something. I'm so confused. "Did you bring me to a live sex show?"

It doesn't smell like sex, though. The air is filled with mildew and rust.

He laughs. "Something better, I hope."

Liam pulls off the blindfold.

We're in the warehouse, I realize. I recognize the pitted cement walls. The room where I saw him torture that guy with a very long knife. That's when I find it, the source of the grunting sounds. It's not people having sex, it's a struggling man zip-tied to a chair.

Lightning flashes outside, brightening the room. The man's face is drawn and pale, but I think I've seen him somewhere.

"Is that...?" He looks familiar. I know he does. Then Liam pulls the rag from the guy's mouth.

"Man, what the fuck is going on here? Do you have any idea what my father will do to you when he finds out where I am?"

Now that I hear his voice, it all pops into place. "The guy from the pool. The one who grabbed me. You said you'd break every bone in his arm." Thinking of it now, I'm a little breathless.

"If I touched him again." The guy jerks from side to side. "You said if I touched him again. I didn't, though. I didn't touch him. I didn't even know where he was. Y-you can't do this."

Honestly, he sounds a little desperate. I turn to Liam. "He's right," I say, almost weirdly disappointed. "He didn't touch me again."

I don't like hurting anyone innocent. Still, I remember the look in this guy's eye. The way he grabbed me. He's at least a bad guy. Maybe even a worse guy.

"He touched a lot of people, baby. That's his entire problem." Liam circles around to the back of the chair. I hear a snap, and the guy in the chair screams a scream so loud it's echoing off the walls.

It rings so loudly I'm tempted to cover my ears. "Are you sure nobody can hear that?"

Liam makes his way over to the wall, knocking gently. "This building may look like it's falling apart, but that's intentional. Unless you're a teenager following someone you shouldn't, nobody would think to look twice at this place. We've got state-of-the-art soundproofing inside these walls, on top of a whole lot of dense concrete."

The guy in the chair looks awfully pale all of a sudden. Awfully worried.

"Okay. Good." Looking from Liam to the guy and back again, I ask, "What did he do?"

"A better question is what didn't he do?" Liam leans down again. There's another snap and another scream. This time I do cover my ears.

"Too much, kid?" Liam steps back, looking concerned.

"Huh-uh. No." I drop my hands from my ears and shake my head. "I can handle it. Tell me what he did."

Whatever it is, I know this man is no good. For all the burden Liam places on himself, I know he takes what he does seriously. He wouldn't bring someone here who didn't deserve it.

Liam squeezes the guy's nose shut until he's forced to take a breath and then shoves the rag back in. "Sorry, man. My baby doesn't like the screaming."

Then he comes over to me, taking hold of my hand. "This guy, aside from being an entitled, gropey douchebag, participated in parties hosted by that guy who tried to buy you before the auction. Parties where people were chained to a wall and forced to participate in hell only knows what kind of disgusting acts. Found out when we were trying to track down whoever Dylan Beck was working with. No news there yet, but we'll keep digging."

He pauses, leaning in to press his lips against mine. I melt into him, almost forgetting where we are until he pulls away again.

"There's also—was it two or three...?" He looks at the guy in the chair, who grunts and squirms again. "Right. It was four exes who filed assault charges and his daddy made it go away with his money. Then kiddo here harassed them continuously, even after NDAs were signed and promises were made."

My fingers tighten into fists. "I don't want you to call him kiddo," I blurt.

Maybe it shouldn't matter, but I don't like it. I'm the only one he can call kid, or any variation of that. He definitely can't say it about this sack of human trash.

Liam brushes his palm across my cheek. "Sorry, baby." He clears his throat. "Moving on. There were also a few times in high school when fellow students lodged charges of sexual harassment or sexual assault."

Oh, I don't like that. I don't like that at all.

The guy's thrashing so much he's making the chair jump. He's obviously trying to say something, but he's still got the rag in his mouth.

Liam hooks his thumb. "Our friend here's probably trying to say those charges back in high school were sealed because he was a juvenile. You know Bev, though. She can hack into all sorts of things."

I can't hold back my grin. "She's good at that, yeah."

"Not sure you want to hear the rest," Liam adds quietly. "There were also a few things in the juvenile records about animal abuse." His face softens. "Baby animals."

My breath catches in my throat. My fingers clench and release. I've never been violent. But I can't stop the furious tornado swirling inside me.

The force of air through my nose is the only thing I'm aware of before I pick up a hammer from Liam's shiny table full of tools and start swinging.

"What the fuck is wrong with you? Using people like that? Rape? Abusing baby animals? Do you have any idea what it must be like for a tiny helpless baby to be taken from its parents a-and hurt and hurt by some power-drunk asshole?" I'm shaking. Shaking, but I can't stop. "How would you like to have no idea what's going on and no parent to protect you? You sick fucking—"

Liam's hands come down on my shoulders. I don't realize I'm crying until I step back, my breath sawing in and out so hard that it burns my chest. I haven't cried like that since I lost my parents.

Since that bitch killed them.

Oh.

I really am angry, huh?

"Was this a bad idea, baby?" Liam's arms come around me.

"No. No, it's... I didn't realize all of that was in there."

The guy in the chair, honestly, his face looks a little messed up.

"Did I do that?"

The backs of Liam's fingers stroke down my cheek. "You did that, kid." He leans down, laughing quietly in my ear. "Awfully bloodthirsty for a vegan."

Bloodthirsty. I've never thought of myself that way. I try to wipe the tears from my face. "I can't stand it when people hurt someone who can't fight back."

The guy's protesting, or he's trying to. It's impossible to understand him.

"I know, kid." He picks up a knife from the table. One I've seen him use before, with a long, curved blade. "Your friend Simon was here recently. We'd picked up a member of that trafficking ring that he had some history with, and his boyfriend beat the shit out of him while he watched. It seemed like a good gift. Better than a gift certificate, maybe."

Simon? I had no idea.

He slides a finger under my eye and wipes the rest of my tears away. "Always wondered when you'd finally let out some of that rage."

My body is vibrating. I can't believe this, but I think I liked it.

"It was a good present," I whisper.

Liam's right. Now my birthday will be a day when we stopped a bad guy from hurting others. That's good.

I'm still shaking. I don't realize how much until my legs give way under me. Luckily Liam is there to catch me before I fall.

He always catches me these days.

"You want me to finish this?" He uses the knife to gesture to the bad guy in the chair.

"I don't want to punk out or anything, but I do feel like I should sit down."

"This ain't for the faint of heart, kid. I can finish." He points to another metal chair over by the door. "You can wait over there if you want. I want you to see what I'm going to do to him for you, but you can wait outside if you'd rather. Brennan should be here soon."

I perk up. "Brennan's coming?"

"He's coming to take care of the body. Said he has a place." Liam rolls his head from side to side and jiggles his arms a little, almost as if he's limbering up before a workout rather than torturing a bad guy to death. "The rest of my team is busy this week, and I figured it would be more romantic if it was only the two of us anyway."

I find my footing, rising up on my toes to kiss him. "It's romantic, Daddy."

Maybe it shouldn't be. It's not as if either of us are into candles or flowers, though. And it means something, Liam sharing this with me.

The chair guy's eyebrows shoot up. He coughs and sputters, managing to spit the rag out of his mouth. "You guys are fucking sick, you know that? You think I'm—"

Liam shoves the rag back into his mouth. "Spit it out again and I'll make it hurt more."

I guess it makes sense that the worse guy doesn't think this is romantic. He doesn't know us. And he isn't going to.

My friends would probably be shocked. I don't like suffering, and that's what Liam is inflicting. When it's a worse guy though, so I understand. "When's Brennan coming?"

"Soon," Liam confirms. "Apparently he feels like he owes me for sparing that Jacob kid who was following you around. So I called in his favor."

The chair guy's gone even more pale. His eyes are so wide; if this were a cartoon, his eyeballs would have popped out. Good. Let him be scared. He deserves it after everything he's done.

"Brennan's not so bad, you know. I'm happy to hear the two of you are getting along."

"Don't get ahead of yourself," he grumbles. Then he

leans down to kiss me. "Go and rest. I'll break some more of this guy's bones for you."

"Say please."

"Please, brat."

"I love you, Daddy. Can we go for burritos after this?"

"I love you too, kid. Whatever you want." Then he turns back to finish what he started.

And I settle in to watch.

CHAPTER THIRTY-SIX

RAVI

ONE MONTH LATER.

It's Liam's first time coming to the gym with me, and I can see now why he's been going by himself.

"You're overdoing it, Daddy."

He gives me his usual pissed-off glare, but he ruins it by sticking his tongue out at me.

It's fine. I'm not afraid of him anymore, anyway.

Liam's gotten sillier lately. I'd like to think that's because of me. Or maybe it's because he finally stopped fighting against himself.

"Stop treating me like an old man."

"Stop pushing the weight too high."

The bullet graze in his leg and the stab wound are healed, but he still has some pain. Especially where he got stabbed. His doctor keeps telling him to take it easy, and he keeps swearing he is. I can tell you from the way he fucked me over the sofa last night that he definitely is not.

"Wait, how did this geezer even get in here?" Troy and Adam elbow each other. They're supposed to be lifting weights, but it always seems more like this is some kind of social hour for them. They both work out for about thirty minutes, and then they sit around and talk. My mother would have said in a past life they were gossipy aunties.

Liam opens his mouth to answer, but then he sort of freezes in the middle of his rep on the leg press, grimacing in pain. Very manly, stoic pain, but clearly still pain.

As he eases the weight back down, I explain to the guys. "Liam's company consults for campus security, so he has a pass to come in whenever he wants. He's also allowed to get free food at the dining hall. All the watermelon sorbet we want on Tuesdays."

Adam and Troy look dubious, but that stuff is delicious.

Then I reach over to the weight stack on the leg press and pull the pin out, dropping the amount Liam's been pushing by twenty pounds. "Told you. Stop overdoing it," I murmur into his ear.

"And I told you, if you keep giving me lip, you're going to get a spanking."

"Spanking. Really?" I bend down to pick up the water bottle sitting by my feet. On the way back up, I whisper in his ear, "Bring it on, Daddy."

It's fun when I can make his face turn red.

"Wait, how do you two get in here?" Liam asks Adam and Troy. "You're not even students."

"Oh, we get in anywhere," Adam says. Troy responds with a fist bump. They do seem to be... I don't know. Popular? I feel like everywhere we go they're flirting with someone.

Mr. Monroe comes wandering in, setting up on a nearby treadmill.

"Hey, Mr. Monroe. Where's PJ?"

"He's with his foster brother, Evans, working on their new ice cream shop. I'm here to work out with my brother, though he seems to be running late today. And, Ravi, I told you—"

"Nope." I say unapologetically. "Maybe eventually I'll get used to it, but you were still my teacher practically five minutes ago."

Mr. Monroe smiles. "Okay, Ravi. I can respect that."

Liam gets this look on his face. I've seen it plenty before. The kind of look where if people are unkind to me, then he's going to hurt them, which is sweet, but... I mean, really? Mr. Monroe is the nicest guy.

So nice he probably wouldn't ever even murder someone. Smiling, I give Liam's hand a squeeze. I'll stick with my killer daddy.

"At least the semester's over, right?" Mr. Monroe pushes his treadmill into a light jog.

Yes, and thank God. Ever since PJ's birthday party, when I got lost on the way to the bathroom and accidentally walked in on PJ fucking Mr. Monroe with his hands around his throat, it has felt super awkward to sit in his class. Trying to focus through a lecture on Toni Morrison's second novel when you've seen your teacher's O-face? I'm glad that's done.

"Which reminds me. We're doing a cookout next weekend, Mr. Monroe, if you and PJ want to come?"

"I'll talk to PJ," Mr. Monroe says. "My brother invited me to go bowling, but things between him and PJ are still pretty tense. Every time I think they're finally tolerating each other, one of them blows their stack. PJ would probably love to come as long as he can bring his friend Evans."

Maybe that explains why Mr. Monroe is planning on working out with his brother while PJ's not around. The, uh, stack-blowing thing.

"Evans is welcome. The whole escort group is invited." Brennan too. Hopefully he and Liam can manage to get along. "We built this whole entertainment area on the back of the house. Brick patio, swimming pool, and a fire pit. The weather's supposed to be cool, and the pool is heated, so we're going to do it out there."

I ignore Liam's grumbles about how the whole thing was a waste of money. If I can't use my millions for something fun, then what's the point? Besides, he grumbled a whole lot less when I batted my eyelashes and told him how happy it would make me to have a place to hang out with my friends.

I did try at first to give the money back. He wouldn't let me.

Liam finishes up his leg workout and groans as he leans down to pick up his own water bottle. I'd get it for him, but I feel like this is a good reminder for him about taking things easy.

Adam pulls his phone out of his pocket, frowning at the display. Then he nudges Adam. "Your blood sugar's a little low. Let's go grab you a smoothie, huh?"

I'm selfishly really glad Adam's not checking his blood sugar the old-fashioned way anymore. It was only a little drop of blood, but now that he's got a glucose monitor, I don't have to see it. Why it doesn't bother me when Liam tortures someone, I don't know exactly. Except, it never bothers me when it's a bad guy. Liam only ever bleeds the bad guys.

"We're taking off too, I think. Going to the grocery store." I do a little hand clap. Grocery shopping is fun. All the bright colors and stuff.

Adam laughs. "Awfully excited about that, huh?"

I shrug. "I like doing couple things."

"He likes it when people look at us funny in public," Liam grumbles.

"He's right. I like that too." The last time we went out to eat together, the waiter, who was on the older side, asked if I was Liam's son and then asked if I wanted the children's menu, so I may or may not have told the dude to get an eye exam before climbing into Liam's lap and making out with him.

Now Liam says we can't eat there anymore, which is fine. Mama Elisabetta's is too stuffy for me.

"Oh, also, I get to draw Liam tonight for my art portfolio."

After spending most of the semester barely staying afloat in my science classes, now I get to do something I actually enjoy. I'm looking forward to the spring when I can show my portfolio to my new advisor.

Besides, I know what my mom really wanted was financial independence for me. Being married to a struggling art professor wasn't easy for her. But between Liam and me, we've got enough to be able to do whatever we want. Mr. Monroe even said he'd put me in contact with some art gallery friend of his.

Adam and Troy snicker, probably about the portfolio thing.

"Cool, cool. Well, you two crazy kids have fun," Troy says

as he tows Adam out of the room. "Don't do anything we would do, Rav. We'll see you this weekend."

"You know," Liam tells me as we walk toward the gym exit, "I was thinking instead of the grocery store, we could go home, get showered, and watch a movie."

"But we're out of those things you like."

"Mm-hmm. But InstaDelivery recently expanded their delivery radius, so if you order everything you want to get on the drive home, I can tie you up when we get there and try out that thing you wanted to do."

Ooh. "Clothespins?"

It sounded decidedly unsexy at first, but after some research I think I see the appeal.

"That one." He leans down to put his lips to my ear, giving me a shiver. "Sex is a couple thing too, you know."

Right in front of a gaggle of tennis players who just came streaming in from the outdoor courts, I turn to give him a kiss.

"Okay then. Take me home, Daddy."

EPILOGUE

Wes

I'm running late when I burst into the locker room to get changed. I hate being behind schedule, especially now. Fallon's been barely tolerating me lately, and I can't say I blame him. Honestly, I know my head's a mess. That doesn't mean I want to lose my brother.

Our mom couldn't take it. Neither could I.

I'm hoping that Ravi kid is still around. Fallon mentioned his former student's new boyfriend does something with security, and I think I need to talk to someone about that. Something weird is going on at the hotel I help manage, and frankly? I'm not sure I trust our in-house staff.

At least the gym is quiet now. Most students are gone for winter break. Unlucky for me, I happened to run into one of my mine on my way here, who wanted a reference for a job at the Belle Argo Premiere. One thing I've learned as the night manager of that place? She does not want to work there.

Not that I could really tell her so.

I've never been terribly comfortable getting naked in front of strangers, so I head to the far back corner of the locker room. There's usually nobody there. I also keep my head down, so nobody ever thinks I'm gawking like a perv.

So, I only have myself to blame when I run into someone. "Sorry, I—"

I step back when I see who it is. My mouth keeps working but I can't manage to make sound. Because I know this guy I bumped into, and I know the one standing next to him.

"Hey, Brunch Daddy. How's it going, Westy?" the one I bumped into says with a weird grin. Troy, I think? These two guys always seem to be together, and I tend to get them confused.

Oh hell. A cold sensation fans across my back.

"It's Wes," I tell them. "Just Wes. My mom calls me Westlake. Nobody calls me Westy."

"Oh, yeah, Westham," says the one with the shoulder-length hair. He takes a big drink of the smoothie in his hand. I think that's Adam? Every other time I've seen him he's got it pulled back in one of those man buns. My soon-to-be ex would probably scoff and say man buns are out of style. Then she'd probably fuck him anyway.

Our boss has long hair, and she seemed to like fucking him just fine.

"I like Westy better," says the one who might be Troy.

"It's Wes," I grit out.

The part I'm not confused about? These guys are sex workers. Like my brother's boyfriend used to be. I've seen them skulking around the hotel when I'm working. I'm forced to tolerate my brother's boyfriend, but I don't have to tolerate these two.

I grip my duffel bag tighter and try to squeeze past them. "Look, never mind. I'm late meeting Fallon. We're supposed to be working out while his boyfriend is fixing up his little ice cream stand."

I'm not saying it's the worst job, but how much money can he really make serving ice cream on a beach that's routinely mauled by hurricanes?

"Oh, right," Maybe Troy says. "That why you're in a hurry? Don't wanna have to deal with PJ? We've noticed you seem to have a real beef with our friend."

I look down at where Maybe Troy has wrapped his hand around my upper arm. The last thing I want is to make a scene, but I also don't want to keep standing here talking.

"There's no beef." There absolutely is. I've made it abundantly clear that I'm not comfortable with the way Fallon lets his boyfriend treat him, but I can't exactly say so to PJ's buddies.

My brother's boyfriend used to be in one of his classes as a student. He's over a decade younger. Worse, he seems to have the same kind of dominant nature as Fallon's late wife had. Not exactly the same, but enough that it makes me itch to be around the two of them.

With a tug of my arm, I pull out of Maybe Troy's grip and head back to my usual locker. I don't realize they've followed me until Maybe Adam says, "You homophobic or something?"

"Hom—what? No. Of course not. I'm the one who set up PJ and Fallon on their first date. Would I do that if I was homophobic? What I am is control phobic."

"It's just that we remember the day you came storming into our brunch place looking ready to throw down with PJ." Maybe Troy gestures between the two of them.

Guess that's why they call me Brunch Daddy?

I'd been trying to get the sex worker I hired to fuck my brother to leave him the hell alone. A situation that's been biting me in the ass since it first put me on these twenty-something thugs' radar.

"Right," Maybe Adam agrees between gulps of smoothie. "And then there was the way you lost your shit at the birthday party last month."

"I walked in on them fucking when I went to ask if we had more ice," I insist in a harsh whisper. "Nobody wants to see their little brother getting choked by his twenty-year-old boyfriend."

"Pretty sure PJ's, like, twenty-three. Twenty-four?" Maybe Troy nudges Maybe Adam.

"Twenty-four, I think," Maybe Adam agrees. "Or twenty-five? No, I think he's around a year older than you, so that would be twenty-four."

Jesus, my head is spinning. "Look, guys. This is pointless. I told you I don't have a problem with—"

Until I stumble backward, I hadn't realized they'd been advancing on me. And I'd been retreating. Like they're the predators and I'm their prey. Like raptors, I guess sex workers also hunt in pairs.

A bead of sweat trickles down my back.

Somehow I've let them back me all the way into the far corner, where there's a bench seat running between the lockers for people to sit on. That I've awkwardly sort of landed sideways on.

"What the fuck are you...?" I don't finish the sentence because I don't think I want to. What are they doing? They're probably about to beat the shit out of me—some sort of fucked-up payment for me being a dick to their friend.

I glance toward the opening to the bank of lockers, but there's nobody. It's why I like this spot. The only person I ever see back here is someone from custodial services, and that's only if it's late in the evening.

"Look, whatever this is—"

Maybe Adam's hand comes down on my shoulder. He's got an alarmingly strong grip for kind of a lean guy, and his fingers dig solidly into my muscles.

It gets extra confusing when Maybe Troy straddles the bench in front of me, pulling on one of my legs to make me straddle it as well. Then he scoots forward, hooking each of his legs over each of mine, trapping me in place with his crotch practically mashing mine.

I blame the fact that Gina hasn't wanted to have sex with me in almost a year for the reason I start to get hard. Skin on skin feels good, right? Even if it's someone you can't stand. Even if it's someone who looks as if they want to punch you in the face.

Totally normal.

I cough to cover the groan I almost let out when his fingers press into my leg.

Maybe...maybe this is not entirely normal.

"Adam, keep a lookout."

The words "Got it" come from behind me, followed by the slurp of a smoothie. Okay, so the one in front of me is Troy. I'm oddly gratified to know for certain, in spite of the complete and total *what-the-fuck* of this entire situation.

I'm not expecting it when he reaches for my fly.

"What the hell are you—"

With head-spinning efficiency Troy's pulled my cock out, and he's stroking me with his hand.

And I try to tell myself I don't want him to, until a strained "Oh, God" comes out of my mouth.

Nobody's touched me in so long.

That little thing doesn't satisfy me. It never has.

Remembering Gina's hurtful comments makes me move to cover myself, but Troy only bats my hands away. "Chill, Westy. Lemme make you feel good."

Do I protest? Do I ask him to stop?

Do I tell him I want more?

"It's Wes" is all I say. Frankly, it comes out embarrassingly like a moan.

It's a little painful as hand jobs go. The skin on his hands is a bit rough and he's not using any lube, but my dick doesn't seem in the mood to be choosy.

"Got a live one here, Adam."

Behind me, Adam's heavy breaths puff against my ear. He's leaning down to get a better look, I realize. He slides one hand over my shoulder, stroking my nipples through my dress shirt.

"That's a pretty looking cock you've got there, Westy," Adam breathes.

"It's not—*oh God.*" My protest is cut off by Troy staring me dead in the eyes as he leans forward and lets an obscene drizzle of spit from his mouth land right on my hard cock, and then resumes stroking me.

"Somebody likes this," he quietly sing-songs. "Don't worry. We won't tell. You sit there and fuck my fist like a good boy, and we'll let you come."

The sound that comes out of my mouth, it's one I've never heard before. I'm fucking his fist exactly like he wants me to. Like *I* want me to. Even though I shouldn't.

It takes a shamefully short amount of time before my orgasm shoots through me like lightning. I'm shaking with the force of it, unable to control my limbs. For a moment I forget myself, opening my mouth to let the whole damn locker room know what's happening over here, but Adam clamps a hand over my mouth from behind.

I wind up biting down on his fingers as he tries to keep my cries muffled.

In front of me, Troy only chuckles. Then he presses on my leg to let me know he doesn't want me to move yet. The other hand, the one that's covered in my body fluids? He stares me down as he licks every drop from his fingers.

If anyone had ever told me someone licking jizz from their hands could look like a threat, I wouldn't have believed them. Until now.

"What the fuck was that?" I whisper. I don't know if I'm asking them or myself. God, maybe? The old professor in the next row of lockers who's always heading to the pool in his Speedo around this time?

I'll take any answers at this point. Any at all. I'm at a loss.

Somewhere nearby, a locker slams, and I nearly jump out of my skin. Except I still can't move, because Troy's got me pinned. He's clearly stronger than I am, but he's also not in a post-orgasm daze.

"That?" Troy tucks my cock back into my slacks. Gently, almost politely, given the situation. "Just showing you how letting someone control you can be sexy, babe. Fun even. It was fun, right?" He leans forward, lips against my ear. "Imagine what we could do to you if you weren't so embarrassed by your own dick."

Fuck me.

"It was—" I don't know what the hell that was.

But clearly Troy takes my broken-off answer as agreement, because he only gives me a smug grin.

"Thought so. Kaybye, Westy."

By the time I've remembered how to use my tongue again, they're long gone.

"It's Wes," I whisper to no one but myself.

The next thing I know, I'm stumbling over the bench, rushing to follow after them. I have questions. And I need answers.

THANK YOU FOR READING GUARDIAN!! I hope you loved this dark guardian/ward romance.

Find out what happens next with Wes, Adam, and Troy, in DUBIOUS, an MMM bi-awakening age-gap romance...

(Scan below to order Dubious)

A DIVORCÉ *and two male escorts walk into a luxury hotel...*

Wes

I feel like my life is falling apart.

At forty-two my wife is divorcing me, my brother barely tolerates me, and my new boss? He's the one who took my wife.

On top of everything else, employees at the hotel I work for seem to be disappearing.

I don't know how much longer I can go on like this.

A lifeline comes from the most unexpected place. Two twenty-something friends of my brother, who happen to be male escorts.

To be honest, I thought I was straight. But they make me...feel things. Amazing things. Terrifying things.

Then, disaster strikes. The three of us get kidnapped together.

To survive, I do things I never thought I would. With them.

After, I'm not the same. And they're the only ones who understand.

Adam and Troy

Since high school, we've been each other's ride or die.

We helped each other run away from dangerous homes. Kept each other alive. Comforted each other, in any way we could.

There was always something missing. Or maybe that was some*one.*

When we first meet Wes, we're only messing with him for fun.

But then we all need each other.

Which is when we realize.

He's the something we've been missing.

Tropes: bi awakening, throuple, age gap, enemies to lovers, dude in distress, forced proximity, power dynamics, trauma bonding, repressed desires, strategic seduction, unhinged heroes vs innocent hero, kink awakening, found family, older submissive, late queer awakening

Possible triggers include: homophobic slurs, patricide, drugs, kidnapping, troubled pasts, consensual noncon play, car accident, attempted murder, actual murder, and, well, some of the consent is a bit dubious

(Scan below to order Dubious)

Want to read what happens after Ravi ties Liam to the bed from Liam's POV? Scan below...

Sign up for my newsletter to stay in the loop about future releases.

ALSO BY BETH CHRISTOPHER

The Belle Argo Escorts

1. Blackmail (enemies to lovers, hurt/comfort, brat/a-hole)

2. Switch (age gap, teacher student, Dom awakening)

3. Guardian (age gap, guardian, power dynamics, vigilante)

4. Dubious (MMM, age gap, queer awakening, trauma bonding, older sub)

ACKNOWLEDGMENTS

Thanks most of all to those of you who made the decision to pick up this book and read it to the end! You are my sort of people and I'm so happy to have you here.

Thank you to all the reviewers and influencers who got excited about this series and helped to spread the word. I'm truly honored and grateful.

Thank you to Elizabeth Babski at Babski Creative Studios for all the amazing cover art in this series. Thank you to Sydney Feron **@editivepublishing** for keeping me honest and pushing me to do my best work. Many thanks to Lea Vickery and Kate Wood for proofreading and advocating for these characters, and to AJ Rose, thanks so much for supporting and cheering me on.

Most of all, thanks always to my husband and kids for their support, and for keeping me humble with your jokes about "those gay books you write." 🙄 I love you anyway.

ABOUT BETH CHRISTOPHER

Beth Christopher is not part of the cool kids club. She's part of the "went to bed early with her dog and a book" club, the "said something awkward in public again" club, and founding member of the "got distracted thinking about ramen again" club (the meetings involve sitting lost in thought while her cats judge her). She writes down the stories in her head when she remembers to, and when she's not writing she's likely doing weird kitchen things (like making cheese out of cashews) or watching Ted Lasso (the Christmas episode is the best episode and she will die on that hill). She lives with her family and her fur babies in Belle Argo, Florida.

Sign up for her newsletter or keep in touch on Bookbub Instagram, and Threads to stay in the loop.

www.ingramcontent.com/pod-product-compliance
Lightning Source LLC
LaVergne TN
LVHW041110080826
845145LV00007B/1750

* 9 7 8 1 9 6 9 8 1 0 0 9 1 *